SATAN'S
HARVEST

Books by Ed and Lorraine Warren:

Graveyard: True Hauntings from an
Old New England Cemetery
(with Robert David Chase)

Ghost Hunters
(with Robert David Chase)

The Haunted
(with Robert Curran and Jack & Janet Smurl)

Werewolf: A True Story of Demonic Possession
(with William Ramsey and Robert David Chase)

In a Dark Place
(with Carmen Reed and Al Snedeker with Ray Garton)

SATAN'S HARVEST

ED & LORRAINE WARREN

MICHAEL LASALANDRA

MARK MERENDA

MAURICE & NANCY THERIAULT

GRAYMALKIN
MEDIA

Published by Graymalkin Media

www.graymalkin.com

Originally published by Dell Publishing

This edition published in 2014 by Graymalkin Media

ISBN: 978-1-63168-016-8

Printed in the United States of America

3   5   7   9   10   8   6   4   2

Book design by Timothy Shaner

For Anne

ACKNOWLEDGMENTS

WE WOULD LIKE TO THANK the following people for their cooperation in the creation of this book: Ed and Lorraine Warren, Maurice and Nancy Theriault, Jerry Seibert, Bishop Robert McKenna, Father Galen Beardsley, Joey Taylor, Karen Jaffe, Fred Salvio, Jessica Spellman, Chris McKenna, Benjamin Massey, Joe Sciacca, and Debbie Noland.

The authors also wish to acknowledge several books that contributed to their research into the unfamiliar world of paranormal phenomena: *Hostage to the Devil* by Malachi Martin (Harper and Row Publishers, 1976); *People of the Lie, the Hope for Healing Human Evil* by M. Scott Peck (Simon and Schuster, 1983); *Witchcraft at Salem* by Chadwick Hansen (George Braziller, 1969); *The Encyclopedia of the Occult* by Lewis Spence (Bracken Books, 1988); *Strange Beliefs, Customs and Superstitions of New England* by Leo Bonfanti (Pride Publications, 1980).

—M.L. and M.M.

May, 1989

INTRODUCTION

I WAS a general-assignment reporter at the *Boston Herald* in the late winter of 1985 when I was asked to check out a story that was developing in the town of Warren, a little more than an hour's drive west of Boston. There were reports that the Catholic church was planning the exorcism of a farmer there. The *Herald* was known for offbeat stories and I had received more than my share of strange assignments in the time I had been working there, but this one was perhaps the strangest.

Naturally, being a reporter, I was skeptical. But I headed out to Warren anyway. It turned out that what I found in Warren was more than just a good story. It was something that has bothered me from that day on. And it is something that has bothered a great many others, causing several people great harm as it touched them in different ways.

What follows is a reconstruction not only of the events that took place in Warren, Massachusetts, in 1985, but also of the events that led up to that time and those that have followed. The names of a few minor characters have been changed to protect their identities. In all other respects, the story remains as it was told to us by the people who lived it. The story is a shocking and frightening one, but one that, in a time when satanism and satanic cults are on the rise all over America, must be told.

—M.L.

May, 1989

POLICE CHIEF JERRY SEIBERT wondered why he was out freezing his ass off on this bitterly cold morning, instead of being back at the station, nursing a hot cup of coffee.

He was sitting behind the wheel of his cruiser, uncomfortable because he was wearing two layers of clothing, which made it hard for him to move freely. He stretched out his long legs and arched his back. The upholstery squeaked as he stretched. He thought about what it might be like in Florida this very moment.

His toes were numb. His salt-stained shoes were still wet from the slush that had covered the streets of Warren, Massachusetts, since the previous Tuesday. Aside from the accident reports every time somebody drove down the steep slope of Coy Hill and skidded past the stop sign at the bottom, nothing much lately had drawn the attention of Warren's tiny police force.

Seibert was fairly certain that one of his men would be called to the Depot, a seedy bar on Main Street, to break up a fight later that evening. The Bruins were playing and the bar's patrons, mostly unemployed laborers and bikers, could be counted on to draw inspiration from the hockey players and try to rearrange one another's dental work.

Keeping the peace in Warren was a rather predictable business. The most dangerous moments usually occurred at the annual town meeting, Seibert thought. Getting an extra thousand dollars out of the tightfisted town fathers could be a real blood-bath.

Warren, population 3,800, was not the kind of town that produced a lot of exciting police work. What it did produce was plenty of small-town politics. The Board of Selectmen that governed the town was often composed of three local merchants, each with his own interests, personal loyalties, and enemies. Seibert thought of them as Moe, Larry, and Curly. It didn't help any that one of the chief's four patrolmen was also Curly's nephew.

You give an inexperienced group of men a million-dollar budget to run a small town, and they'll screw it up every time, Seibert thought bitterly.

The ex-marine had been police chief for almost five years; and each time he was reappointed for a one-year term, it was a battle. Seibert longed for the day when he could quit his job and hang out his shingle as a private investigator. Rousting bored teenagers out of the town square at the complaint of the local shoe-store owner was not his idea of glamorous police work.

In any case, this was not the kind of morning he wanted to

spend paying a visit to Frenchy Theriault, whom Seibert suspected of being an arsonist and who had recently taken to telling people some very tall tales.

Theriault was a local tomato farmer, best known in the area for the little wooden stand that sold farm produce in the autumn months to tourists passing through on their way to see the annual explosion of foliage in the Berkshire Mountains of western Massachusetts.

Unfortunately the man now seemed to be retailing bullshit as well, the police chief thought. Lately, Frenchy had taken to telling folks in town that his house was possessed and that his family was being haunted by the spirit of his wife Nancy's mother.

Seibert, who had his own mother-in-law, was perfectly prepared to accept the story—if Nancy Theriault's mother had been alive. But Nancy's mother had died over fifteen years earlier.

Seibert couldn't help smiling a little, despite his irritation, as he recalled his own report on an incident at the station house a week before.

"On February 24, 1985," he had written, "Maurice 'Frenchy' Theriault came into the Warren Police Department asking that the department take custody of several rifles he owned. Asked if there was any problem, Mr. Theriault said he was seeing a psychic, and he had been informed by the psychic that he was possessed and should bring all his firearms to the police station. Mrs. Nancy Theriault was with her husband and informed the officers that she was the only one who could pick up any of the firearms from the police station, and not her husband. Mr. Theriault informed us that under no circumstances was he to be given the rifles, because he might not be himself. He may look like that person, but it might not really be him."

Seibert had suppressed a snort of laughter, glad enough to get the guns out of Frenchy's hands. He had duly recorded two Winchester rifles and a shotgun.

Seibert had nothing against Frenchy. In fact, he kind of liked the little guy. Theriault was only about five and a half feet tall and wore a thin mustache. His face and hands were lined from a lifetime of labor and the sockets of his eyes were deep-set, giving him a tired, brooding look that put a lot of people off. But once you got to know him, Seibert thought, he was nice enough. Last Thanksgiving, Frenchy had come to the station house with turkeys for each of the officers on the force.

But since then Seibert had ticketed Frenchy twice because his dilapidated truck, which he used to haul the tomatoes he grew, was nowhere near roadworthy. And then there were the fires in the Theriault farmhouse. Dan Prescott, at the state fire-marshal's office, suspected Frenchy had started the small blazes himself in order to get the insurance money. Seibert was inclined to agree with him.

In any case, he thought, that certainly seemed more likely than Frenchy's explanation. When he'd reported them, Frenchy had said the fires were caused by mysterious forces that invaded the house and caused objects to fly around on their own. But cops don't buy supernatural excuses for suspected crimes.

That's a laugh, Seibert thought. Frenchy had undoubtedly concocted this nonsense to sidetrack the arson investigation. Pretty original though.

At least Frenchy added a bit of local color to Warren.

■ ■ ■

But Seibert wasn't in the mood for it today and was none too pleased to find himself driving up to Frenchy's house. Nancy Theriault had called the station in a panic, screaming that she needed help. She had said she was afraid not only for herself but also for her three young grandchildren who were visiting them at the time. Seibert could only imagine what might be going on there. Rumors of weird events at the house had been circulating in the village and were growing more and more bizarre with each retelling. Seibert had decided to take a camera with him. Maybe some photographic evidence might quash the ridiculous stories, he thought.

Things had gotten to the point where Frenchy was being shunned. Seibert had been in the diner two weeks before when Frenchy came in and sat down for his usual midmorning cup of coffee. The other five customers looked at one another and quickly got up to pay their bills. Within two minutes the door had slammed shut, ringing the little brass bells that hung on the door. The diner was empty except for the cop, the tomato farmer, and Sam Davis, the owner.

It wasn't the first time Frenchy had caused a mass exodus from the diner.

Davis frowned and came over to say something to Frenchy when Seibert waved him off.

"Look, Frenchy, you're ruinin' Sam's business," Seibert had said. "You're gonna have to stop this bullshit about your house bein' possessed, or you're gonna have to stop comin' here. You understand?"

The farmer hadn't replied. He merely nodded his head and stared into his coffee cup.

Seibert's recollections were interrupted when his two-way radio crackled.

"Jerry, you need any help with that domestic?"

Seibert recognized the voice of Massachusetts State Trooper Colin Kerns. Trooper Kerns was assigned to the nearby Brookfield state police barracks, and the two men had a good working relationship. It was common practice for them to respond to emergency calls together. Local residents who had seen them in action often remarked on the striking physical contrast: Seibert, the tall French-Canadian, and Kerns, the tall, rangy black man.

Seibert suspected this morning's call was more of Frenchy Theriault's effort to cover up his role in the fires at his own house, but in the back of his mind he felt a squirm of uneasiness over the wild rumors and talk of supernatural events. Although he was a skeptical and case-hardened police officer, he was also a practicing Roman Catholic. It wouldn't hurt to have a witness in addition to the camera, he convinced himself.

The police chief picked up the microphone on his mobile police radio. "Yeah, Colin, come along for the ride," he said. A minute hadn't passed before he saw Kerns's blue-and-gray state-police cruiser fall in behind him.

As they approached the Theriault property, Seibert couldn't help thinking that if the farmhouse *was* haunted, it was certainly in the perfect spot for it. Perched on a knoll, just off quiet Brimfield Road, the house stood alone, with no other houses in sight. The bare oak trees and slate-gray clouds above lent a desolation that gave Seibert a shudder.

The simple New England frame house was rickety and badly in need of repairs. Especially, Seibert thought, since the fires that had been "mysteriously" started in recent months.

About two hundred yards from the main house was a one-story greenhouse with a tin roof. Fifty yards farther on was a storage shed in the shape of a huge aluminum barrel set into the ground. The fields around the house bristled with short sticks that in a couple of months would support the vines that produced Frenchy Theriault's juicy red tomatoes. Completely encircling the open fields was a thick forest of pine trees, enclosing the farm from the outside world.

It saddened Seibert to see the once-proud farmhouse running to ruin. But that wasn't so unusual these days in Warren. Farming just didn't support a family the way it used to, and the central Massachusetts village had seen better days. The high-tech boom that had sparked Massachusetts's economic revival, bringing new jobs and prosperity to the state, had bypassed small farming towns like Warren.

Seibert had been to the house on several occasions. Frenchy Theriault had twice called the station in the middle of the night to complain of strange noises outside his house.

The police chief's subsequent investigation had turned up no evidence of any noises—or of anything that might be causing them—and Seibert was inclined to think that this problem, too, was largely in Frenchy's head.

Seibert's investigation hadn't reassured the farmer. He kept insisting he'd heard the noises and talked darkly of other things done to "torment" him. Theriault's wife, Nancy, clearly frightened, had supported her husband's story. The law officer thought she was mainly scared of what Frenchy might do to her if she didn't agree with him.

Theriault did have problems. And they were not just in his head, as the police chief was about to find out.

■ ■ ■

As Seibert passed the ramshackle farm stand that stood at the entrance to the Theriault driveway, he slowed to make his turn. He couldn't count the number of times he had seen Frenchy, Nancy, and one or more of her kids weighing tomatoes at the stand, most of the time for city dwellers who were just passing through and had rarely tasted a real farm-grown tomato. Those damned things in the supermarket didn't taste any more like a tomato than a baseball did, as far as Warren's chief of police was concerned.

Seibert swung past the stand and pulled up near the house. Getting out of the cruiser, he buttoned the top button of his jacket against the icy air and slammed the door shut. There, he thought. Another strange noise for Frenchy to complain about.

Nearing the house, he heard something that made him look up toward the clouds weighing down on the farm and darkening the late-morning sky. The weather vane at the top of the Theriault home was spinning wildly, yet there wasn't a hint of breeze.

That's weird. It's as if there's a hurricane blowing, Seibert thought.

He heard another car pulling up on the frozen gravel driveway. Wheeling around, he let out a sigh as he recognized Trooper Kerns. For a moment he had forgotten he was being followed.

"What do we have, Jerry?" Kerns rolled down the window and called out.

"I dunno," Seibert replied. "Maybe Frenchy's beating his wife or something. Come on, let's go in."

The two officers made their way along the path to the darkened side entrance of the Theriault house. It was a distraught Nancy Theriault who opened the ripped screen door. She was clutching a multicolored crocheted blanket, which was wrapped around her shoulders.

Forty-three years old, Maurice Theriault's wife was known in the town as a pleasant, quiet woman who sold tomatoes with her husband and accompanied him to St. Paul's Catholic Church when they made one of their infrequent Sunday appearances. With cascades of curly reddish-brown hair and—in normal circumstances—a ready country-style smile, people often told her she looked like singing star Loretta Lynn.

"Yeah," Nancy would say. "She's the coal miner's daughter, and I'm the tomato farmer's wife."

Whatever he thought of Maurice, Seibert resolved to be gentle with Nancy, who was shaking uncontrollably, her face streaked with tears.

"He's in there," she cried, pointing toward the kitchen.

The officers stepped heavily in their boots down the hall. Seibert went first, with Kerns a step behind.

"Be careful," Nancy whispered in a frightened voice.

■ ■ ■

Maurice Theriault was sitting at the kitchen table, with a dazed expression on his face. Blood streaked the black-and-gray stubble on his chin. He looked at the two officers as if he was exhausted and surprised to see them.

"What's going on, Frenchy?" Seibert asked.

"I dunno, I dunno," the farmer replied in a voice that seemed to come from far away.

Nancy Theriault pointed mutely at the bathroom door just

outside the kitchen. Kerns hesitated and looked twice at Seibert before stepping forward and spinning the well-worn glass door-knob. The door was stuck, so he gave it a kick. It groaned and flew open.

For an instant both men stood paralyzed. The black-and-white tile floor of the tiny, stark bathroom was smeared with blood. The old-fashioned bathtub was streaked with it. The medicine-cabinet mirror was flecked with it. The bathroom even smelled of blood.

Seibert instinctively reached for his gun. He was blocking the door and Kerns wanted out of the gruesome bathroom.

"This didn't happen 'cause he cut himself shaving," Kerns muttered to Seibert.

"Nancy, what happened here?" Seibert demanded.

"I can't tell you," she choked out. "You'll think we're crazy or criminals or something. Just like when we turned in the guns."

Seibert did his best to reassure Nancy that he only wanted her statement for his report. Finally she agreed to tell him what had happened.

Maurice had gone into the bathroom after breakfast. A few minutes later, Nancy said, she became worried and knocked on the door. She heard bizarre sounds coming from the other side, and fearing for her husband, she pushed the door open.

Then she had screamed.

In the middle of a pool of blood Maurice Theriault, his face contorted beyond recognition, was lying on his back in a fetal position, gyrating like a top. His tobacco-stained teeth were bared in a wolfish grimace and his eyes were rolled back, exposing only the whites. He was emitting a mournful wail and babbling what seemed to be words, but were not in any language his wife had ever heard. Red froth bubbled from the corner of his mouth.

Petrified as she was, Nancy grabbed Maurice under each arm. He seemed to weigh a ton. But she managed to drag him out of the bathroom and into the kitchen, leaving a sweep of blood on the hardwood floor of the hallway.

As soon as she had touched him Maurice calmed considerably, although he continued to mutter incomprehensible sounds.

"That's what happened," she said. "That's the honest truth."

As she was telling the officers the story, Maurice sat propped in a rusted folding chair. Although no one had noticed it at first, blood was seeping from his eyes.

"Holy shit," Kerns said, his uniform soaked with sweat. He wiped perspiration from his upper lip and shook his head. "You ever seen anything like that?"

Nancy Theriault, trying to control her trembling, dabbed at Maurice's eyes with a tissue, even as her own continued to stream tears.

Seibert, who had gone to the sink for a glass of water, was trying to decide if he should call for an ambulance. As he turned to Maurice, the glass of water slipped from his hand and shattered on the floor. All the others, except Maurice, jumped at the sound.

"Colin, come here," said Seibert in a strangled whisper. "Look at his back!"

From the rear the blood on Maurice's T-shirt formed a pattern the two officers instantly recognized. They looked at each other in disbelief.

"Let's get his shirt off," said Seibert.

With no resistance from the semiconscious farmer, the two men peeled off his shirt and stood back.

Nancy Theriault had seen it all before. But that didn't make it any less frightening. She started to scream. "Oh, Frenchy, not again!"

The two policemen didn't even hear her. They were staring at the crimson lines on Maurice's back. Lines that any Christian would recognize.

Lines in the sign of the cross.

"Nancy, what *really* is going on here?" Seibert demanded when she had calmed down enough to talk.

The police chief had taken Polaroid photos of the farmer's back, photos that clearly showed the marks. Seibert was a cop, and despite the weird happenings in the Theriault home, he tried hard to think like a cop.

He knew that in any crisis a police officer has to be aware of his surroundings, the possibilities, and the probabilities. The probability was, he thought, that Nancy Theriault had scratched her husband or that he had fallen down and bled a lot from superficial wounds, although Seibert had yet to see any. The possibilities, on the other hand, were endless—and Seibert didn't like to think about them.

"I—I don't know...I don't know what's g-going on," Nancy stammered. "Strange things have been happening to Maurice. Awful things. I've been so frightened. I know you don't believe us about the sounds, but we hear them every night now. And the other day Maurice was standing there, right there where you're standing"—and she pointed at Kerns—"and suddenly he flew across the room as if he had been hit by a truck."

Trooper Kerns, hardened cop though he was, did a quick side-step off the spot where Nancy said Maurice had been standing.

"It was like he was a little doll and somebody had flung him against the wall," Nancy continued. "Sometimes his face changes and I don't even know who he is. Last week he picked up our tractor by himself."

The two policemen looked at each other. The Theriaults' tractor weighed almost two tons.

Kerns sensed that something else was bothering Nancy. "Is there something you're not telling us?" he asked.

"You'll think I'm crazy. I don't want everyone to say I'm crazy," Nancy sobbed.

"Just tell us about it, Nancy," Kerns said, putting his muscular arm around her shoulder. "Nobody's going to say anything."

She took a deep breath that was interrupted by little gasps from crying. It felt good to have the police here. They could protect her and the grandchildren if Maurice were to go off the deep end again. Yet she didn't know how much of the story to tell them. She didn't want to see them haul her husband—or her—off to the nuthouse. But she couldn't help but blurt out another incident anyway.

"Well..." she said, glancing nervously at Maurice. "Last week I saw two of him."

"What?"

"Two Maurices."

"What do you mean? He looked different?"

"No! No! There were two of him! I saw them. There's a word for it, doppel-something."

Kerns sighed. What with bleeding eyes, crosses, unknown languages, and double apparitions, it was turning into quite a morning. He was not looking forward to writing the report on this one.

While Maurice sat staring into space, almost as if he wasn't there, the two cops sat down at the kitchen table and took notes while Nancy told them more of her story:

"My daughter and I were sitting in the living room watching TV. This was last month, before I sent her away to New York to live with her father, and you remember how cold it was, maybe ten degrees. Suddenly Maurice walked by in his jeans and under-shirt, heading out the front door. I called out to him that it was too cold, but he kept on going, right out the door. My daughter ran back into her room to get her coat—she was going to catch him—but when she passed the door to our bedroom, I heard her scream, so I ran up there too. There was Maurice, sitting on the bed, putting on his shoes!"

Nancy insisted there was no possibility Maurice could have doubled back down the hall. She hadn't removed her eyes from the front door. Besides, only seconds had elapsed.

Maurice was as bewildered by the incident as Nancy was. He insisted he hadn't gone near the living room or the front door but was just getting ready to go out.

The two policemen questioned Nancy repeatedly, and although skeptical of her account, were convinced she was sincere. Turning to Maurice, Kerns felt nausea welling up inside. Blood was still seeping from Maurice's eyes. He stared at the trooper with a grotesque leer. Kerns nearly knocked over a jar of instant coffee that was sitting at his elbow.

"Jesus Christ!" the startled cop shouted. He watched, horrified, as Maurice's expression turned to one of demented fury.

"What the hell do we do, Jerry?" asked the shaken Kerns.

Seibert had been wondering the same thing. But he had an idea. He had seen enough.

"We're going to call Father Beardsley."

■ ■ ■

On the other side of Warren, Father Galen Beardsley, a rotund, elderly parish priest, was eating his lunch—a tuna sandwich, a pickle and chips, and a cup of milk. Beardsley had been pastor of St. Paul's in Warren for five years and was nearing retirement age. He already had his mobile home down at the trailer park and was dreaming of the day he would move into it. When the telephone rang, he gazed regretfully at his tuna sandwich, and a flash of apprehension went through him.

Father Beardsley had a premonition that the phone call had something to do with Frenchy Theriault, and unlike the local police chief, the priest was certain Frenchy's problems were genuine. He had already been out to the Theriault home on more than one occasion and blessed the house. But he had seen enough in those visits to know that whatever was going on was more than he was equipped to handle.

The parish priest who had preceded him in his post had been called out one night to visit the home of a man who claimed to be possessed by demons. According to the local records, the man had tried to kill the priest when he first visited. With holy water and prayers, the man's bizarre behavior had ceased. But it was too late for the priest. He died shortly afterward at the young age of fifty-five.

That's why, a few weeks earlier, Father Beardsley had called in a pair of demonologists, Ed and Lorraine Warren, to investigate what was going on with Frenchy Theriault.

So as the phone rang he thought it might be the Warrens calling. They had promised to come up to Warren again over the weekend to continue their investigation of the phenomena that had been plaguing Frenchy Theriault.

Father Beardsley picked up the phone and listened intently

for several minutes as Seibert recounted the morning's events.

"Chief," said the priest, taking a deep breath, "there's nothing you can do. This thing is bigger than you. In fact, it's bigger than both of us. But there are some people who are trying to help. Their names are Ed and Lorraine Warren. They're demonologists. They're already familiar with what's been going on. In fact, they've been up here a couple of times."

"Oh?" said Seibert.

"They're supposed to come back again soon," Father Beardsley said. "They're trying to decide if Frenchy needs an exorcism. I think I'll call them again right now and see if they can come up here tonight. I don't know if we can wait any longer."

"That's for sure," said the stunned Seibert. "Somebody's got to do something soon."

After hanging up, Beardsley gazed out of the rectory window for several minutes. Then he reached for his Rolodex, flipping through it until he came to the W's. When he found the number for the Warrens, he slowly reached for the phone and dialed the number in Connecticut. As he dialed he thought about what Chief Seibert had told him. It seemed as if things were getting worse for Frenchy. He hoped that the Warrens could get back up here quickly. The situation was definitely out of control.

As he listened to the ring of the phone, Father Beardsley looked up at the crucifix above his desk.

"We're going to need your help on this one, Lord," he whispered.

TWO

FALL IN MAINE. The leaves turn from green to a patchwork of colors. The trees explode into a canvas of brilliant hues—red, then orange, yellow, gold, and finally brown, before they drop to the ground.

Ten-year-old Maurice Theriault was trudging through the fallen leaves that had gathered along the side of St. John Road on his way home from school. There was a pleasing scent of burning leaves in the cold air. Maurice's cheeks were ruddy and his nose was runny.

He was small for his age, but muscular. Perhaps it was the line of his jaw that made him seem older, or his tired eyes. His neck and shoulders were well developed from working in the potato fields and the barn for as long as he could remember. He always wore the same blue-plaid shirt and jeans, which his mother carefully patched and repatched at the elbows and knees.

Poverty was a way of life among the farmers in tiny Van

Buren, Maine, in 1946. Located directly on the Canadian bolder in rural Aroostook County, Van Buren, population 4,500, was home to many of Maine's potato farms. Even in the midst of postwar prosperity, life was hard for those who had to scratch a living out of Maine's rocky soil.

St. John Road ran alongside the St. John River and eventually connected to Main Street, the heart of what passed for downtown in tiny Van Buren. As he walked Maurice spotted a group of boys playing in a pile of leaves in a field where the road bent. He quickened his pace, secretly wishing he could join them but hoping they wouldn't see him.

Sometimes some of the other boys made fun of him when they spotted him coming, because he usually stank of cow dung. They teased him unmercifully and he hated it.

Even though the other kids also lived on farms, their fathers let them enjoy their childhoods. Maurice didn't have that luxury.

Their lives seemed so different from his. For one thing, most of the boys his age were in higher grades. They didn't have to miss school as often as he did in order to help their fathers out on their farms. Of course they had chores to do, but the other boys weren't expected to do nearly as much as Maurice had to do. It hurt Maurice to be different, and he felt like an outcast.

He continued to walk home as he usually did, head down, looking at the pavement.

As he walked Maurice thought back to the day the previous spring when his father had bought a new tractor. "Drive it, or else," his father had threatened. The child tried his best but couldn't master what was really a man's job. His little legs couldn't reach the pedals. Short legs were no excuse, as far as Philippe Theriault was concerned. He was determined that Maurice would work as a full-fledged farmhand. When his son failed in a task, even one a grown man might find difficult, Philippe would respond with a stinging smack in the face or a humiliating kick in the behind.

Philippe Theriault didn't have a loving bone in his body. He towered over Maurice, his menacing presence much taller than his actual five feet nine inches. His mouth was a permanent scowl, formed by the deeply etched lines from his nose. His thick wire-rimmed glasses made his eyes a tiny blur. The few times Maurice saw his father without his glasses, he seemed almost human.

It was a cruel illusion. Philippe would just as soon slap Maurice as say hello to him. For Maurice, there were no fatherly hugs or pats on the back. Philippe had little use for his other children either, but Maurice, as the eldest, bore the brunt of his abuse. By the time he was ten Maurice already had nine brothers and sisters. Eventually there would be fifteen children in all.

But there was no even division of labor—or abuse—around the Theriault farm.

Maurice was followed by three girls, Jean, Pam, and Sue. But because they were girls, Philippe didn't expect them to help out much, especially with the hard chores. He pretty much ignored them.

After the three girls came Philippe, Jr., called "Phil." He was

Philippe's pet. Whatever affection Philippe could muster went to Phil. Then came Betty, Judy, and Anne. Philippe ignored them as he did the other girls.

Seven more children would eventually follow, but none would ever get the treatment that Philippe had reserved for his first-born.

Even as a toddler in St. Agatha, where the Theriaults had lived before Philippe purchased the farm in Van Buren, Maurice hid under his bed, hoping his father wouldn't find him and hit him. At first Maurice just feared his father. Before long he hated him with a burning passion.

But as much as he hated the coldhearted farmer, Maurice would not think of disobeying his father's commands. If he did, he knew to expect a blow—from the back of his father's hand, his fist, or even a two-by-four if that was nearby.

If he was late coming home today, he thought as he hurried, head down, past the children frolicking in the leaves, he shuddered to think what his punishment would be. It was harvest season and Philippe had a full afternoon's work planned for Maurice. One quick look at the boys jumping in the leaves and Maurice speeded up his pace for home.

When he reached the weathered brown farmhouse little Maurice looked for his mother, hoping she might be in the kitchen baking some of the French-Canadian pastries that he loved so much.

Alice Theriault was a short, slender woman, with a long brown braid down her back that was turning frosty gray at her crown.

Her round brown eyes and oval-shaped face reminded Maurice of an angel he had seen on a stained-glass window in church. He thought of it whenever he saw her hair unwound from its braid. Maurice marveled at how neat and clean she looked despite the hours of drudgery in the farmhouse and the even more grueling days out in the fields. But her hands were rough and calloused. The nails were short and the knuckles were reddened, swollen from hours of pounding a washboard, doing laundry by hand for her large family.

Since his brothers and sisters were too young to stand up to Philippe, Alice was the only person on earth Maurice could turn to for help. She tried to protect him from Philippe's rage, often standing between them and taking a blow herself. Maurice wished he could stop that from happening, but it was impossible. All he could do was weep for his mother. But they never discussed his father's violence. Never.

To his disappointment, his mother was not in the kitchen when he arrived home. Most likely she was out in the field, picking potatoes, following Philippe's orders.

Gulping down a glass of milk, Maurice went looking for his father. He wasn't aware of the milk mustache left on his upper lip. Better not to dawdle and incur Philippe's wrath.

Maurice looked downhill toward the barn and saw his father entering it. Probably going to fix a piece of machinery or tend to a sick animal, Maurice thought. The boy wanted to watch, hoping he could learn something useful. But he also knew that if he asked his father to teach him, his reward would be a curse or a beating. Maurice decided to slip into the barn and secretly watch from behind a bale of hay. Maybe if he learned something on his own, his father would be pleased.

The boy took his time walking to the barn, trying to drum up enough courage to spy on his father. He tried to anticipate his father's unpredictable rages, and in his head he continually heard Philippe's booming voice screaming at him. No matter what the circumstances, Maurice just couldn't win.

When Maurice reached the barn door, he grabbed the old iron handle and pulled quietly. The familiar warmth of the barn and its smell enveloped him as he slipped inside. The light from outside poured into the barn and seemed to shine like a spotlight into one of the stalls. He heard some shuffling in the hay.

When he saw what his father was doing, his jaw dropped and his eyes opened wide.

The boy wasn't quite sure what was going on, but he knew he shouldn't be there. He tried to run, but he was frozen, as in a nightmare. A hot flash raced through him as he imagined himself being spotted.

Maurice wondered if he should stay put or get out of there as quickly as possible. He pondered the alternatives for a moment, gulped, and made his decision. Turning to sneak out, Maurice didn't see the black pitchfork that had been leaning against the bale of hay. He only brushed against it, but that was enough to send it clanking noisily to the ground. The sound startled

Philippe, who immediately stopped what he'd been doing and looked around. His eyes locked on Maurice and the boy froze with panic.

"Maurice."

Philippe's voice sounded like thunder.

Maurice trembled. "Yes, Papa." He could hardly get the words out of his mouth.

"Maurice, come here."

The boy hesitated.

"Maurice, come here or I will kill you," Philippe said, his eyes still riveted on his frightened son.

Maurice walked slowly toward the stall.

"I want you to watch me," Philippe said, resuming what he had been doing before he was interrupted.

Maurice could hardly bear to watch, but he didn't dare look away.

A few minutes later Philippe was finished.

Maurice turned, poised to run, but his father's voice held him in place. "Now do what I was doing," his father commanded.

Maurice closed his eyes and tried to imitate his father, all the while wishing he were anywhere else.

After a few minutes Philippe told him to stop. "If you're going to watch me, then you're going to have to do what I do," he said. "Next time maybe you won't watch me. And you better not say a word to anybody about this. If you do, you'll die. And I'll bury you in a manure pit."

With that, Philippe strode out of the barn, bellowing a depraved laugh.

Maurice began to cry, not sure what it was that he had just done but understanding that it was somehow evil. What he didn't know—couldn't have known—was that with this act, he had opened the door to a lifetime of torment. And that the perpetrator of that torment would make Philippe seem like a pussycat.

Maurice kept his terrible secret for three years. During that time Philippe continued his forays into the barn and often forced Maurice to join him. Maurice knew what he was doing was sick and terrible, and he hated himself for doing it. He always felt an evil presence in that barn.

Maurice was growing up sullen and introspective. His posture was changing. His once erect frame was now stooped, and his head was bowed from continually looking at the ground.

Only with his mother did Maurice feel safe, but he was betraying her by keeping his terrible secret, and he felt overwhelmed by guilt. He thought of confessing his sin to Father Mainard, but he was too ashamed—even in the dark privacy of the confessional. He felt too ashamed to even look at the cross.

His mother asked him several times what his father did in the barn, but Maurice couldn't bring himself to tell her either. The boy did his best to hide his torment, but inside he imagined he was already in hell.

One day he was enjoying a piece of fresh apple pie with his mother in the security of her kitchen, when he decided to be brave. "Mama," the boy whispered. "You know how you're always asking me what Papa is doing when he goes to the barn? If you want to know, why don't you watch?"

That was as close as he could come to telling her.

Alice Theriault knew that her thirteen-year-old son was troubled, but rather than press him she decided to act on his suggestion. She dreaded what she might discover. Worse, she dreaded that Philippe might find out she was spying on him. That would mean a certain beating. But she had to discover her husband's secret.

Maurice waited upstairs in his room as his mother headed for the barn. He was so apprehensive he could hardly breathe. Please, God, he prayed, don't let her get caught.

He opened the window and breathed as silently as he could in order to hear better. He sank to his knees and recited the Lord's Prayer. His knuckles turned white from being squeezed so hard.

Before he could finish he heard his father's voice—and he knew the worst had happened.

"You bitch! You fucking bitch! What the hell do you think you're doing in here?"

Maurice heard a sharp crack, then a scream.

Oh, God! Oh, God, I hope she's all right, the boy prayed as a chill went up and down his spine.

"I'm going to kill you someday, woman!" he heard his father scream. "I swear I'm going to kill you someday."

Maurice sobbed. There was something in his father's voice that made him sure it was more than just an idle threat.

But Maurice didn't have time just then to dwell on the threat on his mother's life. The barn door burst open and Philippe was already on his way to the farmhouse to hunt for him.

"*Maurice, tu vas payer pour ça!* You're going to pay for this!"

Maurice thought about running and hiding, but where would he go? Philippe would find him and beat him even worse.

The door burst open. Philippe stood there bare-chested, in his dirty workpants, his hair a mess. The veins in his face seemed as though they would burst, and his eyes seemed to pop through those thick glasses.

"You little bastard," he screamed. "I told you not to tell her."

"I didn't tell her, Papa," Maurice whimpered. "Ask her if you don't believe me..."

But Philippe didn't even hear Maurice's answer. He had pulled his belt out of its loops and was already waving the strap around like a madman. A strange gurgle was coming from his throat.

Philippe attacked his son furiously, whipping him repeatedly all over his body. The razor-sharp belt sang through the air with each blow, drawing blood as Maurice curled into a ball and cowered under the assault.

By the time he had stopped, Philippe's belt was dripping with blood. He wiped it off on Maurice's quilted bedspread and put it back on before heading downstairs.

Maurice lay on his bed, sobbing, aching with pain. He cried from his gut, and wondered why he'd ever been born. He cried until there were no more tears, until he had no more strength. He stayed in a fetal position for hours, staring at a bloodstain that Philippe's strapping had left on his bedspread.

I hate him, I hate him, I hate him, he thought. I've got to get out of here.

Maurice's thoughts drifted back to a frigid February afternoon seven years earlier. He was walking home from school in a raging blizzard that started at eleven A.M. Most of the other children had been picked up by their fathers that day, but six-year-old Maurice was left to fend for himself, as usual. The howling wind and snow cut into his face. He pulled his hat down over his ears and wrapped his scarf across his mouth, but he couldn't escape the bitter cold. He could hardly see in front of him. Snow was swirling madly and the landscape was quickly turning white. His face stung and his fingers and toes were going numb.

The snow piled up fast. By the time Maurice was halfway home it was up to his knees. To escape the biting wind he took cover behind a snowbank that must have been five feet high. He crouched down to keep warm, and within minutes he was covered with snow. He began to cry. Unable to move his arms or legs, he slipped toward unconsciousness.

Maurice no longer felt the cold. Everything was white. Then the face of a man appeared. He had long brown hair, a neat brown beard, and soft, warm eyes. Instead of a plaid woodsman's jacket or a down vest, he wore only a white robe. The man looked at Maurice and smiled.

Despite the freezing weather the man didn't appear cold at all.

In fact, he seemed to radiate warmth.

Leaning over, the man extended his hands. He picked Maurice up almost without effort and began carrying him away. The man never said a word to Maurice.

The next thing the boy knew, he was home in bed. His mother fed him a bowl of hot soup and told him that he had somehow appeared safely on the porch of the farmhouse.

"It was Jesus who saved me, Mama," Maurice said.

Alice Theriault had not seen the man who had dropped her son off at her doorstep in the middle of the raging blizzard. But she had no doubt that Jesus was responsible. When she had seen how bad the storm was, she'd said a prayer, asking God's protection for her son on his way home from school. Jesus had answered her prayer by having one of the townspeople give her son a ride home, she was certain.

"I'm sure He did, Maurice," she said. "I'm sure He did."

Once Maurice had snapped out of his daydream, his tears had dried and his anger subsided. Just remembering that day had calmed him down. Perhaps Jesus would come and save him again.

■ ■ ■

By the next spring things had only gotten worse around the Theriault farm. It was planting season and Maurice was being made to work harder than ever. Whenever it was planting- or harvest-time he'd be forced to quit going to school for weeks at a time. As a result, he was far behind in his studies. Although he was thirteen, he was only in third grade. Some of his younger sisters, who weren't forced to work around the farm as if they were adults, had already passed him in school.

Maurice wasn't stupid, but everybody treated him as if he were. When Philippe did allow him to attend school, he'd still have to work each afternoon after classes and all day on weekends. Even though the other kids picked on him at school, it was better than staying home to work with his father. Working alongside his father meant being yelled at for the smallest mistake and being slapped or kicked. Philippe Theriault hated his own existence and took it out on everyone, especially his eldest son.

Maurice got to the point where he'd do anything rather than work with his father. One day Maurice was having trouble starting the tractor when his father exploded at him. "Maurice, you no-good bastard, can't you even start the machine?"

"I'm sorry, Papa. It must be broken. I'm doing it the way I usually do it."

Philippe charged at his son, huffing and snorting like a bull. He jumped up onto the tractor and pushed him as hard as he could with both hands, knocking the boy off his seat and onto the ground.

Maurice fell with a thud, his head landing against a boulder. He got up slowly and began walking, dazed, toward the farmhouse, trying to stop the bleeding by holding his T-shirt tight against the gash in his scalp. Philippe took no notice. He had gotten the tractor started and was already driving away toward the potato field.

As he stumbled toward the farmhouse, Maurice's hatred for his father consumed him. He turned around and looked at Philippe disappearing into the distance.

"I'd rather work for the devil than work for you!" the boy shouted.

He felt a little better when he said it, so he said it again, this time louder. "I'd rather work for the devil than for you!" Maurice repeated it loudly, over and over again, as he neared the house.

In the kitchen Alice had just taken a strawberry-rhubarb pie out of the oven and was putting it on the windowsill to cool. Maurice's voice was ringing out across the yard:

"I'd rather work for the devil than for you!"

Alice shuddered when she overheard her son's sacrilegious oath.

Somewhere, someone else was listening too.

THREE

THE FOLLOWING DAY Philippe thumped up the stairs and barged into Maurice's bedroom, well before daylight.

Snapping on the ceiling light, he barked, "Let's go, Maurice, now! We've got some fields to plow."

Maurice groaned from under his pillow. "Can't I sleep a little longer, Papa?" The sudden flood of light was painful for Maurice's sleepy eyes.

Waking was always a disappointment because his dreams, when he could remember them, were so much more pleasant than real life. Sometimes he would try to retain the plots of his dreams and elaborate on them during the day. This particular morning he was dreaming about kissing a girl from school when the rude interruption came.

"I guess you didn't hear me, you lazy bastard. I said get out of bed *now*."

Philippe started to take out his strap, but Maurice was already out of bed, had pulled on his jeans, and was on his way downstairs to the kitchen. He gulped down a glass of milk, grabbed a croissant, and headed out the door toward the tractor.

"Maurice, you start up the tractor. And today I want you to do it right."

The boy grimaced. He dreaded what would happen if he failed again. He walked slowly toward the intimidating machine, going over in his mind the proper way to start it.

The seat squeaked as he climbed into it. He extended his left leg as far down as he could, using every ounce of strength he could muster to push the clutch to the floor. Then he turned the key and quickly put the gas pedal to the floor, while lifting his left leg off the clutch. This was where he usually got into trouble. He just couldn't seem to do all those things in a fluid sequence so that the machine would go forward without stalling.

But this time he had no trouble at all. Somehow his legs seemed longer. He hardly had to strain to keep the clutch down and when it came time to hit the gas and let go of the clutch, he did it easily. The tractor lurched slightly, then moved forward without a hitch, almost as if it were moving on its own.

This is easy, Maurice thought to himself, steering the tractor downhill toward the main potato field. The motion of the big tires over the rows of spring mud jostled his head and shoulders in syncopation with the motor. The sweet spring air, coupled with this new accomplishment, made Maurice feel heady. He felt older.

Maurice never had trouble starting the tractor again. And plowing the fields was no longer the torture that it had always been. Maurice couldn't figure it out. It seemed almost as though somebody were next to him, helping him do the work. It was an easy spring.

By fall he was running the tractor like a man. He harvested so many potatoes that even Philippe had trouble finding fault with him, although he certainly tried.

One day in late October Philippe and Maurice were boxing potatoes, and Philippe actually warned his son that he was working too hard. But it wasn't Maurice's welfare he was looking out for.

"Maurice, you're going too fast," Philippe said over his shoulder. "Take it easy. I don't want you to wear out now. We're just about finished harvesting. Next week we start hauling logs. You'll need all your strength for that."

Philippe was glad his son was now doing the work of a man, yet it bothered him to see the boy growing up. It might not be so easy to push him around anymore. Ah, what am I worrying about? he thought. The kid's only fourteen. I'm still in charge around here. And besides, I'll use his strength for hauling.

Every winter, between harvest and planting seasons, Philippe hauled logs to help make ends meet. It was the job Maurice dreaded most. The logs were so heavy that grown men often had trouble lifting them. And it was usually so cold that a few hours of work would leave his fingers numb, and his neck sore and stiff, so that lifting the logs became twice as difficult.

One December morning Philippe and Maurice were getting ready to haul a pile of logs to Paul Courcy's farm across town. The temperature had dropped to zero and the snow was falling hard.

Maurice was reaching for the snow chains. "Papa, they say we're going to have a blizzard," he said. "Maybe we should wait until the storm is over."

Philippe glared at his son. "That just shows how stupid you are," he shouted, curling his lip with disgust and shaking his finger at him. "If there's a storm, Paul's going to need his logs, isn't he? Now, start loading these fucking logs on the flatbed. And don't question me again."

It was the coldest day of the year so far. Maurice placed his hands against the muffler of the tractor to try to keep them warm. The freezing air stung his face, so he breathed through his scarf. Not daring to look at his father, he looked at his hands.

Maurice felt fire at the pit of his stomach. He hated his father so much. It was as if he were screaming inside at the very top of his lungs, but his voice was absolutely paralyzed, out of fear of his father's vicious temper.

Maurice got up and trudged over to the enormous woodpile, then reached for a log. To his astonishment, it seemed no heavier than a baseball bat. Yet the log was about three feet long and a foot in diameter.

Maurice tossed it onto the flatbed and reached over for another.

Again the log seemed as if it were balsa wood, except it was a log of sturdy pine. He picked it up without effort and placed it next to the first one.

At the other end of the woodpile, Philippe Theriault was huffing and puffing as he loaded log after log. Clouds of steam from his breath hung around him in the freezing air. "These goddamn things get heavier every year," he muttered.

Philippe hadn't been watching Maurice, but when he finished with his pile he looked over at the boy and saw that he had loaded every one of his logs. "Hey, since when are you able to keep up with me?" he said, looking sidelong at the boy.

Maurice didn't know what to say, so he just looked down at the ground and shrugged his shoulders. Inside, he wondered how he'd been able to lift the logs so effortlessly. It was almost as if he'd had help, he thought.

Maurice didn't know who'd been helping him, but he was appreciative. He started giving thanks each time he got help. *"Merci,"* he would whisper. *"Merci beaucoup."*

From then on Maurice would ask for help whenever he faced a difficult task. "Please, if there's somebody next to me, help me," he'd say. "I want your help."

More often than not he'd get it.

Maurice's mysterious ability to work as if he were a grown man—a very strong grown man—proved to be as much of a curse as a blessing. Philippe realized that he could now rely much more heavily on his son to help him run the farm. Late the next summer he decided that Maurice would have to quit school and begin working for him full-time. He told the boy over dinner one cool night in late August.

"Maurice, you're wasting your time at school," he blurted out as Alice passed him the bowl of mashed potatoes. "You're fifteen now and you're only goin' into fifth grade. You ain't never goin' to be nothin' but a farmer, boy. Face facts. So you may as well start working for me full-time. I need the help and you can do the work of two men. So you won't be goin' back to school next week."

Maurice was stunned. He didn't really like school, mostly because the other kids made fun of him for being so far behind, but he had been doing better toward the end of last year. He was studying hard and was starting to read a little. Every now and then he'd pick up a newspaper to look up the hockey scores.

Before he could say anything, his mother interjected on his behalf. "Philippe, *chéri,* I think Maurice would be better off in school," she said quietly. "I could do his work for him."

"Shut up, woman," Philippe shot back very loudly, pointing his finger at her. "I've made up my mind. The boy's school days are over. Starting now he's working for me full-time. End of discussion."

Maurice looked around at his brothers and sisters, hoping that somebody might say something, but it was not to be. They were all too scared to utter a sound.

Maurice felt as if he were burning inside again. He wanted to say something but knew it was hopeless. He'd become too useful around the farm. His father would never change his mind. He pushed his plate away, excused himself, and went up to his room. It seemed as if he were in a deep, dark hole from which there was no escape.

Later his mother came up the stairs quietly and knocked softly on the door. She came in and sat next to him on the bed.

"I'm sorry, Maurice," she said, putting her warm arms around him. She was wearing a smooth white sweater that felt so soft to Maurice. He put his head on her shoulder. "Maybe you can study a little at home. You can get some help from your brothers and sisters."

His mother made things a lot better. At least she was on his side, he thought. Maurice let out a big sigh.

"Don't worry about it, Mama," he answered. "Papa's probably right. I can barely read. I'm never going to amount to anything, except as a farmer or a workman, so I may as well get used to it. If only I could get away from him, I'd be all right."

So Maurice's school days were over. His fourth-grade education would have to do. He was no longer a kid. He was a farmer. He was going to bide his time until he could be on his own.

Maurice hated working with his father, but he actually enjoyed the work. Farming was satisfying. He liked to plant seeds and watch them grow. Sometimes when he was pulling out weeds, he would think of them as being evil, strangling what was good. He planted a bumper crop of tomatoes that year.

For the next three years he learned as much as he could about farming while he counted the days until his eighteenth birthday. On that day he'd be eligible to enlist in the army. He'd finally be free of Philippe Theriault's reign of terror.

Finally the long-awaited day came. July 13, 1954. Maurice was up early. It was a hot, sunny day, a perfect summer's day in Maine. Vacationers were heading to the St. John River to do some fishing. Maurice Theriault was on his way downtown to the army recruiting office. It was a five-mile hike from the Theriault farm into downtown Van Buren, but that didn't bother Maurice. He walked briskly. Today he would begin a new chapter in his life.

By the time he got to the recruiting office, Maurice was dripping sweat, but he wasn't tired. He was excited. His hands trembled as he filled out the stack of papers. By the time he was finished, Maurice was dreaming of the day when he'd be wearing army green, stationed maybe in Germany or France. Philippe Theriault would be far, far away.

The sergeant told him that his papers seemed to be in order and that all he needed was to pass the physical exam and he'd probably be inducted within two months. He passed the physical with flying colors.

Maurice was elated, but he knew the worst was yet to come. He'd have to tell his father what he had done. But this time he had the U.S. Army behind him.

When Maurice got home that afternoon Philippe was standing in the driveway, waiting from him. He was clearly upset.

"Where the hell you been all day?" he boomed.

Maurice looked down at his feet. In his mind he was seeing them in army boots. He decided to get right to the point. "I joined the army today, Papa," he said. "I'm goin' to be a soldier."

"The hell you are," Philippe said, his eyes narrowing.

"But, Papa," Maurice said, his face flushing. "I already signed the papers and passed the physical. I'm going to be inducted in two months."

"We'll see about that," Philippe said. "Right now, you've got some grass to cut. Now, get the hell out of here and do it, or I'll knock your goddamn block off."

Maurice went about his chores and managed to avoid his father for the rest of the day. The next morning, when Maurice awoke, Philippe wasn't around. Maurice was relieved not to have to face him.

"Where's Papa?" Maurice asked his mother, who was busy fixing oatmeal for the rest of the children.

"He took the pickup and went into town," she replied. "I don't know where he was goin', but it seemed important. He didn't even wait to have breakfast."

Maurice began to worry. A bad taste crept its way up his throat. "Do you think he's going to try to stop me from joining up?"

His mother sat down next to Maurice and gently held his hand. She looked him in the eye. "Maurice, he told me before we went to bed last night that he'd stop you from leaving the farm if it was the last thing he ever did. He needs your labor here. He can't afford to lose you. I don't want to lose you either, but I know that you need to get away from him. *C'est dommage,* it's too bad, his mind is made up. I'm sorry, *mon chéri.*"

It was about noon when Maurice heard his father's pickup coming up the driveway. He hopped out of the truck, a smug look on his face, and headed right for Maurice, who was fixing the barn door.

"You can forget about the army, you no-good bum." Philippe chuckled with evident satisfaction. "You ain't goin' *no*where."

He handed his son a piece of paper. Maurice could barely read it, but he didn't have any trouble recognizing a number and letter stamped at the top: 4-F.

"But...but I p-passed the physical," he stammered. He felt as if the wind had been knocked out of him.

"That's not what the army doc says today." Philippe was poking his pointed finger deep into Maurice's left shoulder. "You are out, boy. I told you that you're a farmer. And you'll be farming with me until you're at least twenty-one. If you try to leave, I'll get you. *C'est vrai.* That's a fact."

Maurice was crushed. He walked slowly into the house and up to his room. He threw himself down on his bed and started to cry. He cried until he had no voice.

The next morning Maurice woke up to his mother's opening the curtains in his room. She had made him some hot tea and cinnamon toast, which she placed next to him on the bed. Maurice was sorry to be awake.

"I'm sorry, Maurice," she said. "I wish I could have stopped him."

"How did he do it, Mama? How did he get me changed to 4-F?"

Alice Theriault put her arms around her son. "You know Papa and that army doctor go way back, Maurice."

Maurice faced three more years before he'd be free. It wasn't a pleasant thought, but he decided to make the best of it. Maybe he'd join the National Guard. At least he'd be able to get out of the house a few nights a week and an occasional weekend.

When fall finally rolled around, Maurice did just that. But after he attended just three meetings, Philippe started interfering. After dinner one night Maurice dressed up in his uniform, waiting outside for his friend Girard Laurent to pick him up for the meeting.

Philippe came out of the house. "Maurice, I want you to clean up the barn tonight," he said, taking a swig from a bottle of beer.

"But, Papa, I have a Guard meeting tonight. Why didn't you ask me last night?"

Philippe came up right next to him. Maurice could smell the beer on his breath. "I don't need a reason, boy," said Philippe. "Now get to work."

"But I'll get in trouble. You just can't miss a Guard meeting without a good excuse—"

"Look, you little shit, I didn't want you to join, but you did it anyway. Now, don't disobey me again, or I'll fuckin' flatten you."

Maurice turned around and walked slowly upstairs. The familiar sense of hopelessness hung in the air. He carefully took off his brand-new uniform and put it in his closet. He got back into his jeans and trudged out to the barn. It was the last time he would put on that uniform.

From then on Philippe would always find something for him to do on meeting nights. Maurice went to see his unit commander.

"I—I can't continue in the Guard, sir," Maurice said, a sheepish look on his face.

"What do you mean, son?" asked Captain George Thibadeau. "You can't just quit the Guard."

"I can't help it, sir," Maurice said, looking down and speaking in almost a whisper. "My father wants me home and I can't go. I wish I could, but I can't." His face was red with shame.

"I'll talk to him," Captain Thibadeau replied.

Maurice shrugged his shoulders. He knew better than to hope. Somehow Philippe always won.

The next day Captain Thibadeau drove out to the Theriault farm to talk to Philippe.

Maurice saw the two of them talking out by the barn. A few minutes later Thibadeau got back into his Jeep and drove off.

Philippe gave Maurice the news at dinner. "Talked to your captain today," he said, stuffing a forkful of meatloaf into his mouth. "You're no longer in the Guard."

Maurice wasn't surprised this time. Nothing his father did surprised him anymore. He knew Philippe would find a way to

stop him. About all that was left to do was to feel sorry for himself and go through the motions.

■   ■   ■

He was still feeling bad the following Saturday as he drove the
truck back to the farm after having hauled a load of logs all the
way to Ashland, a sixty-mile drive. He still didn't have his driver's license because Philippe wouldn't let him go for the test. But
he insisted Maurice haul the logs anyway. He told him to use the
back roads so he wouldn't be spotted by a cop. Ashland was the
farthest Maurice had ever driven, but he had no problems with
the haul.

On his way back home he stopped in downtown Van Buren
to buy a chocolate for his mother. She loved chocolates, but
Philippe would never buy her any. He would never get her anything. So Maurice would sometimes get her one when he had a
spare nickel, which wasn't often. Despite all the work he did at
the farm, Philippe refused to pay him. "I feed you, don't I?" was
his usual reply when Maurice would ask for a dollar or two so he
could go out to a movie. "That's all I gotta do."

As he walked out of the candy store with his mother's gift,
Maurice spotted Josette Vallery, a girl he used to know at school.
She had always been nice to him.

Josette was short, with very white skin, blond hair, and large
almond-shaped brown eyes. Her face was framed by a white silk

scarf, and she wore a green loden coat. He wanted to talk to her, but he was too shy. He put his head down and started to walk the other way.

"Maurice..."

He heard Josette call his name.

"Maurice, is that you?"

He turned around. She had a big smile on her face.

"Hi, Josette." He felt uncomfortable talking to girls, but she was so easygoing.

"Maurice, its nice to see you. Where have you been?"

"I had to quit school, Josette. My father is making me work for him."

"Is he still as mean as ever?" Philippe was famous in town for being someone to avoid.

"Worse. Working for him is like working in hell."

"I'm sorry to hear that. Maybe you should move off the farm. Work for yourself."

"If only I could. But he won't let me leave until I'm twenty-one."

"I know how you feel, Maurice. My parents are very strict too. But they finally said I could start going out on dates. I just wish someone would ask me."

Maurice may have been uneducated, but he wasn't a fool.

"Uh, uh...maybe, you know, maybe you and me, we could go out to a movie or something sometime," Maurice blurted out.

Josette's eyes lit up. She was glad Maurice had taken the opening she had given him. She had always liked him and she felt sorry for him because of how his father treated him.

"How about tonight? There's a new movie in town at the Bijou. It's a John Wayne movie. You'd like that."

Maurice could hardly believe his ears.

"You bet, Josette! I'll pick you up at seven."

He almost skipped back to the truck. When he got home Maurice was in a good mood. He felt that maybe things were beginning to go his way.

"Hi, Mama," he said, bounding up the stairs to his room. He made a beeline for his top dresser drawer, reached inside, and felt around for his money. He always kept it in an envelope way in the back corner.

Then a sinking feeling came over him. There wasn't anything in there but a handful of change. He counted it. Only seventy-three cents. Admission to the movie was fifty cents each, and he'd need at least a buck to take Josette out for a Coke later at the soda fountain.

He'd have to ask his mother.

He ran down the stairs. "Mama, Mama," he yelled excitedly. "I got a date with Josette, a girl I know from school! We're goin' to the movies tonight. But I don't got enough money, Mama. Can I please have a couple dollars? Please, Mama?"

Alice Theriault was happy for her son. He had been moping around for so long, she was pleased to see him excited about something. She went to the cookie jar, but when she reached inside, it was empty. She'd had five dollars in there the last time she'd looked. Philippe must have taken it. She'd seen him come home with two six-packs of beer the day before.

She had to fight back the tears. She was planning to buy some material for a new dress. And she dearly wanted Maurice to go on his date tonight.

Alice went up to the bedroom and found Philippe's pants. She looked inside the pocket and found one dollar and a receipt for a five-dollar purchase of beer at the food store. She decided to take the dollar and give it to Maurice. She'd have hell to pay, but she wasn't going to sit by and have all her son's happiness taken away.

"Maurice, I can only give you one dollar," she said. "That will get the two of you into the picture show. You'll have to figure something else out if you want to take her for a soda afterward."

"*Merci,* Mama," Maurice said, laughing. "Thank you. I love you." He gave her a big hug and they both laughed.

It wasn't much, but maybe he could borrow a buck or two from his friend Girard. If not, he'd just have to explain to Josette that he was a little short this week. She'd understand.

He was still in a good mood when he came downstairs whistling. Philippe was in the living room, cleaning his hunting rifle.

"Cut out that goddamn whistling," he barked. "Can't a man have some peace and quiet?"

"Sorry, Papa. But you won't be bothered tonight. I'm...I'm going out—on a date."

"Oh, yeah?"

Maurice felt that panicky feeling in his gut.

"Is that okay? I'm going to the movies with Josette, a girl from school. Can't I go?"

"How you gonna get there?"

"I was gonna ask you if I could use the truck. I'm drivin' it real good now. Drove it all the way to Ashland today. No problem."

"But you ain't got a driver's license, Maurice. I can't let you take the truck."

"Please, Papa. I really like this girl. You make me drive the truck for work. What's the difference?"

"The difference is that I need you to drive it for work. You can walk to the movies. Now, get the hell out of here."

"God, that *bastard*! I hate his guts! Why do I ever hope for anything? Why do I deserve this life? I hate this!" Maurice said to himself between his clenched teeth. His heart felt as if it had been ripped in half. He thought about the situation: He couldn't ask Josette to walk all the way into town. He'd have to cancel the date, but he didn't want to hurt her feelings. He decided to call Girard and ask him if he'd take Josette to the movies. Later, Maurice found out the two of them had hit it off. They started going out together and eventually got married.

Maurice decided he would not try to date a girl until he was off his father's farm. What would be the use? This wasn't the first girl that he'd had to give up because of his father. He would face life as if he were a prisoner in jail.

■ ■ ■

The time passed slowly, but it passed. On Maurice's twenty-first birthday his bags were already packed. Philippe Theriault was out in the field early, so Maurice didn't have to worry about saying good-bye to him.

He dressed quietly, taking a final look around his room. Bad memories came immediately to mind. He thought about the dozens of times he had been whipped with his father's belt, and a hot flash raced through his body. He walked slowly downstairs, trying to focus on the good times with his mother and his brothers and sisters.

In the kitchen Alice Theriault was making Maurice's favorite breakfast, crepes. His brothers and sisters were gathered around the table, waiting for him to come down.

As he entered the room Alice began to cry. She hadn't noticed how her boy had grown. Although he was only five feet six his body was stocky and muscular. He looked bigger than he was. Suddenly he was a man and he was leaving. If only Philippe wasn't so damned hard on him, her son wouldn't be leaving. She thought about her first son and her mind drifted off for a moment to the day of the blizzard when Maurice had been rescued by a Good Samaritan.

Maurice put his arms around her. "Mama, don't worry," he said. "I'll be all right. I'm going to Connecticut. I got a buddy down there. He works in a silver factory and he told me he can get me a job."

Maurice hugged each of his brothers and sisters and then kissed his mother good-bye. *"Au revoir,* Mama," he said. "Good-bye."

His eyes welled up with tears as he walked out the door for the last time. He looked over his shoulder at his father's chair one last time. "I swear I hate you, you bastard. Curse you! I hope the devil takes his pitchfork and sticks it in your heart!"

Alice looked down and shook her head.

Girard was waiting outside in his car. Maurice threw his bags into the trunk and hopped into the front seat. Out of the corner of his tear-blurred eye, he saw his father working in the field. The old man didn't bother to say good-bye or even look up.

"Good riddance," Maurice whispered as Girard started the engine. "Good riddance, you bastard. I hope you rot in hell."

Girard dropped Maurice at the Greyhound station, where he boarded a bus for Boston. There he would change buses and catch one bound for New Britain, Connecticut. There he would make his own life. He was finally free.

FOUR

JUST A FEW MILES southwest of Hartford, Connecticut, lies New Britain, a gritty factory town that bears the fitting nickname "the hardware city of the world." Maurice spent a grim two years there, laboring in a machine shop, but he never got used to factory work. He disliked being indoors for so many hours a day. He lived in a tiny apartment over a bar that had a flashing neon light and the back of a billboard for a view. He was always homesick.

Although he never wanted to see his father again, he sorely missed his mother, his brothers and sisters, and the country life he loved. He decided to go back to Van Buren. What did he have to lose?

When he returned, Maurice looked up a girl he had gone out with a few times a couple of years before. Christine Harper had always liked him, but he'd had to stop seeing her for the same reason he was unable to date Josette—no money and no transportation. Christine had been hurt when he dropped her, but she hadn't blamed him. She knew it wasn't his fault.

Although it had been two years, Christine was thrilled to see Maurice. She hadn't changed at all. Very mature-looking for her age, she could pass for a woman in her twenties. Christine was what some would call buxom. She wore her ash-blond hair long and straight, and she liked to dress simply, in solid colors. When she found out that Maurice was back in Van Buren and had no place to stay, she invited him to stay with her. Christine lived with her grandfather, Hubert Emery, and they had an extra room. She was hoping the old man wouldn't mind having a boarder.

When she approached Hubert with the plan, he rejected the idea immediately. But when Maurice offered to help out with the chores and pay a few dollars a week in rent, it seemed to sway him. The extra money would keep Hubert in liquor through the long, cold winter. And since winters in Maine were extremely long and extremely cold, Hubert needed all the whiskey he could get his shaky hands on.

Hubert was a grizzled old Frenchman who always had a couple of days' growth of white beard and seldom bothered to wear his teeth. He often misplaced them when he got drunk, which was most nights. He was a bourbon man and usually smelled of it. He always wore a green plaid jacket and brown corduroys that were fastened at the top with a big safety pin. The snap fastener had broken years ago, but Hubert liked to get a lot of mileage out of things.

Maurice and Christine were getting along wonderfully. Although they weren't lovers—she was only sixteen—they were becoming close friends. For the first time in a long, long time, Maurice was feeling happy. He was developing a life of his own. He'd just had to wait for it longer than most people.

But something about Hubert made him feel uncomfortable. The old man seemed jealous of the time Maurice was spending with Christine, especially when he was drunk. He would mumble to himself and peer at the two of them, then mumble some more.

But what could they do? Christine was still attending school. She was too young for them to move in together, even if Maurice could afford his own apartment, which he couldn't. His job as a farmhand in a potato field didn't pay much.

They decided they had to put up with Hubert at least until Christine graduated. By this time Maurice had gotten good at waiting for things he wanted. He could do it again.

But one day Maurice came home from the field a little bit early and found Christine on her bed, sobbing. "What's the matter, Chris?" he said, taking her hand and sitting down next to her.

"Nothing, Maurice," she whispered. "Nothing." She was lying facedown, her face buried in the crook of her arm.

Suddenly Hubert opened her bedroom door and walked in. When he saw Maurice he stopped dead in his tracks and just stood there. The usual smell of bourbon was in the air. He peered down at Maurice and asked, "What you doin' home so early, boy?"

"I wasn't feelin' so good. What's the matter with Chris? She's been cryin'."

"I dunno. Don't worry about her. She's okay. Sometimes she gets crazy. You know women."

He turned around, slammed the door, and stomped off into the living room.

Maurice looked at Christine. "What's he so mad about?"

Christine looked away from Maurice and began crying again.

"You want to talk about it, let me know," he said, closing her door gently behind him as he went off to his own room, wondering what had caused her tears.

The next day Maurice was still not feeling well and stayed home from work. After Christine had left for school, Hubert came into his room. "Boy, I think it's time you moved outta here," he said. "This place just ain't big enough for the three of us."

Maurice was beginning to feel the same way. Hubert had become more and more possessive of his granddaughter and Maurice felt as if he was competing for her affection. He packed his bags and headed down the stairs with a suitcase in each hand. He was angry and confused. What's wrong with me? he was thinking. Why can't I keep a girl?

There was a loud knock on the front door just as he reached the bottom of the stairs.

"Police, open up."

As Maurice moved toward the door Hubert shot up out of his

easy chair and ran into the kitchen. Maurice had never seen the old man move so fast.

When he opened the door a burly police officer was standing there impatiently. "Where's Hubert Emery?" he demanded. "I got a warrant for his arrest."

"He just ran into the kitchen," Maurice answered. "What's going on?"

The officer brushed past Maurice through the living room and into the kitchen, where he found Hubert behind an open drawer. Bullets were strewn out all over the counter. He was trying to load his hunting rifle, but his shaky hands had knocked the bullets all over the place. The officer rushed forward, knocked the gun to the floor, and shoved the old man against the wall. He put handcuffs on Hubert and led him away through the back door.

Maurice followed them outside, but the cop told him to go back into the house and wait for Christine to come home. Maurice was puzzled, but he did what he was told.

Ten minutes later a green Chevrolet pulled into the driveway. A middle-aged woman was driving, and Christine was sitting in the passenger's seat. There were tears streaming down her face.

"Hubert's just been arrested!" Maurice shouted. "What's going on?"

Christine walked toward Maurice, her reddened eyes looking down at the ground. "Oh, Maurice, I'm so sorry."

She stood facing Maurice, holding on to his shoulders. Then

she blurted it all out. Hubert had been forcing her to act as his wife for years. She had to sleep with him whenever he demanded it. She hated it, but she was afraid to say anything.

"But then you came back, Maurice," she said, looking into his eyes for the first time since she started telling her story. "And I fell in love with you again. And I thought you would take me away from him...."

Later another policeman came to the house. He wanted Maurice to come with him to the station. "We just want to ask you some questions," the cop said.

So Maurice went with him. At the station he was taken to a hot room bathed in bright lights and questioned about his relationship with Christine, about Hubert's relationship with Christine, and about his relationship with Hubert Emery.

"Did you know he was bangin' her?" the cop asked, handing Maurice a cigarette.

"No, of course not," Maurice answered, a little incredulous. "If I knew, do you think I'd have stood for it?"

"Then were you bangin' her?"

The cop's voice got louder, and his eyes peered straight into Maurice's.

"No," Maurice said without hesitation. "I never did. We're not like that with each other...we're more like friends."

Maurice was telling the truth, but not all of it. He and Christine had never made love—that was true. But they were more than friends. She loved him, and although he had never admitted it to himself or anybody else, he loved her. The revelation that she had been forced to have sex with her own grandfather hadn't changed his feelings about her. He knew how it felt to be a victim. If anything, she would need him more than ever. He wasn't going to let her down.

"You got to believe me," Maurice insisted. "I wouldn't do nothin' to hurt that girl."

The cop asked him a few more questions and decided to call it quits. He didn't know Maurice well, but he felt the young man was sincere. It was something about the look in his eyes. He could tell that Maurice loved Christine and wanted to protect her. He figured she needed somebody to protect her.

"Okay," he said. "You can go now. But we're going to need you to testify, so don't go far."

Maurice picked up his blue peacoat from the back of the chair, stamped out the cigarette on the floor, and headed out the door in front of the cop. He took a left down the corridor and began walking toward the front door, when he was startled by the sight of Hubert Emery being led past him, hands cuffed behind his back, shuffling toward an empty cell.

Hubert had a crazed look in his eyes and was muttering something under his breath. When he saw Maurice he stopped and stared at him. Maurice felt scared and tried to look away but couldn't. It was as if Hubert were controlling him with his eyes. Then Hubert opened his mouth to speak.

"I'm going to haunt you for the rest of your life," he said, speaking slowly and deliberately.

The words came from Hubert's mouth, but the voice didn't sound like his. It was deeper, more guttural.

He spoke again. "You two will never be happy together. You'll never make a life together. I curse you to the devil!"

Then two officers grabbed the old man and dragged him down the corridor to the cell. As he was being dragged away he spat on Maurice's shoe.

Maurice just stood there, shaken.

"Don't worry about him," said the officer who had just finished questioning Maurice. "He's goin' away for a long, long time."

But Maurice was frightened. The words rang in his ears over and over.

■ ■ ■

The next day Christine's mother showed up in Van Buren. She was living down in Portland, and after hearing what had happened, had decided to take Christine away. But instead of taking Christine to live with her, she was going to have her daughter placed in a foster home.

Maurice was determined not to let that happen. As soon as he found out, he rushed down to Beneficial Finance to get a loan. He needed a car, and fast. Although his job at the potato farm didn't pay much, the loan officer knew Maurice and trusted him. He approved a five-hundred-dollar loan on the spot.

Within an hour of receiving the money, Maurice was the owner of a white '49 Mercury. It was banged up and needed a paint job, but it seemed to run pretty well. The salesman at Don's Car Lot said it had a lot of miles left in it.

Maurice had rented a room about a block from Hubert's old house after Christine's mother ordered him out. He drove straight from the car lot to the rooming house, a brown-shingled triple-decker, stopping only to fill the tank with gas. When he got home he burst through the front door and ran up the stairs to his room, not bothering even to say hello to the landlady, fat old Mrs. Picard, who was very interested in all the excitement.

He stuffed some clothes into an overnight bag and rushed back downstairs to the pay phone in the hallway. He fished around in his pocket for a nickel and the receiver slipped out of his hands, which were sweaty by now from nervousness. His throat was throbbing with the beating of his heart. He dialed Christine's number as fast as he could. Please, God, let Christine answer, he prayed.

The phone rang only once before he heard her familiar voice. "Hello."

"Christine, it's me. Get your clothes together. We're getting outta here. I got a car. We'll go up to Canada and get married. How quick can you be ready?"

Christine was stunned. She hadn't known if she was ever going to hear from Maurice again. "Maurice, I can't believe what you're saying...."

"Well, are you coming or not?"

It wasn't something Christine had to think about for long. "You bet I am!" she gushed, quickly lowering her voice to a whisper so that her mother wouldn't hear. "Be outside in fifteen minutes. My mother is taking a nap. She won't even know I'm gone. And, Maurice...I love you. You've made me the happiest girl in the world."

Christine tiptoed into her room, barely able to contain her excitement. She packed a bag, being very careful to place her best dress on top, to make sure it wouldn't get wrinkled. She peeked in on her mother, who was sound asleep, still tired from her grueling three-hundred-mile drive the day before. Christine felt as if she were walking on air. Trembling with anticipation, she placed her bag outside the front door and waited excitedly for Maurice to show up. Looking up at her mother's window, she bit her lip. Oh, God, Mother, don't you wake up! she was praying. Don't you dare wake up and spoil everything!

It seemed as if she'd been waiting for Maurice forever. She looked at her nails, then traced a heart in the gravel over and over. "Maurice. My love," she wrote with the toe of her black pump.

In about ten minutes the Mercury pulled into her driveway. When Christine got in she showered Maurice with hugs and kisses. He put his arm around her as they drove off. She was thinking this was the first scene in her life that felt like a fairy tale. It hardly felt real.

It didn't take long to cross the border into New Brunswick.

They stopped in the town of Edmundson and found a justice of the peace who lived in a little white cottage surrounded by tall pines. Before the afternoon was over they were man and wife.

They spent their honeymoon night at a tiny motel and drove back to Van Buren the next morning. Suddenly everything felt different for Maurice and Christine. The air was crisper and cleaner. Nature was more beautiful. It seemed as though all their senses were heightened and that everything took on a new meaning. At last life belonged to them.

Later that day, over grilled cheese and Canadian bacon sandwiches at a cozy roadside diner near the Maine border, they discussed their future. Maurice was very earnest about his role as the provider, and Christine felt safer with him than she had ever felt before. They agreed they should move out of Van Buren for good. Maurice said he had some friends in Holyoke, Massachusetts. They decided to go there.

■ ■ ■

Holyoke was a medium-sized mill city in the Bay State's rural Pioneer Valley. Maurice figured it was as good a place as any to make a new start in life. With a population of about 60,000, Holyoke was closer in size to New Britain than to tiny Van Buren, but the central Massachusetts city seemed closer in spirit to Maurice's hometown in northern Maine. For one thing, there were plenty of French-Canadians in Holyoke. That made Maurice feel at home. And the fact that Holyoke—known as "the paper city of the world"—was full of paper mills also provided a link to Van Buren, settled by lumberers from French Acadia, where lumbering remained a major industry.

So Maurice felt comfortable in his new surroundings right from the start. And the fact that Holyoke was about five hundred miles away from two people Maurice wanted nothing more to do with—Philippe Theriault and Hubert Emery—made it almost perfect.

Maurice's old buddies quickly found him work in a paper mill, and he and Christine settled into married life. Maurice seemed happy, although he sometimes got annoyed at Christine for being lazy around the house. She wasn't working, yet she rarely dusted, swept, or tidied up. Maurice had to talk to her about it repeatedly. Each time she promised to do better.

Maurice and Christine began working on a family right away and had a child before their first wedding anniversary. They named him Adam. Two more children followed in rapid succession: a girl, Nicole, and a second boy, Marc. Friends joked that Maurice was working in a paper mill during the day and in a baby mill at night.

One hot and sticky August night, as he and Christine were lying awake in bed after having put the kids to sleep, they began to argue. It was the usual argument:

"Woman, I told you to clean the house today. What happened?"

"Maurice, I didn't have time. The kids keep me busy every second."

"You better find the time. I work hard at the mill all day, and I don't like coming home to this. The place is a shithouse. Dirty clothes everywhere. Dust piling up. I don't even have any clean clothes."

"I'm doing the best I can," Christine answered, her face reddening. Couldn't he understand that she was working too?

"My mother could do it," Maurice shot back. "Why can't you?" Maurice was shouting now.

Christine was getting tired of the same speech. She had been through it so many times before. She turned over and faced the wall. What she saw startled her. "Maurice, look at the crucifix!"

The panic in her voice got Maurice's attention. He looked over at the crucifix on the wall over their dresser, blinked his eyes, and looked again. A red streak was making its way down the yellowing flowered wallpaper. Blood was dripping from Christ's hands and feet.

Shaken, Maurice put his arms around Christine. Suddenly he forgot what they had been arguing about. They both dropped to their knees in prayer.

When they looked up, the blood was gone.

"You saw it, didn't you, Maurice?" Christine whispered, her voice barely audible but her eyes still wide and glued to the cross.

"I dunno," he answered. "I think I did. The cross was bleedin'. But now it ain't."

Christine curled up next to her husband. "I'm scared," she said.

"Aw, we probably imagined it," he told her, patting her shoulder. "Don't worry."

But inside, Maurice was scared too.

■ ■ ■

Maurice and Christine tried to forget about the frightening incident, but the very next Sunday after attending church they began to argue again. Maurice had asked Christine to fix him a pot roast, but she had forgotten to defrost the meat. When she brought out a plate of leftovers from the night before, he exploded. "Where's the pot roast I wanted?" he demanded,

Christine looked down at the table. "I didn't take it out in time," she said. "I forgot. I'll make it tomorrow night."

"That's it!" Maurice shouted, slamming his hand down on the wooden table. "I've had it!"

He stormed off into the bedroom. As soon as he passed through the doorway he saw it.

"Jesus!" he said, doing a double take. "Christine, come quick—it's happenin' again!"

In the kitchen Christine stopped her sobbing. This time she knew exactly what Maurice was talking about.

Hesitantly she walked into the bedroom and looked at the wall over the dresser. Once again blood was gushing from Christ's hands and feet. "What is this? What's going on?" she cried.

This time the frightened couple approached the cross. Maurice reached out his hand and touched the blood on the wall. The blood came off on his finger.

He dropped quickly to his knees and began to pray. Christine did the same. By the time they had finished the Lord's Prayer, the blood had disappeared from the cross, the wall, and Maurice's finger.

But it had not disappeared from their minds.

The crucifix would bleed in front of Maurice and Christine again. It was to happen often—usually when they were in the middle of one of their increasingly frequent arguments.

To Maurice it was a sign that his marriage was in trouble. Each time it would happen it would shake him up, and then he'd try to straighten things out between them.

But Christine didn't need a bleeding cross to tell her they were in trouble. Maurice, she felt, was becoming impossible to live with. He was yelling at her all the time—just the way he told her his father used to yell at him.

Maurice thought his wife was always against him. He couldn't see how she could ignore her household duties while she stayed at home all day. After all, she only had three kids to take care of. His mother had had ten—and she hadn't had much trouble keeping house.

"She won't provide a proper home," he told his buddy Steve at the mill. "What does that woman do all day? She's not workin', so why's the house always a pigsty? I told her things have got to straighten up. I'm layin' down the law. If they don't straighten up, I'm gonna leave her. I don't want to, but I'm gonna have to. I ain't got a choice."

The strange thing was that Maurice felt that he still loved Christine, and Christine was certain that she still loved Maurice, even though he didn't understand her one bit. Each one seemed to be moved by some outside force to believe that the other was turning against the marriage. Maybe, she thought, Hubert Emery was right. Maybe they would never be happy together.

At the same time Maurice and Christine found they had another outside force to contend with. Maurice's father had decided to pack his family up and move them to Massachusetts. Philippe's farm was failing, and like many of the French-Canadians in poverty-stricken Aroostook County, he decided that he'd move on to greener pastures. Most of the others who had left Van Buren had gone to Massachusetts, so that's where Philippe decided he'd go too.

To Alice it was a dream come true. She missed Maurice and her grandchildren badly and had secretly hoped they would move back to Van Buren one day. The prospect of moving near her first child was just as good. And maybe they'd find some better land to farm.

When she suggested to Philippe that they move to Holyoke, he surprised her. He said that was where he wanted to move too. He had some friends in the area. The fact that his son also lived there barely crossed his mind. In fact, Alice wasn't even sure Philippe knew that Maurice was living in Holyoke.

Alice was thrilled that they'd be near Maurice again. And although she was worried about how her son would take the news, she was hopeful that things would work out. Maybe time had healed some of those wounds.

For his part, Maurice was happy to have his mother around. He missed her too, and she'd be able to help out with the kids from time to time. As for Philippe, he would just stay clear of him. Since Maurice wasn't going to be living with his father, there was no way the old man could boss him around.

As it turned out, Philippe's return had little impact on Maurice's life. The two avoided each other as much as possible. Philippe had plenty of other children to make miserable. And Maurice was too busy raising his own kids and trying to keep his failing marriage together to think much about his father.

If anything, it was his mother, not his father, who had the worst effect on Maurice and Christine's marriage. Although Alice was always as sweet and helpful as she could be, her presence seemed to add to the stress of the already shaky union.

In Maurice's mind Alice Theriault was like a goddess hovering over his life with a gentle presence. Her house was always immaculate, her children well fed with delicious food prepared from recipes handed down to her from her own mother. There was no way Christine could measure up to his mother.

Within a year of his parents' arrival Maurice and Christine had split up, convinced their marriage had been cursed by the ghost of Hubert Emery. Although they remained friends, they decided it would be better to go their separate ways.

Christine agreed that the children would remain with Maurice. She would go to Maryland to stay with her aunt Constance for a while. Then from there they would figure things out.

■ ■ ■

A few months after moving in with Aunt Constance, Christine fell ill with pneumonia and had to be hospitalized.

Maurice was worried. The illness made him realize how much he loved her. Although he and Christine were no longer man and wife, he still cared for her and knew she needed him. He wanted desperately to visit her in the hospital, but how could he? He couldn't get time off from work.

During this time he went to see his mother. When she opened the door Alice Theriault's face turned white. "Maurice, what are you doing here? I thought you were in Maryland visiting Christine!"

Maurice scratched his head. "I had a feeling like I was there too," he said. "But I thought it was just a dream."

Alice scrunched up her eyebrows. "It's so strange! I just got off the phone with Christine at the hospital in Baltimore. She said you had just left her room. Why would she tell me that lie? Her aunt Constance also spoke to me and was telling me how sweet it was of you to come, and that you looked a little pale."

Maurice's head began hurting. "I feel weak," he said.

"Maurice, you better sit down," Alice said, taking her son's arm and leading him to the couch in her living room. "You don't look too good. Let me get you some chicken soup."

Maurice sat down as his mother went to the kitchen. By the time she returned he was fast asleep.

When he awoke, Alice Theriault demanded an answer. "Will you please tell me what's going on here?" she asked her son.

But Maurice couldn't explain it. As far as he was concerned he had only visited Christine in a dream. "How could I have just been in Baltimore and be here with you now? It's impossible."

■ ■ ■

In room 208 at Baltimore City Hospital, Christine Theriault was feeling better. She looked over at her aunt Constance and smiled. "I knew he'd come," she said, clutching the bouquet of flowers he had given her.

Constance smiled back. "He still loves you, Christine.

It was not the last time Maurice Theriault would appear in two places at once.

FIVE

MAURICE LIVED AIMLESSLY for the next several years, kicking around from job to job and from town to town, but mostly staying close to his mother in Holyoke. Without Alice, Maurice would have been lost. She would look after the kids for him almost every day. She was like a mother to them.

Maurice often thought that Adam, Nicole, and Marc ought to be raised by their own mother rather than his, but all attempts at reconciling with Christine proved fruitless. When she up and moved to Texas, he knew it was over for good. The thought saddened him because, down deep, he still loved her. And he felt that she still loved him too. She had said it many times in letters and phone calls over the years. But whenever one of them suggested giving the marriage another try, the other would back away. Maurice blamed it on Hubert Emery's curse. Eventually he realized that the curse was stronger than their love. Finally he stopped trying.

Maurice held a number of factory jobs, but none of them amounted to much. Since he couldn't read or write very well, he was constantly passed over for foremen's jobs. And his thick French-Canadian accent didn't help matters. Some of his bosses made fun of him because of it and called him "Frenchy."

In time the nickname stuck. Even his friends started calling him Frenchy. But to them it wasn't a putdown. And he didn't take it as one. He kind of liked it. After all, he was proud that he was of French descent. And it gave him a new identity. Not long after his nickname had caught on, Maurice started growing one of those pencil-thin mustaches like the one worn by the then popular French actor Charles Boyer. If they were going to call him Frenchy, he thought, he might as well look the part.

But the new nickname wasn't putting dollars in his pocket. It seemed he'd never get out of his rut. In frustration he left his kids with his mother and went back to Van Buren one last time. He thought maybe he could get some cheap land and resume farming—something he had never gotten out of his blood. He had no trouble finding work on a potato farm, but as always, he couldn't make enough money. And Maurice was lonely. He missed his kids. He missed his mother. And he missed Christine.

Just when life seemed to be at its lowest point, Maurice met Erica. She was working in the potato fields with him. Petite and slim, with red hair and green eyes, Erica seemed the answer to his dreams. He needed a wife and his children needed a mother. He quickly asked her to marry him. Erica, who was raising a small boy on her own, was equally lonely and agreed to assume both roles. They married and moved back to Massachusetts, to a farm in Belchertown, a little village a few miles east of Holyoke, where they began growing fruits and vegetables.

But their marriage proved to be little more than one of convenience. There was no passion in it, and the nine-year union produced no children. It turned out that Erica and Maurice had almost nothing in common, and they lived from day to day in their own separate worlds. During the years he was with Erica, Maurice found himself turning inward more than ever before. He couldn't share his feelings with Erica and felt more and more isolated in the marriage. Strange things would happen to him, but he never told her about any of them. He never told anybody, preferring to keep it all to himself.

For instance, in the fall of 1965, he was once out walking through his tomato patch when he almost tripped over a wooden cross. "Where the hell did that come from?" he muttered to himself.

When he reached down to pick it up, Maurice's eyes began to get blurry. He started to rub them but stopped when he felt a gushy liquid on his fingers. When he pulled his hands away he noticed his fingers were covered with blood. He hadn't remembered cutting himself, but he ran into the house and headed straight for the bathroom to check himself in the mirror.

He could hardly believe what he was seeing. Blood was seeping from both eyes. Maurice tried to clean the blood up with a tissue, but he couldn't get it to stop. The funny thing was that he couldn't find a cut or a scrape around either of his eyes. He thought maybe he should get himself to a doctor, but for some reason he stayed right there. He continued to stand in front of the mirror and watch as the blood poured from his eyes down his face, onto his shirt and into the sink.

Maurice was transfixed as he watched his eyes bleed. He felt no pain or fear. It was almost as if he had gone into a trance. He was in the bathroom for about twenty minutes when Erica began banging on the door.

"Maurice, you all right? What's the matter?"

Startled, Maurice emerged from his trancelike state. He looked at himself and noticed some dried blood on his face and shirt. He quickly cleaned himself up.

"I'll be right out," he said, taking off his shirt and throwing it into the hamper. "I just cut myself shaving. It's nothing."

Erica was glad that Maurice wasn't sick. They were going to a dance at the Elks Hall that night, and she didn't want him to back out again. He did that all too often.

When Maurice came out he seemed unusually quiet, as if he was deep in thought. Erica wanted to ask if something was bothering him, but she decided not to. He's been a little touchy lately, she thought. Better not to start an argument.

They left for the dance about eight that night, but Maurice had barely said a word since he'd come out of the bathroom. Inside the dance hall he sat down at a corner table, not bothering to say hello to anybody, not even to some of his pals from the factory. And he never even asked Erica to dance.

She didn't know what to make of his strange behavior. Maurice wasn't what she would have called outgoing, but he usually enjoyed these dances. He liked country music and even though he wasn't much of a dancer, after a couple of drinks he would be up stomping his feet, especially if the band was playing one of his favorite songs, such as the "Orange Blossom Special."

Invariably Maurice and Erica would stay at the Elks Hall until last call at one A.M. and then head over to a friend's house for one or two more before calling it a night. But tonight Maurice would have none of that. It wasn't much past ten when he announced to Erica that he wanted to leave, that he had something important to do.

Naturally Erica was upset. She had been waiting all week for this evening, and now Maurice was going to spoil it. She started to argue, but Maurice seemed in no mood for a fight. He simply said he was leaving and that she'd better come along because he wasn't going to wait for her.

Erica swallowed hard and gave in. She could tell Maurice wasn't in the mood to be persuaded to stay. As was usually the case when they disagreed, Erica gave Maurice the silent treatment. She got into the Chrysler New Yorker without saying a word, slamming the door behind her.

Most times Maurice would try to smooth things over, making a joke or promising to do something to make it up to her, such as take her out to lunch at Freddie's Diner or to the Dairy Queen for a sundae. But tonight he seemed to be giving her his own version of the silent treatment—except that he didn't seem at all angry or upset with her. He just wasn't talking.

He drove quietly, staring ahead as they drove down Route 202. There was a fork in the road about two miles from home, and it required slowing down to take the left turn. Directly in the middle of the fork was a sturdy old oak tree.

As Maurice approached the fork Erica noticed that he wasn't slowing down. She wanted to say something, but was still giving him the silent treatment and didn't want to break it. Yet Maurice continued to drive straight for the tree, and he showed no signs of turning or stopping.

"Frenchy!" she shouted.

But Maurice didn't even hear her. He continued to head for the tree. He seemed to be transfixed, in some sort of a trance. It was as if he was determined to crash.

Seconds before the car went off the road and straight for the tree, Erica reached over and grabbed the wheel, turning it quickly toward her. The quick action probably saved their lives. Instead of hitting the tree head-on, the car careened sideways into a stone wall that ran along the side of the road. The crash was loud, as metal crunched and glass shattered. But when it was over neither Maurice nor Erica had received even a scratch.

Erica was practically hysterical. "Maurice, what were you trying to do, kill us both? Are you insane?"

Maurice turned toward Erica and pulled her toward him.

"What happened?" he asked.

Maurice didn't even remember having left the dance. He had no recollection of driving home. All he knew was that the crash had startled him out of what seemed to be a deep sleep.

Erica didn't want to hear it. She figured her husband was losing his mind. There were other things, but she had tried to dismiss them. There was the time their pet beagle, Peter, was killed, for instance. Maurice told her he had been hit by a car, but later she found a bloody pick in the area where he'd said the accident had occurred. It was Maurice's pick.

But it didn't make any sense that he would kill Peter. Maurice loved that dog and took him out hunting nearly every Sunday during the season. And the day after the dog had been killed, Maurice had buried him in the woods, crying all the while as he dug the grave.

Then there was the time she had watched out the kitchen window as Maurice beat his riding horse, a pinto named Bar Coda, with a stick after the horse had failed to learn a trick Maurice was trying to teach him. When Erica chastised Maurice about being too rough with the animal, Maurice professed not to know what she was talking about.

"I would never hit Bar Coda," he said. "I love that horse."

Erica believed him. She knew that he did love that animal. But she also knew what she had seen.

But Maurice would not accept responsibility for his bizarre

behavior. He blamed Erica, claiming that she put him up to the violent acts.

It made no sense, but there were simply times when Maurice made no sense—not to Erica, not to anybody. It was as if there was another person inside him. When that other person took over his personality, anything was possible.

Maurice's strange behavior was taking its toll on the marriage. Twice Erica left him and went back to Maine. Both times Maurice went up and brought her back. Eventually, though, she left him for good.

"You're crazy," she said as she walked out the door. "You ought to see a headshrinker."

This time Maurice didn't even try to get her back. He knew he was wrong, that he had caused Erica to leave, and that she had good reason for leaving. He decided he'd just have to carry on alone. He had been through this before. He'd manage without her. But he wondered if she was right. Maybe he was going crazy. But farmers didn't see psychiatrists. Whatever was bothering him, Maurice thought, he'd figure it out. Maybe that mysterious force that he'd called on for help in the fields would come to his aid again.

■ ■ ■

Alone again, Maurice decided he needed a plan of action. And as had been the case so many times before, Maurice's plan involved a change of scenery. This time he decided to leave Massachusetts for upstate New York. He'd stay with his uncle Kevin Ferrand in the town of Greenfield, outside Saratoga Springs, site of the famous health spa. He had always liked Uncle Kevin and knew the old man could probably use some help cutting wood for the winter.

When he got there Uncle Kevin was happy to have him, but there wasn't much work to be had on his tiny farm. Maurice had to look around for additional work and found it on Simon Junot's farm. He helped in the fields and cut wood too. Simon let him sell some of what he cut, to make some extra money. It was a good arrangement for Maurice and Simon didn't mind. He liked Maurice and wanted him to stick around. The two men had become drinking buddies and liked to stay up late at night, sitting around the pot-bellied stove in the kitchen, drinking whiskey and beer and swapping stories.

One chilly night in November of 1979, Maurice showed up, as usual, with a bottle of Jim Beam bourbon for himself and a six-pack of Genesee beer for Simon. But before they could get down to some serious drinking, the old man asked Maurice for a favor. "Frenchy, can you help me out? Give my daughter a ride to work, okay? Her car's busted."

Simon's daughter, Nancy, was working the night shift at General Foods. She would go in at eleven and work until seven in the morning. It wasn't ideal, but as a divorced mother of three girls Nancy couldn't be choosy.

Maurice had seen Nancy many times around the farm, but he had never gotten to know her. Usually she was sleeping when he was working in the fields, or heading out the door to her job when he came over at night to drink with Simon.

Nancy was an attractive woman of forty, with curly red-brown hair and hazel eyes. She had a deep, sexy voice and was very articulate and outspoken. She had been married to a policeman for thirteen years before her divorce three years earlier, and was used to hanging around with cops, not farmers.

Maurice couldn't help being captivated by Nancy from the first time he saw her, but he never made a move for her. For one thing, he didn't know how Simon would feel about it. Second, he was a little intimidated by her. He was still basically shy when it came to women, and he noticed that she wasn't afraid to voice her opinions—probably from hanging around cops for so many years. He figured he wasn't her type.

But he was glad to give Nancy a ride to work. They didn't say much on the way to the plant where she worked as a packer, but Maurice enjoyed the few minutes they spent alone together. She seemed genuinely interested in him, and it turned out that she didn't look down on him at all because he was just a farmer. After all, she was a country girl.

Maurice decided to make a pass at her. He was forty-three years old and he'd been lonely in the year since he and Erica had been divorced. But it was more than that. There was something about Nancy. She moved him as he had never been moved before. She was strong and smart and wouldn't take any guff from anybody. She would make a good partner.

The next night, Maurice came over earlier than usual and offered right away to drive Nancy to work. When they got into his pickup, he breathed deeply and announced, "You can move over, closer, if you want."

Nancy tried to stifle a laugh. "That's okay, Frenchy. I'm fine right here."

And she remained leaning against the door, not budging an inch. But inside, she was glad he had asked. She was wondering if he would ever make a pass at her. Now that he had tried, she wanted to take it slowly. She had been burned before. No reason to rush into anything. There was plenty of time.

Maurice gave Nancy a ride to work for the rest of the week. He wanted to make another move the entire time but he was afraid he'd be rejected again. She hadn't exactly jumped at the offer to sit beside him that second night. But he decided that if he didn't do something by Friday, he might not get another chance. She was due to get her car back from the shop on Saturday.

On his way back home Thursday night he devised a plan. The next day he'd load up the front seat of his pickup with tools, lodging them up against the passenger-side door. And when it came time to give Nancy a ride to work that night, he'd tell her the passenger-side door was jammed and she'd have to get in through the driver's side. If she did, she'd have to sit in the center of the seat, right next to him.

The plan worked to perfection. Nancy got in without hesitation and she sat right by his side. Of course, she knew that it was all a ruse, but she didn't mind. She had been waiting patiently for him to make another move, and she thought his trick was pretty clever. By the time they got to the factory, Nancy was hugging Maurice.

As he dropped her at the gate Maurice asked if he could pick her up in the morning and take her to breakfast. Usually Nancy got a ride home with one of her girlfriends. She was thrilled that he'd asked and told him so.

When her shift was over at seven in the morning, Maurice was waiting by the gate and he was wearing his best Western suit. It was gray with black lapels. He wore a white shirt with silver tips on the collar, and a string tie.

"Frenchy, I think this is the beginning of a beautiful friendship," she said, quoting a line from her favorite movie, *Casablanca.*

From then on they were inseparable. Soon afterward they moved back to Massachusetts with the intention of buying themselves a small farm. This time Maurice was certain that things were going to work out.

■ ■ ■

Maurice and Nancy moved to the town of East Longmeadow, a small farming community just south of Springfield. For the first time in a long time, things were really going well for Maurice. His relationship with Nancy couldn't have been any better. Their little rented farm was prospering, so much so that they were thinking of buying some property of their own.

They were again living close to Maurice's mother, and he was glad of that. He always missed his mother when he wasn't living nearby. Now he was only about fifteen miles away. It wasn't quite the same as when they were in the same town, but they were still near enough for frequent visits.

Maurice and his father were even beginning to talk to each other. They weren't exactly close—that would have been impossible, considering the way Philippe had treated Maurice as a child—but at least they no longer openly hated each other. When Maurice would drop by to visit his mother, Philippe would sometimes come over and make small talk. Usually he'd ask Maurice how his tomato plants were faring. Once in a while he'd even ask about his grandchildren.

Maybe it was because so many of his other kids had moved far away, to Oklahoma City. First it was Philippe, Jr., known as "Phil." He was five years younger than Maurice and always seemed to have been Philippe's favorite—if there was such a thing. However, even Phil eventually fell out of favor with Philippe. It happened when Phil's car—which Philippe had signed for—was repossessed. Philippe exploded at Phil with a fury that he usually reserved for Maurice. Phil moved to Oklahoma not long afterward.

After Phil left, several more of the family followed him out there. First Lucy, then Betty, then Julie, and then Jason. The thinning out of his flock seemed to make Philippe more reflective.

He still had his moods though. It was just that he would no

longer explode the way he used to when Maurice was a child. These days Philippe seemed to keep his hostility inside. Maurice could sometimes see the anger building up in him. He had good built-in radar for that. But instead of lashing out at the nearest person, Philippe would just stomp out of the room, slamming the door behind him.

Although he was glad that his father seemed to be making an effort to make amends, Maurice was troubled by Philippe's new pattern of behavior. At least in the old days he knew what to expect. Now he compared his father to a ticking time bomb. Maurice feared that if his father didn't let his anger out, he might one day go off the deep end and do something really hideous.

But Maurice tried not to dwell on those fears. After all, he was just a tomato farmer, not a psychiatrist. And he had his own problems to deal with. While the strange events that had ruined his marriage to Erica had, for the most part, subsided, there was still an occasional incident that caused him to worry.

There was the time he and Nancy had gone to look at a farm in Warren, Massachusetts, about twenty-five miles northeast of Longmeadow. They were standing on the porch, discussing the pros and cons of buying the property. In the middle of their talk Nancy took out the cross that she always wore around her neck, a cross given to her by her mother.

"Let's ask Jesus to help us decide, Maurice," she said.

All of a sudden Maurice's eyes widened and looked as if they were on fire. He stared at Nancy as if she had done something terrible. Then he reached over, and using both hands, pushed her off the porch.

Before Nancy could say anything, Maurice had leapt off the porch and was on top of her. He yanked the cross, chain and all, from around her neck and threw it into the woods.

Nancy was crying. "Maurice, what did you do that for? That cross was a gift from my mother. What's gotten into you?"

But Maurice was already back on the porch and was mumbling, "I have her by the hand...I have her by the hand."

Nancy came over to him, but he seemed to have forgotten the incident.

Nancy tried to get him to talk about what he had done with the cross, but Maurice insisted he didn't know what she was talking about.

The next night, however, Maurice told Nancy he had something for her—and he reached into his pocket and pulled out the cross.

"Maurice, you went back to get it for me," Nancy said, astonished. "I'm so glad. But how did you find it? Those woods are thick with brush."

"I didn't find it," Maurice said. "A lady found this cross. A lady in white. She took me by the hand and led me to where this cross was. I don't even remember where. But she showed me right where it was."

"What lady? Who?" Nancy asked.

Maurice hesitated. Then he blurted out something that frightened Nancy. "I didn't get a good look at her face, but I think it was your mother."

Nancy sat down. "I think I need a drink of water," she said. She didn't know what to think of Maurice's story. Her mother had been dead for fifteen years. Maybe, she thought, her husband had seen her spirit. It was her mother's cross and chain. Maybe her mother had come back to help him retrieve it. Nancy figured anything was possible. She had a spiritual nature and a lot of faith. Maybe spirits do exist, she thought. After all, the Holy Ghost is a spirit, right? She had never seen a ghost, that was true. And neither had Maurice, as far as she knew. But there was always a first time for everything.

On the other hand, it was also possible that Maurice was crazy.

She decided to try the spirit theory. It gave her hope that she might see her mother again, which felt very comforting.

"Yes, Maurice," she said. "It was probably my mother's spirit."

She said it, but unconvincingly. She just didn't know what to believe.

■ ■ ■

Despite the strange incident Maurice and Nancy decided to go ahead and buy the farmhouse in Warren. Not long afterward Philippe announced, out of nowhere, that he was moving his family to Oklahoma, to be closer to Philippe, Jr., and the other children who had moved there over the past few years.

Maurice was upset. He didn't want to be so far from his mother. But something else bothered him even more. He didn't know why, but he had a sinking feeling that he would never see Alice again. He begged his father not to pull up and move west, but it was no use. Once his mind was made up about something, there was no changing it and Maurice knew that.

After they had gone Maurice's mother was constantly on his mind. A feeling of doom came over him whenever he thought about her living out there in the middle of nowhere. His father's hasty decision to move to Choctaw, Oklahoma, just didn't sit right with him. Just what had been going through Philippe's mind?

A year went by. Maurice called his mother long-distance from time to time, and things seemed to be going okay. Maurice's fear—that his father might revert to his old violent ways—hadn't come true. Instead he was only getting more sullen and depressed, Alice reported. Sometimes, she said, it was more frightening than when he used to throw a chair or lash out with a belt.

So the nagging worry continued to weigh heavily on Maurice's mind.

One night in June 1982, Maurice and Nancy were getting ready to go to bed when they heard a strange noise in the house. It sounded like somebody mumbling downstairs. "Maurice, did you hear that?" she asked.

"It sounds like somebody talkin', but I can't make it out," he answered. "I'll go down and take a look around."

Maurice came back up a few minutes later. "Nobody down there," he reported. "We must have imagined it."

They got into bed and heard the sounds again.

"Maurice, there's definitely somebody down there. In fact, I hear two voices. A man and a woman. It's like they're arguing. Shhh, listen!"

Maurice had heard it too. He got out of bed and ran down the stairs again, but when he got to the living room the noises had stopped. He looked around everywhere but found nobody. They were both a little frightened but figured it had to be their imaginations. Sometimes the wind can play tricks.

He climbed back into bed and told Nancy there was nothing to worry about. Before he drifted off to sleep he had worried thoughts about his mother. For some reason he thought she was in some kind of danger. He thought of calling her, but it was late. He'd call her in the morning.

■ ■ ■

Maurice and Nancy were awakened before dawn by a loud pounding on the front door.

"Open up, open up!"

Maurice kicked off the sheets and grabbed a robe before heading down the stairs. He opened the door and saw a somber-faced police officer standing there. "We tried to call you, but nobody answered," the policeman said.

A cold chill raced down Maurice's spine. "What's the matter?" he demanded.

By this time, Nancy had rushed downstairs and stood by Maurice's side. "What's going on?"

"You better call your sister Lucy in Oklahoma," the cop replied. "There's been a terrible accident. I'm sorry." Then he turned and walked to his cruiser.

Maurice's heart sank. The sense of doom was so real that he could almost taste it. Something horrible had happened. The cop hadn't said so, but he knew somehow that his mother had been involved.

He held his breath while he dialed Lucy's number in Choctaw. Before the end of the first ring, however, Maurice's palms got sweaty and his head began spinning. Everything turned white. He dropped the phone and fell to the floor.

As Nancy grabbed the phone, Maurice's brother-in-law Ken Paxton answered at the other end. "Ken, this is Nancy," she shouted. "What happened out there?"

"Nancy," he said, his voice almost a whisper. "You better sit down."

SIX

IN JUNE, 1982, the following article appeared in the Holyoke *Tribune-Transcript:*

> *Police in Oklahoma expect a final report Wednesday on the apparent murder-suicide of a former Holyoke couple living in Choctaw, Okla.*
>
> *Choctaw Police Chief Randy Holt today said only technical reports from the medical examiner's office, ballistics office, and the Oklahoma State Bureau of Investigation need to be finished.*
>
> *"We expect the final report to go along the lines of the preliminary ruling from the medical examiner's office and our investigation, which ruled it a murder-suicide," Holt said.*
>
> *Philippe, 69, and Alice (Pelletier) Theriault, 64, of Choctaw, were found dead in their bedroom Friday morn-*

ing. Police said the cause of death was gunshot wounds.
The Theriaults' daughter, Lucy Waldrop, of Nicoma Park,
Okla., with whom the couple was staying, found the bod-
ies after hearing shots.

Police said three shots were fired by Mr. Theriault.
They said the first shot missed and lodged in the head-
board of the bed, while the second struck Mrs. Theriault in
the right side of the head. Mr. Theriault then shot himself
in the chest, according to police.

Funeral services for the couple will be Wednesday
morning at the Messier-Farrell Funeral Home, Chestnut
Street, Holyoke, followed by the liturgy of Christian burial
in Our Lady of Perpetual Help Church here. Burial will be
in Notre Dame Cemetery, South Hadley. Calling hours at
the funeral home are Tuesday from 2 to 9 P.M.

Maurice had scarcely gotten up from his chair since he came to
after the phone call to Oklahoma. Suddenly life seemed to have
lost all meaning. His beloved *maman* was gone. Nancy had come
over to him several times, trying to comfort and console him,
but it was no use. He didn't want to talk, he didn't want to eat. He
didn't want to do anything. All he could do was think about what
had happened out there in Oklahoma.

He had worried for years that Philippe might snap and do
something like this. Maybe I could have prevented it. Why didn't

I call last night? he thought. He tortured himself by imagining his mother's last few violent moments of life. He played the scene in his mind over and over again. There must have been a struggle. He probably had been beating her. She was shot at a close distance. "Oh, poor *Maman*. My beloved, poor sweet *maman!*"

Finally, after darkness had fallen, Maurice, his mind exhausted, fell off to sleep, still in the same easy chair he had been sitting in all day. And he began to dream...

■ ■ ■

In Maurice's dream Alice Theriault woke slowly in the early-morning light in Nicoma Park, Oklahoma. Even though she knew she was awake, she kept her eyes shut. She could hear her husband, Philippe, moving around the bedroom of their daughter's house, and she had no desire to see him right away. It would automatically turn into a confrontation. She didn't want to spoil this visit with Lucy. It had been such a long time since they had been together. And if Philippe started cursing or hitting her, a family scene was sure to follow, as was usually the case. She smiled a little to herself to think that she'd always had the notion that her "golden years" would be easier.

After more than forty years of marriage to this volcanic personality, Alice still never knew where or when one of his maniacal outbursts might occur. There were days when he might not bother to wake her, preferring to have a solitary coffee in the kitchen, and other days when, if she didn't get up and prepare his breakfast, his face would turn purple with rage and he would take off his thick leather belt and whip her out of bed.

Having suffered almost half a century of abuse, Alice had stopped asking why Philippe could be so angry about something one day and not notice it the next. She had stopped asking, as well, why it was her lot to suffer abuse from such a man. She was simply grateful for the few isolated moments like these when she could lie in bed and drift, the light from the windows suffusing the inside of her eyelids with a warm glow that gave her thoughts a rosy hue.

Lying under the heavy coverlet that protected her from the brisk weather that had lingered into June, Alice let herself enjoy her dreamy state. She pictured her parents, whose warm example of love and mutual respect had stayed with her, in bitter contrast to her own marriage. *Maman* and *Papa* had been so happy together when she was growing up in Van Buren, Maine. She had thought all marriages must be the same. With Philippe Theriault she had found out just how different some unions could be.

As an adolescent Alice had worked as a seamstress. There had been such fun when she could work and giggle with the other girls in their homes, doing the piecework that often gave them cramps in their hands and didn't pay enough to buy one of the dresses they were making. Still, she had loved the companionship, and she and her special girlfriends had often walked arm in arm to downtown Van Buren for a movie or soda.

When Philippe Theriault had begun courting her she was afraid of him. He was five years older than she was and already had the rugged build and dark beard of a man. Alice still felt, in many ways, as if she had just become a teenager.

But the other girls thought him strong and handsome, and her parents, loving as they were, did nothing to discourage a match that might mean she would marry and leave the house. After all, there were too many mouths to feed and too many daughters to marry off.

So she had married and had regretted it, and continued to regret it every day of her life. Philippe had quickly proved himself to be a bully of the worst kind. Alice realized within weeks that the hulking farmer had married her just to have a maid who would cook and clean and sleep with him.

On Saturday nights when she knew that her girlhood friends were at the movies, as she herself had been such a short time ago, she would have to sit quietly in the corner while Philippe got viciously drunk. She had asked once if she couldn't go out with her old friends, but her husband had called her a tramp and forbidden it. In any case, she couldn't afford it, since Philippe gave her no money.

No, her best hope was to be quiet and hope that Philippe would drink until he passed out, before becoming physically abusive. He had hit her on their wedding night, and although the blows were rare, the threat of them had never abated.

She had thought at first to leave him, but she had become

pregnant almost immediately after the wedding. Seven sons and eight daughters had followed, and any thought that she might escape her disastrous marriage had vanished in the avalanche of work involved in taking care of her children. Philippe had never considered pregnancy a reason for her to stop her daily chores, and the number of children to be cared for made that an impossibility, in any case.

But she did love being a mother, despite the work, and found some fulfillment in having loving relationships with each of her children.

Alice's thoughts turned to Maurice, her eldest. Although she had special feelings for each of her children, there was no denying that her relationship with Maurice was unique. He was a fine boy, a sweet boy, she thought, and she hoped that he might one day become a priest, one of God's chosen ministers.

She had done her best throughout his childhood to protect him from Philippe's murderous tantrums, to see that he was clean and well fed and that he got a good education. When Philippe forced him to quit school, she had been as heartbroken as her son.

She remembered tenderly the tranquil moments the two had shared when Philippe wasn't there. Most of those moments seemed to have taken place in the kitchen when Maurice was still very young. Surrounded by the smells of traditional French-Canadian dishes, mother and son enjoyed what were perhaps the most loving moments in their lives for some twenty years.

Alice remembered just as vividly the pain she had felt when Maurice had cursed his father in the field, and again when he'd left the house. She understood why he had to go, but it still removed one of the bright spots in her own existence, which was otherwise so hard and dreary. She also knew that, no matter how justified it was, no good could come of such a sacrilegious oath.

Alice was convinced that now, with Nancy, the forty-three-year-old Maurice had found safe haven, had found the peace that had eluded him all his life. She thought of the mysterious stranger who had once picked Maurice out of a snowbank during a raging blizzard and delivered him safely home.

Guard him all his life and bring him safely home to You, she silently prayed.

Alice heard Philippe leave and then quickly re-enter the room, opening and shutting drawers as if he was looking for something. She shut her eyes more firmly and feigned sleep. Lost in her few good memories, she had no desire to replace them immediately with the hard reality of Philippe Theriault and the state of Oklahoma.

Alice did not like Oklahoma. The American West—with its windswept plains, rolling clouds, and harsh landscape—seemed so alien after a lifetime in New England. Here there were no little villages with picturesque churches, no stone walls, no apple trees, no familiar faces. A woman of French-Canadian descent who spoke English with a decided accent, when she spoke it at all, did not fit in a land of oil rigs and cowboys. Alice loved visiting her children, but lying there in the guest room of Lucy's house, she couldn't help but wish they were all back in Maine.

Alice could not have known that she would never see the region of her birth again, would never see her children again, would never see another morning.

■ ■ ■

Maurice's dream continued. In it, Alice was back in her parents' living room in Van Buren, trying to guess whether the delightful odor coming from the kitchen was her mother's *pain complet,* wheat bread, or a *baguette,* the long, thin loaf of French bread that accompanied all family dinners. It seemed to her that she could hear the voices of her brothers and sisters running and laughing about her. Large families were normal among the staunchly Catholic French-Canadian families of Maine, and hers was no different: five brothers and four sisters made for a very lively household indeed.

But even as these memories surrounded her, she was suddenly overcome by an overpowering stench, something acrid, putrid, as if all the animals in her father's barn had defecated there in her parents' living room. But as soon as this absurd thought presented itself, she realized it could not be, that the smell was here, here in Nicoma Park, Oklahoma, here in the room with her.

She opened her eyes. What she saw was so utterly terrifying, a scream throbbed in her throat. Philippe was kneeling on the edge of the bed, leering down at her. He was dressed normally, wearing his habitual blue jeans and a plaid work shirt, but it was a Philippe she had never seen, not even in his wildest rages. His brow was so swollen that it was apelike, and his lips were drawn back over his teeth, giving his jaw the look of a muzzle. His eyes were black, like two bottomless holes.

Alice knew she was in grave danger. She could not see Philippe's hands, which seemed to be holding something under the folds of the coverlet, but she was sure he was holding his belt and was going to beat her.

"*Good morning,*" he purred.

Alice gasped. The voice had come from Philippe, but it was not his voice. "Philippe, why are you talking like that?" she asked.

"*We are not Philippe,*" he replied.

"We? What do you mean 'we'? Who are you? What are you?" she whispered in French.

"*Nous sommes des vieux copains de Philippe,*" the voice replied. "*We are old buddies of Philippe's.*"

The temperature of the room, which had been chilly but nothing more, now became freezing and Alice shook under the covers, whether from fear or from the cold, she could not tell.

Alice, who was both deeply religious and a bit superstitious, did not want to ask the next question, but searched instinctively to keep this, this *creature* talking.

"What is your name?"

But it didn't answer. Instead, a steady stream of talk—disjointed, bizarre, blasphemous—came forth.

"*Mrs. Stickney, Mrs. Stickney...in cowl and beads and dusty garb...the eel is credited with the possession of many marvelous virtues...the power of transformation is shown in a multitude of cases...fuck, fuck, fuck...Joan of Arc was married to the fire...hideous...wolf, cat, dog, griffin...Uriel...the nails...Sextus reigned six years...Ooooaaaaaaaaaaaaaaaah...Stick together now, mates...The Claimant, the Daring One, Mr. Homunculus...You ask me to tell you how we know the Ruler of Seven Chains.*"

"What is your name?"

"Toise."

"Who are you?"

"Not your mother." And the creature with her husband's face began to cackle.

"Astaroth, Baal, Cozbi, Dagon, Aseroth, Baalimm, Chamo, Beelphegor, Astarte, Bethage, Phogor, Moloch, Asmodaeus, Bele, Nergel, Melchon, Asima, Bel, Nexroth, Tartach, Acharom, Belial, Neabaz, Merodach, Adonides, Baemot, Jerobaal, Socothbenoth, Mahomer, Beelzebub, Leviathan, Lucifer, Satan! Recognize us now?"

"Who are you?"

"We're the devil."

Alice fainted. Instantly she felt herself being shaken so hard she thought her neck would snap.

"Wake up, bitch," the creature snarled.

Opening her eyes again, Alice tried again to scream but felt her cries cut off as a hand closed around her throat. Leaning close to her ear, the creature uttered a warning so absolute, in a voice that carried such pure menace, that Alice simply stared terrified at the ceiling.

"*Shut up, bitch, or we will kill you now,*" it hissed.

The animal-like face, barely recognizable as her husband's, was in front of her again, only inches from her eyes.

"*That's better,*" he said. "*Much better.*"

"What are you going to do to me?" she quavered.

"*We are going to kill you, then we are going to kill this disgusting worm that we have used for so many years,*" he said, pointing at his own chest. "*Don't you think that will be a fitting conclusion to all the years we've tortured you and your family? We've even tortured him*"—he pointed again to himself—"*if the truth be told, which it can be now, because you aren't going to be telling anybody.*"

He laughed, snorting in a repulsive way, snot dripping from his broad nostrils, foamy spittle collecting in the corners of his mouth. Blood began to seep from his eyes. Gazing at Alice, who lay paralyzed on the bed, he continued:

"*Yes, we've even tortured this worm,*" he said, his voice constantly changing—now a guttural snarl, now a crooning singsong. "*So now his time is over. We're going to kill you and then we're going to kill the worm. The police will come and rule it a murder-suicide. What else could it be? The police don't believe in us, which is very convenient indeed for us. After that we will go and pay a visit to your dear son Maurice.*"

Alice closed her eyes. "Holy Mary, Mother of God!" she whispered.

The creature looming over her giggled.

"*Chaire Miryam, kecharitomene,*" he said in a strange language.

He grabbed Alice by the shoulders, pulled her toward him, and slammed her into the bed over and over again. *"Don't say that, bitch! Don't say that, bitch! Don't say that, bitch!"*

Finally, panting for breath, the creature who called himself Toise and said that he was the devil stopped his beating. But the covers on the bed were completely pulled loose, and now Alice could see her son-in-law's gun lying among the sheets.

The gun was left over from Ken's days on the Louisiana police force, and last night when he had come in he had hung it on the fireplace. Now she stared at it the way someone on the top floor of a tall building stares at the pavement below: dizzy at the idea of what would happen if she fell, wondering in horror if she would feel anything.

Through her terror she sensed that her only hope was to continue talking to the creature, even though she felt she would endanger her soul by doing so.

"Are you really the devil?" she asked.

"The devil, a devil, what do you care, you ugly old cunt? The main thing is, we're going to kill you and then your husband and then your son."

"Why?"

"Why not? Weren't we invited in? Didn't this worm we are inhabiting like to curse everyone and everything? Didn't your son invoke our name?"

His next words made Alice, for the first time, start to sob, for they came out of his mouth in the voice of Maurice.

"I'd rather work for the devil than work for you!" he mocked.

The tears ran down Alice's cheeks as she remembered Maurice's curse on his father.

"*Too bad he's not here, eh?*" said the creature. "*He could work for us both at once!*" And he let loose his demented laugh, strands of saliva hanging from his foul mouth.

Grabbing the gun from the bed, he began to stroke it lovingly. "*My lovely pet, my lovely pet! I want to fuck you, my lovely pet gun....*"

Alice thought for an instant of lunging for it, but her husband was far bigger and stronger than she, a condition that had forced her to passively accept his abuse all her life. She could not now, at this final moment, summon the courage to attack him in this horrible incarnation.

"*Maurice is almost awake,*" crowed the creature. "*We mustn't be late. The early bird gets the worm.*" And he laughed hysterically again. "*Toise must be going to visit your son.*"

Alice saw the death's head that now grinned down at her and began to pray:

"Our Father, Who art in heaven, hallowed be Thy name..."

Her prayer was cut off by the blast of gunfire and the *thwack* of a bullet crashing into the headboard beside her. As she started to rise and scream the second shot caught her in the right temple.

There was a bright burst, and the world went black before her eyes. As she rocketed down the long tunnel leading to death, the last thing she heard was the third gunshot and a voice gurgling, "*The worm...the worm.*"

Nancy and Maurice Theriault *(Photo by Mark Merenda)*

The Theriault farmhouse in Warren, Massachusetts *(Photo by Ed Warren)*

ABOVE: Father Galen Beardsley in front of St. Paul's Church in Warren, Massachusetts *(Photo by Mark Merenda)* RIGHT: Bishop Robert McKenna in front of Our Lady of the Rosary Chapel in Monroe, Connecticut *(Photo by Mark Merenda)*

Ed and Lorraine Warren

SEVEN

The Devil hath power to assume a pleasing shape.

—William Shakespeare, *Hamlet*

How are you fallen from Heaven,
Lucifer! Son of the Dawn!
Cut down to the ground!
And once you dominated the peoples!

Didn't you say to yourself:
I will be as high as Heaven!
I will be more exalted than the stars of God!
I will, indeed, be the supreme leader!
In the privileged places!
I will be higher than the Skies!
I will be the same as the Most High God!

But you shall be brought down to Hell,
to the bottom of its pit.
And all who see you,
    will despise you...
                    —Isaiah 14:12–19

■   ■   ■

AT THE END of Stephen Vincent Benét's famous short story "The Devil and Daniel Webster," the Prince of Darkness is forced to promise that he will never again show his face in the state of New Hampshire.

It is nowhere recorded that any such promise was made about Massachusetts. The Bay State's history is rife with documented cases of devil worship, witchcraft, and black magic. The state that is known for producing presidents and scholars is also known for Lizzie Borden, who "took an ax and gave her mother forty whacks/ Then when she was good and done/ Gave her father forty-one," and for being the home of Albert DeSalvo, the "Boston Strangler."

But there could hardly be a more unlikely spot for the dramatic events of 1985 than Warren, Massachusetts.

On the western border of Worcester County, Warren is a rural town of seventeen thousand acres (twenty-nine point five square miles) of scenic hills and valleys bisected by the Quaboag River. Located on Route 67, which connects with Routes 9 and 20, the town has access to the Massachusetts Turnpike eight miles to the east and ten miles to the west. It is equidistant from Worcester and Springfield (Massachusetts's second- and third-largest cities, respectively), each twenty-five miles away. The Quaboag River, which still bears traces of industrial dams of a century ago, recently has been favored by canoe and kayak enthusiasts. There is a pond and a swimming beach in Warren, and parks and playgrounds for the good-weather months.

Situated some sixty-five miles west of Boston, the town is buried in the southwestern angle of Worcester County, hidden far from the intense spotlight that shines on "dear old Boston, home of the bean and the cod/ Where the Cabots speak only to the Lowells/ And the Lowells speak only to God." This characterization of Boston by John Collins Bossidy, in his toast at the Holy Cross College alumni dinner in 1910, and known to all in the Boston area, certainly had nothing to do with Warren.

Warren's prominence in the news was not to come from intellectuals like Bossidy, or from celebrated sports teams such as the Red Sox or Celtics, or from famous sons such as John F. Kennedy, or from a dramatic role in American history. When Warren made headlines it was to be for something sinister.

Originally part of the Quaboag Plantation (later called Brookfield), Warren was settled in 1727, and incorporated in 1741 as Western. In 1834 the name Western was changed to Warren in honor of the Revolutionary War hero General Joseph Warren.

Many prosperous dairy farms were the economic backbone of the community for its first one hundred years. Warren's history as a mill town began in 1815 with the first cotton-yarn factory, and shortly afterward, the first woolen mill. By the 1800s the community had switched from its agricultural base to a manufacturing economy, which it maintains today. Descendants of the original English, and later, Irish, French-Canadian, and Polish settlers comprise the majority of its current residents. There are only one or two black or Hispanic families living there.

Major industries employ more than fifteen hundred people in the town. Some fifty-seven percent of Warren adults are employed in manufacturing, compared to twenty-five percent of Massachusetts workers. Among the town's biggest employers are a manufacturer of commercial, military, and industrial pumps; a company that makes power presses; another that finishes and dyes cloth; and another that launders clothing and industrial linens.

As is the case with many industrial towns, Warren's population is not an educated one. Of all residents twenty-five years old and older, thirty-seven percent have an elementary-school education or less. Fifty-four percent have never finished high school.

Slightly to the northwest of present-day Warren is the town of Ware, and a short distance from the road that leads to Ware is what old New Englanders call a "town bound"—a spot comparable to the place in the southwestern United States where the borders of Arizona, Colorado, Utah, and New Mexico meet. One can walk around the town bound and pass through three towns and three counties. Local folklore has it that the spot had special significance for certain local inhabitants and that the remains of campfires and strange animal bones have been found in the area.

In the western part of the town is Colonel's Mountain, which reaches an altitude of 1,172 feet. From the summit there is a commanding view of the surrounding countryside. At the foot of the mountain was the home of the Quaboag Indians of the tribe of the Nipmucks. Scooped-out rocks and pestles that have been found there testify to the Indians' coarse, simple fare—samp or hominy and succotash, with wild meats and fish.

The Indians worshipped a number of spirits, some of them evil. For hundreds of years western Massachusetts rang with their cries, their songs, their dances, and their magic incantations. Among the most powerful members of the tribe was often the medicine man, who had the power to drive out evil spirits.

■ ■ ■

But the Indians were not the last practitioners of strange rites in Massachusetts. The Puritan Pilgrims who founded the Massachusetts Bay Colony governed themselves as a theocracy. Witchcraft and the devil were not mere abstractions to these stern men and women who had fled their own country in the face of religious persecution. Devils and witches were very real to them and there were strict laws to deal with them.

Contrary to popular myth, the cases of devil worship and witchcraft that have made Massachusetts infamous in the annals of the occult did not proceed from mass hysteria, nor were they assumed to be manifestations of the supernatural at first.

"When the devil broke forth again, at Salem village in 1692, he was not immediately recognized," according to Chadwick Hansen in his book *Witchcraft at Salem*. When several village girls began to be seized by fits and to complain of terrible pains, the town fathers first sought a medical remedy. "When these calamities first began," wrote the Reverend Samuel Parris, a clergyman of Salem, "which was in my own family, the affliction was several weeks before such hellish operations as witchcraft were suspected."

It seems also that in the Salem of 1692, as with Warren in 1985, the devil was invited to show his wickedness when human beings, innocently or otherwise, dabbled in the occult and invoked curses in his name.

"I fear some young persons, through a vain curiosity...have tampered with the devil's tools so far that hereby one door was opened to Satan to play those pranks, *anno* 1692," wrote Salem resident John Hale. He was referring to young girls in the village who used occult games (usually involving an egg and a glass) to try to find out the occupations of their future husbands. The rhyme associated with this game is still sung today: "Rich man, poor man, beggar man, thief."

One village girl dabbling in such occult practices was rewarded with the sight of a specter in the likeness of a coffin. "And she was afterwards followed with diabolical molestation to her death, and so died a single person," Hale wrote at the time. He added, "A just warning to others to take heed of handling the devil's weapons lest they get a wound thereby."

Once the evil genie was out of the bottle, it proved, as always, very hard to get him back in. One young woman after another fell ill, and they, in turn, accused neighborhood women of tormenting them and appearing before them with the devil. "The devil hath been raised among us, and his rage is vehement and terrible; and, when he shall be silenced, the Lord only knows," said Reverend Parris.

According to Hansen's *Witchcraft at Salem,* Tituba, a Carib Indian slave woman brought to New England from Barbados to serve in the Parris household, was being examined in court. Perhaps she, as the children's babysitter, would tell what was afflicting them.

"Did you ever see the devil?" she was asked.

"The devil," she replied, "came to me and bid me serve him."

The devil had come to her, Tituba said, in the shape of a man—a tall man in black with white hair. Other times he had come in the shape of an animal. He had told her he was God, that she must believe in him and serve him six years, and he would give her many beautiful things. He had shown her a book and she had made a mark in it, a mark that was "red like blood."

But Tituba said others had made marks in the book, and she, too, named some of the older women in the village. Soon the famous trials were under way, and when it was over more than fifteen people had been hanged as witches. One man, Giles Corey, who refused to answer to the charge, was "pressed" to death. Increasing amounts of weight, in the form of large rocks, were placed on his chest until he was crushed, his tongue protruding from his mouth at the end.

■ ■ ■

Although the devil is not often talked about in modern-day pulpits, almost all theologies recognize his existence. In so-called sophisticated circles, the devil is taken to be a metaphor for the evil that men do or the evil that befalls them.

But hundreds of millions of Christians—mostly Roman Catholics, Anglicans, and Protestant fundamentalists—and Hasidic Jews accept, as part of their faith, the idea that a malign spirit can invade a human being and take over the victim's personality.

Plato in his *Republic* not only speaks of demons of various grades but mentions a method of treating and providing for those possessed by them. Sophocles and Euripides describe the possessed, and mention of the subject is also to be found in Herodotus, Plutarch, Horace, and other ancient authors.

The name "devil" is derived from the Greek *diabolos*, "slanderer." It is the name for the supreme spirit of evil, the enemy of God and man. According to the orthodox Christian belief of the present day, Satan has been endowed with great powers for the purpose of tempting man to prove his fortitude.

The original idea of Satan is that of an "adversary" or "agent of opposition." This fits, of course, with the Christian belief in Satan as Lucifer, one of God's fallen archangels, who chooses to revolt against Him.

The Bible does not really explain Satan's origin. Although biblical scholars have always presumed that the serpent in Genesis who tempts Adam and Eve is Satan or his emissary, Satan does not appear until the book of Job, when Job and his sons are about to make an offering to God. "Satan," it says, "also came among them. And the Lord said to Satan, 'From where do you come?' So Satan answered the Lord and said, 'From going to and fro on the earth, and from walking back and forth on it.'"

In the Bible, Satan appears as a distinct personality, described in the book of Matthew as "Prince of Demons," and in Ephesians as the ruler of a world of evil beings who dwell in the lower heavens. In Revelations the war in heaven between God and Satan is described, and his imprisonment is foreshadowed after the overthrow of the beast and the kings of the earth, when he will be chained in the bottomless pit for one thousand years. After another period of freedom he is finally cast into the lake of brimstone forever.

The ability of demons to invade human beings is an important concept to millions of fundamentalist Christians. Most of them accept, on the basis of the Bible, that a person can be possessed by the devil. And there are people regarded as having special gifts who practice a "deliverance ministry," casting out evil spirits by praying over the victim and commanding the devil to leave.

The Roman Catholic Church is no exception. Pope John Paul II has gone out of his way to acknowledge the existence of the Evil One. In August of 1986 the Pope, in the last of a series of summer sermons, told the faithful that the devil exists and "is a cosmic liar and murderer." The Pope said that, contrary to many recent teachings, the devil is still very much in the world "tempting men to evil...to turn away from the law of God." John Paul invoked stark biblical images that portray the devil as an unclean spirit, tempter, evil one, anti-Christ, lion, dragon, or serpent. The Pope said he wanted to "clarify the true faith of the church against those who pervert it by exaggerating the importance of the devil or by denying or minimizing his malevolent power." The Pope asserted that Satan "has the skill in the world to induce people to deny his existence in the name of rationalism and of every other system of thought which seeks all possible means to avoid recognizing his activity."

According to the Reverend Lachlan M. Hughes, a Jesuit professor of canon law in England, demonic possession is a manifestation of the power that God left the devil after having expelled him from heaven. As the Bible says in I Peter 5:8, "The devil, as a roaring lion, walketh about seeking whom he may devour."

Why God has left the devil with such power is a mystery for those who ponder the nature of good and evil.

Although the Catholic Church is conscious of the devil and his deeds, it regards claims of diabolic possession as it does claims of miracles: with great skepticism. The symptoms of demonic possession closely resemble those of mental illness, so great caution is required before the Church will give permission for its final remedy: the solemn rite of exorcism.

Exorcism has always been a part of the Catholic faith. Jesus says in the Bible that He casts out devils, and the apostles performed exorcisms in His name. In the early Church anyone so gifted could exorcise. In the third century exorcism was restricted to the ordained clergy, in particular to a minor order called Exorcists, which was suppressed only in 1972. A manual for Roman Catholic exorcists was published in 1608 and ran to thirteen hundred pages.

The Catholic rite of baptism includes an exorcism (which does not presuppose possession) to ward off evil. As recently as February of 1986, Cardinal Anastasio Alberto Ballestrero of Turin names six exorcists, priests charged with casting out demons.

Perhaps the foremost authority on exorcism in our time is Malachi Martin, a former Jesuit professor at the Pontifical Biblical Institute in Rome and the author of more than a dozen books, including *Hostage to the Devil,* concerning the possession and exorcism of five living Americans.

Martin writes that Catholic Church authorities "believe that there is an invisible power, a spirit of evil; that this spirit can for obscure reasons take possession of a human being; that the spirit can and must be expelled—exorcised—from the person possessed; and that this exorcism can be done only in the name and by the authority and power of Jesus of Nazareth."

Martin sets forth the characteristics of a possessed person: a peculiar revulsion against symbols and truths of religion ("always and without exception a mark of the possessed person");

an inexplicable stench; freezing temperature; telepathic powers about purely religious and moral matters; a peculiarly unlined or completely smooth or stretched skin, or unusual distortion of the face, or other physical and behavioral transformations; acquired weight, in which the possessed person becomes physically immovable, or when those around the possessed are weighted down with a suffocating pressure; levitation, in which the possessed rises and floats off the ground, chair, or bed without physical support; violent smashing of furniture, constant opening and slamming of doors, tearing of fabric in the vicinity, and other phenomena, equally bizarre.

Possession by the devil, according to Father Martin, may result in such immobility that even the combined strength of several people cannot budge the victim. Or the possessed may reveal secrets he or she has no way of knowing. But the strongest indication of possession is the ability to converse intelligently, without repetitiveness, in a language the victim cannot possibly know.

As Father Martin notes, almost every one of these occurrences by itself might have another, more worldly explanation than demonic possession. Victims of Tourette's syndrome (a neurological disorder due to a chemical abnormality in the brain), for example, will sometimes let forth a stream of exclamations, barks, obscenities, along with facial contortions. Doctors also mention paranoia, epilepsy, Huntington's chorea, dyslexia, hysteria, and Parkinson's disease as maladies or disorders whose symptoms might be mistakenly construed as signs of possession.

. . .

The investigation that leads to an exorcism usually begins because a man or a woman is brought to the notice of Church authorities by family or friends, and these people recount events that, taken together, cannot reasonably be laid at the door of any disease known to modern science. In these cases, there is no other recourse than exorcism. A special man is needed: the exorcist.

There is no official public appointment of exorcists. In some dioceses there is a private arrangement between the bishop and one of his priests whom he knows and trusts. In other dioceses "the bishop knows little about it and wants to know less," as Martin notes.

The Church has not laid down qualifications for an exorcist, other than that he be an ordained priest. There is no official training for an exorcist, although Church authorities find it advisable that a priest attempting an exorcism has already assisted at another. But Father Martin, in his chapter "A Brief Handbook of Exorcism," describes the typical (if there could be such a thing) exorcist:

"Usually he is engaged in the active ministry of parishes," he writes. "Rarely is he a scholarly type engaged in teaching or research. Rarely is he a recently ordained priest. If there is any median age for exorcists, it is probably between the ages of fifty and sixty-five. Sound and robust physical health is not a characteristic of exorcists, nor is proven intellectual brilliance, postgraduate degrees, even in psychology or philosophy, or a very sophisticated personal culture. All have been sensitive men of solid rather than dazzling minds.

"Though, of course, there are many exceptions, the usual reasons for a priest's being chosen are his qualities of moral judgment, personal behavior, and religious beliefs—qualities that are not sophisticated or laboriously acquired but that somehow seem always to have been an easy and natural part of such a man. Speaking religiously, these are the qualities associated with special grace."

When an exorcism is needed, it is the exorcist who makes all the decisions, who chooses an assistant priest, if he wants one, and lay assistants. The time and the place of exorcism is left to him.

The place of exorcism is generally in the home of the possessed person. There is a reason for this: As with the Theriault farmhouse, there is a close connection between spirit and physical location.

"The puzzle of spirit and place makes itself felt in many ways and runs throughout virtually every exorcism," writes Father Martin. "There is a theological explanation. But that there is some connection between spirit and place must be dealt with as a fact."

During an exorcism, Father Martin says, the room must be cleared, since objects—even heavy ones—may move about, rock back and forth, even fly across the room and strike the priest or the possessed person or the lay assistants. "It is not rare," Martin writes, "for people to emerge from an exorcism with serious physical wounds."

Windows and doors are securely closed, both to keep the demonic force from affecting the area outside and to stop the possessed person from attempting to throw himself or the exorcist or his assistants from a window.

The number of lay assistants will vary with the exorcist's expectation of physical violence. Four is typical, and often a medical doctor is present as well. In recent years tape recorders and even video cameras have been used.

The assistants must be physically strong and the exorcist, who has fasted and confessed in preparation for his battle with the devil, must make sure that his assistants are not consciously guilty of personal sins at the time of the exorcism, because they, too, can expect to be attacked by the evil spirit. Any sin can be used as a weapon against them.

"The exorcist must be as certain as possible beforehand that his assistants will not be weakened or overcome by obscene behavior or by language foul beyond their imagining; they cannot blanch at blood, excrement, urine; they must be able to take awful personal insults and be prepared to have their darkest secrets screeched in public in front of their companions," Father Martin writes. "These are routine happenings during exorcisms."

Nor is it unusual for an exorcism to last for days on end, or for the poor victim of possession to require two, three, or more exorcisms before finding freedom from his affliction.

"Possession and exorcism are not themselves mere fads with no interest beyond the bizarre and the significantly frightening," says Father Martin. "They are tangible expressions of the reality which envelops the daily lives of ordinary people."

EIGHT

THE STRANGE INCIDENTS that had plagued Maurice off and on for much of his life seemed to escalate after he, Nancy, and her two daughters, Jenny and Lori, moved into the farmhouse in Warren in May 1982.

That summer they decided to drive to Saratoga, New York, to visit Nancy's father. It was late evening. The sun had just set, leaving a delicate lavender edge on a few puffy clouds in the western horizon. The sky went from orange to deep purple. With the windows down, they were enjoying the balmy air as they cruised along the Massachusetts Turnpike in Maurice's New Yorker, at a steady sixty miles per hour.

Suddenly the car started rapidly accelerating until it was doing about ninety. The pedal seemed to be pushing down by itself, out from under Maurice's foot. He scrambled around for the pedal, trying to pull it out, while steering at breakneck speed. The tires were burning rubber. He felt frozen to the wheel.

He slammed on the brakes, but the car continued to surge forward. Maurice did his best to control the vehicle, but he felt something pulling his hands from the steering wheel.

Nancy was screaming, but her arms and legs were immobilized, as though she were tied down with weights. She shouted, "Frenchy, what are you trying to do? Slow down! You're going to kill us! Stop! Stop it!" It took all her strength to use her voice. It was exactly like a bad dream, only she was awake.

Despite what was going on, Maurice didn't panic. He felt as if there was an outside force in the car with them and that their lives were in that force's hands. "Okay," he said. "If there is somebody in here with us, why don't you just take over completely?"

He took his hands off the wheel and his feet off the pedals.

Nancy was still unable to move. She closed her eyes as the car moved by itself into the passing lane, surging ahead, passing a tractor-trailer truck, and then suddenly pulling back into the cruising lane, finally slowing down to a normal rate of speed.

Maurice took the wheel again and continued driving toward New York.

Nancy regained control of her body. "Maurice, what the hell were you trying to prove?" Nancy shouted, shaking all the while.

"You know I didn't do that," he replied. "I couldn't have done that."

Nancy knew Maurice was telling the truth. She had seen what happened. But she didn't want to believe it.

She cried all the way to Saratoga, until she was hoarse. She stared out the window, trying to figure out what in the world had caused the car to drive on its own.

■ ■ ■

The following year, on New Year's Day, there was a blizzard. Snow had been falling all day and was at least a foot deep. Around the house there were some drifts more than three feet high. It was a major nor'easter, as they say in Maine.

Nancy was sitting in the living room, reading the paper. It was getting dark out and she had just a few moments to sit by the fire and read the weather forecast before she'd have to get up and prepare dinner.

Maurice had been sitting next to her but had gotten up a few minutes before to make a cup of coffee.

"Honey," she called out to him, "they say this snow may last all night."

But he didn't reply.

That's strange, she thought. If there was one thing Maurice liked to talk about, it was the weather—especially storms. Whenever she mentioned the subject, he'd get all excited and animated and go on and on about this storm or that and how the weather in Massachusetts was nothing compared to the weather in Maine.

She yelled out to him again. "Maurice!"

Still he didn't answer.

Maybe he's gone into the bedroom, she thought. He had been shoveling the driveway all afternoon and was probably exhausted. Maybe he was catching a few winks before dinner.

Nancy went through the kitchen and peeked into the bedroom. He wasn't there. There was a strange smell though. A bad smell, like rotten potatoes. "Phew-ee! What's that?" She looked around for the source, but the smell seemed to disappear when she tried to locate it.

She called out to her daughter Jenny to look around for her stepfather. A few minutes later Jenny came back into the living room and reported that she couldn't find Maurice. He wasn't anywhere in or around the house.

Nancy and Jenny were puzzled. They would have seen him if he had gone back outside—unless he'd used the cellar door, but nobody had ever used that before. It was nailed shut.

They went to the front door, where Nancy called out his name. It was still snowing. "Maurice! You out there?" Nancy's voice echoed across the snow-blanketed yard.

Seconds later Maurice popped his head out from behind the barn door. "I'm in here," he yelled back. "Turn on the light. I'm comin' right in."

As Maurice trudged to the house through the knee-deep snow, Nancy noticed something that bothered her. Maurice was leaving footprints as he walked from the barn toward the house, but there were none left from when he had walked from the house to the barn. The snow was falling hard—but not hard enough to cover up a grown man's tracks made only a few minutes earlier.

"Maurice, how come there're no tracks going out to the barn?" Nancy asked.

Maurice looked confused. "What do you mean? I been out there all day," he said. "Those tracks been covered up for hours." He stamped his boots on the porch and made a halfhearted attempt at shaking the snow off his hat and coat before entering the house.

Nancy grimaced and started to say something about not tracking snow into the house, but Maurice was already on his way into the kitchen. She decided to forget about it. The house needed cleaning anyway. A little slush wouldn't matter.

Just then Maurice came back out of the kitchen, holding a cup of hot coffee. That's weird, Nancy thought. He wasn't even in there long enough to boil water, let alone make coffee. And he didn't have a snowflake left on him. Not even a melted one.

She went up to him and touched him. He wasn't in the slightest bit cold. Nancy grabbed his arm and pulled on his sleeve, shouting, "What's going on, Maurice? Why aren't you cold? You've been out in the snow. Why aren't you wet and cold? What's with you?"

The mysterious smell came back for an instant.

Maurice raised his eyebrow and stared at her as if she were from another planet. Then he sat down in his easy chair and lit up a cigarette. 'Yeah, it's supposed to be a bad storm," he said. "But nothin' like the ones we used to get back home. No way."

. . .

During this time Maurice was having trouble sleeping. He'd fall off to sleep easily, as he always had. He was usually tired from a hard day out in the fields. But he'd often wake up in the middle of the night, terrified, from some bad dream. One of the dreams kept recurring. In it a bent-over, evil man was sticking pins in his back and laughing.

On this particular morning Maurice awoke from an especially poor night's sleep. He'd been having that dream again. No matter how many times he woke up and fell back to sleep, he couldn't shake that same awful dream. Maurice didn't know what it was supposed to mean or who the man was who was sticking him with pins. His face was obscured. At first Maurice thought it was his father. But sometimes the face seemed more hideous—like something out of an old horror movie he had seen on television.

As he climbed out of bed, Nancy took one look at him and screamed. "Maurice! What's that on your back?"

Maurice turned around. "What are you talkin' about?"

"Maurice, look! There's some kind of writing on your back."

He thought she was joking. "Stop kiddin' around," he said.

But Nancy wasn't kidding. "Look in the mirror," she demanded.

Curious now, Maurice turned his back to the full-length mirror on the wall, peering over his shoulder to see what his wife was talking about.

"Holy shit!" he said.

Nancy hadn't been kidding. There, clear as a New England spring day, were four words scratched out across his back, as if someone had taken a needle and etched a message: *"La porte est ouverte."*

"What is that, Maurice? What does it say? I don't think it's English."

Maurice had trouble making out the words he saw reflected in the mirror, so he asked Nancy to sound out the words as best she could. "La portay est oovray?"

Maurice thought for a moment. It sounded like French, his native language. Nancy obviously hadn't pronounced the words properly, but he got the message. *"Mais oui,"* he said. *"La porte est ouverte.* The door is open."

"What the heck is that supposed to mean, Maurice? The door is open? To what? What happened to you?"

Maurice knew that the scratchings were somehow connected to his dream. Someone was opening a door for him. He didn't want to go through it. But for some reason he feared his wishes didn't really matter.

He wondered if perhaps it was some kind of warning. He had gotten mysterious warnings in the past but had ignored them, not really understanding them until it was too late. But now he was learning to pay more attention to these warnings. Three years before, in the winter of 1981, he had been given what he and Nancy later figured was a warning about his parents' impending deaths, but at the time they had misinterpreted it.

It had been a typical February day in New England. It was cold, with temperatures in the twenties. And the slate-gray sky that made life so depressing around that time of year seemed to be hanging more heavily than usual. Maurice and Nancy had to ride into town to pick up some supplies. They had just gotten to the pickup when Maurice began to feel dizzy. He leaned against the door.

"Your father doesn't have long to go," he blurted out in a voice much deeper than his own. Then he fell to the ground.

Nancy rushed to his side. "Maurice, are you all right?"

Maurice had passed out for a moment, but was quickly back to normal. "I'm okay," he said. "I just got dizzy for a second. Maybe I need something to eat."

"Maurice, you said something scary just before you passed out," Nancy said. "You said my father is going to die. And you said it in a different voice. It was weird. What did you say that for?"

Maurice looked puzzled. "I didn't say anything," he said.

But as they walked to the farmhouse to get a glass of water, Maurice felt uneasy. He felt death in the air. He could almost smell it.

"Let's call my dad," Nancy said. "I want to make sure he's okay."

As it turned out, Simon Junot was fine. Not long afterward, when Philippe Theriault shot and killed his wife and himself, Maurice and Nancy thought back to that February day. Could it have been a warning? And if so, who was trying to warn them? And why?

These were questions Maurice and Nancy couldn't answer. All they knew was that things were getting stranger and stranger.

Nancy had been jotting notes on these unusual occurrences in a diary that she kept under her bed. She called it her "little black book." After each incident, she would pull out the book and write down what had happened.

Maurice didn't like the practice. He just wanted to ignore what was happening to him, hoping the strange events would stop on their own. But after his parents had died, he remembered the warning and asked Nancy to take out the book and read him what she had written. He especially wanted to hear the part about when he had been warned about his father's death.

Nancy walked into the bedroom and reached under the bed for the book. She hadn't looked at it in quite some time. When she pulled it out she was surprised to see that it was charred black, as if it had been in a fire. "This book's all burned!" she said, looking at Maurice as if to accuse him of having set it on fire.

Maurice looked surprised. "Don't look at me," he said. "I didn't do it."

Nancy opened it and began to cry as she flipped through what was left of the pages. Every one had been charred. Even a photograph of her elder daughter had been burned.

"How could this happen?" she demanded. "We haven't had a fire. You burned it, didn't you? You never liked me writing in it."

Maurice looked at her. "I didn't do it," he said. "You got to believe me."

"You sure you didn't burn this book, Frenchy?"

But Nancy could tell from the fear on his face that he was telling the truth. Besides, she never knew him to lie to her. If he hadn't wanted the book around, he probably would have asked her to throw it out. But he wouldn't have set it on fire. He wasn't like that. He was a good man.

Maurice was telling the truth. He was even more frightened than she was. They were both thinking the same thought at the same time: If someone was setting books on fire, what might be set on fire next?

Strange events such as those that were plaguing Maurice and Nancy would put a strain on any relationship. Maurice and Erica had broken up over similar problems. And the bizarre occurrences prompted many arguments between Maurice and Nancy. But Nancy was made of stronger stuff. No matter what happened, Nancy was determined to stick by him. She realized that her man seemed to be in some kind of trouble, and she was certainly not going to abandon him when he needed her most. She decided that they would have to seek help.

"Maurice," she said one day as they sat at the breakfast table, sipping their morning coffee. "I want us to see a priest."

Maurice didn't say anything, just kept his coffee cup to his lips. But from the look on his face Nancy could tell he was relieved. The events had been taking their toll on him. He was trying not to dwell on them, but the more he did that, the stranger things got. He was clearly frightened. "We'll go see Father Beardsley right after breakfast," she said.

. . .

The kindly parish priest was just finishing saying Mass when Maurice and Nancy pulled up. He recognized them from Sunday Mass. They weren't zealous churchgoers, but they came often enough. He agreed to see them in his study right away.

He brought them into his small, tidy wood-paneled office. The room had a nice reassuring smell. There was a worn Oriental rug on the floor in front of a very comfortable deep-red brocade couch, a glass bookcase stacked with books, and there was a simple crucifix on the wall. He sat down behind his sturdy oak desk.

"Father, you've got to help us," Nancy said as she and Maurice sat down. "Strange things have been happening to us. Maurice has been getting messages, and I think they're from the spirit of my mother. We've been arguing a lot because of it."

Nancy deliberately did not tell the priest everything. She didn't want him to think they were crazy. She held tightly on to her purse handle, nervously snapping and unsnapping the fastener. "W-what can we do?" she asked.

Father Beardsley had heard a lot in his many years as a priest. Messages from "spirits" were nothing new. People thought they heard them all the time. The best way to deal with them, he knew from experience, was to find out what the spirit who was supposedly sending the message wanted and then to comply with the wishes—if they were harmless enough.

"And why would your mother be trying to communicate with you?" Beardsley asked. "What would she be trying to tell you?"

"Well, she wouldn't like it that we're living together when we're not married," Nancy replied. "She'd want us to make it right."

"So why don't you?" asked the priest.

Maurice and Nancy just looked at each other.

"I'll marry you myself," Beardsley said.

The next day they set the date.

■ ■ ■

The marriage took place May 19, 1984, at St. Paul's Church. Father Beardsley performed the ceremony. Nancy wore a simple blue dress with a white lace collar and held a small bouquet. Maurice wore his Western suit with the string tie, the same one he'd worn on his first date with Nancy. The only guests in attendance were Maurice's younger sister, Judy, and her husband, Craig, and Nancy's brother, William, and his wife, Betsy.

After the ceremony the six of them went out to lunch at Maurice's favorite steak house. Afterward, Maurice and Nancy drove down to New Britain to stay overnight at Judy and Craig's house. The four of them went dancing that night at the French Club.

Maurice and Nancy felt good about what they had done. "I think things are going to be okay now, Maurice," she said, giving him a good-night kiss. "My mama's going to be happy about what we've done."

. . .

Nancy couldn't have been more wrong. If anything, the strange incidents that were making their lives a living hell only escalated.

A little over a month later Maurice was out in the field cutting up a big old beech tree that had fallen on his property during a lightning storm. He was using a chain saw, cutting the branches into more portable pieces. The wood and grass were still wet from all the rain, and the going was slippery. He was experienced with a chain saw and was being very careful.

As he worked he kept having a vision of the chain saw slipping out of his hands and cutting him. Suddenly he lost his grip on the saw, and the handle slipped out of his hands. The blade cut right into his work boot, sputtering to a stop halfway through.

Dark red blood began spurting through the hole where the blade had cut through the boot. But for some reason Maurice didn't feel any pain. "I didn't cut myself," he said out loud. "I didn't cut myself." He kept repeating the phrase as he slowly walked back to the farmhouse. "I didn't cut myself. I didn't cut myself." He continued to chant as he walked, leaving a trail of blood behind him.

When he reached the house he sat down on the brick steps and took off his bloody boot. When he peeled off his sock, which was also dripping with blood, Maurice saw that his foot was not bleeding at all. There wasn't even a wound! He should have been horrified, yet he wasn't surprised.

Just then Nancy came out of the house and saw the blood. "Oh, my God, Maurice, what happened? Quick! Let me get some towels! Do you want me to call an ambulance?"

"Don't bother," he said. "It's nothing. I'll be all right. It's only a scratch."

"That's really bleeding! You've lost a lot of blood," Nancy said. "Let me look at it."

But Maurice just brushed by her. "I said it was nothing," he muttered.

Just as he had known it would be, from the moment he'd started his little chant.

■ ■ ■

A few weeks later the first of three mysterious fires broke out at the farm. In the first one a storage shed, located about two hundred and fifty yards from the house, burned down to the ground. Maurice had been working close by in the yard and hadn't seen anyone near the shed.

The second fire occurred just a couple of weeks after that. This time it was the vegetable stand in front of the house, by the side of the road. It was badly damaged, but it was left standing.

The third fire broke out inside the house itself, in Nancy's daughter Jenny's bedroom, in the middle of the night. Again, there was no explanation for it.

Fortunately no one was hurt in any of the fires, but the three blazes in a row set Maurice back financially. And of course they had frightened him and Nancy considerably. For a while Maurice was staying up at night with a flashlight and a gun, waiting to catch whoever was setting the fires. He couldn't imagine who might be doing it. He didn't have any enemies in town.

Of course, he kept thinking that the fires might be related to the other strange events that had been occurring with increasing frequency around the farm. Then he'd try not to think about the unexplained knockings, bad smells, rattlings, heavy breathing, and walking sounds that were repeatedly waking him and Nancy up during the night.

In October Maurice was out in the yard with Jenny's fiancé, Dennis, raking leaves. As he raked, Maurice slipped and fell down next to a stately old elm tree. When he landed on the ground, he noticed he had fallen on a large piece of bark. Maurice picked it up and motioned to Dennis to come and take a look. But Dennis, noticing the unusual shape, just laughed. "Yeah, we can use it for home plate the next time we play softball."

But Maurice did not act as if he had just stumbled onto home plate. He turned deadly serious and began shouting, "Take it! It is a part of me! Take it in the house and shut out the lights and look at it!"

Jenny, who had heard Maurice yelling, came running out of the house toward the two men. Maurice insisted she take the piece of bark inside and look at it in the dark.

By this time Jenny was used to the strange occurrences that had been taking place around the farmhouse, so she took the bark inside. As Dennis passed her in the foyer, she whispered to him, "This is getting a little ridiculous."

"Just do it," Dennis shushed her and whispered back. "Don't get him upset."

So she brought the bark into a darkened bedroom—and couldn't believe her eyes when she saw it. The bark was glowing in the dark. It lit up the room like a thirty-watt bulb. "Jesus!" she said. "How can that be?"

Maurice took the bark and nailed it to the wall next to his bed.

The light continued to shine for the next several days. When it finally darkened he took it down and hung a crucifix in its place.

More strange things kept happening. Usually they were harmless enough, although they did create a lot of fear. Crucifixes would bleed, objects would glow in the dark. Fires would break out, but nobody ever got hurt. Even when things would happen to Maurice—such as the time he cut through his foot—he would survive intact, at least physically. What the incidents were doing to his mind was hard to tell.

It wasn't until just before Christmas of that year, 1984, that events began to pose a real threat to Maurice himself.

Maurice and Nancy decided they would really decorate the farmhouse that year. Normally they weren't big on Christmas. And Maurice hated the idea of putting up lights. But this year the kids wanted the holiday to be special. They were feeling the pressure of all the strange goings-on, and they thought a little extra Christmas spirit might help. What with all that had been happening, Maurice felt he ought to do something religious.

So Maurice made a six-foot wooden cross that he planned to mount on the roof, facing the street. He got out the wooden ladder and leaned it against the roof. Superstitious as always, he carefully avoided walking under the ladder. The cross resting on his shoulders, Maurice began climbing step by step up to the roof, with one hand carefully keeping his balance on the ladder.

Once on the roof, he nailed up the cross. Then he climbed back down the ladder to get the colored lights he was planning to string along the cross. Something happened on his way back up.

Maurice was on the second to the last step of the ladder, about to place his right foot on the top step when he felt the ladder twisting, as if someone at the bottom were trying to make him fall.

"Hey!" he shouted as he grabbed for the roof to hang on. He looked down. That's funny, he thought. There's nobody there.

He shrugged and took another step up. As soon as he took the step it happened again. This time the ladder shook violently. Maurice lost his balance, let go of the cross, and fell to the ground with a thud.

Maurice cried out with pain. He had landed on his shoulder and it hurt. But he was determined to finish the job. He got up, righted the ladder, placed it back against the front of the house, picked up the lights, and began climbing back up, carefully holding on to the ladder and making sure it was lodged more securely against the house.

He had touched the roof with his hand and was about to lift his right foot up and over, when the ladder began moving away from the house. Maurice grabbed for the drain but missed. He fell over backward and again hit the ground, this time landing on his head.

He was dazed but didn't lose consciousness. He was determined to try once more. He wasn't going to let this get the better of him. It was like a spiritual challenge, a fight between good and evil. At least the cross was up there. This time all he had to carry up with him were the lights, a hammer, and some nails.

Maurice strung the lights around his neck, picked up the hammer in one hand and the nails in the other, and took a deep breath. Then he stepped up on the ladder. He held the hammer in his right hand, ready to strike at anyone or anything that might attack him.

But this time he didn't even get halfway up before the ladder tipped over backward. As he fell Maurice could feel the string of Christmas lights tightening around his neck. Once on the ground he tugged at the lights, prying them away from his invisible assailant. "Get away from me!" he shouted. "Leave me alone!"

The lights loosened their grip around his neck and Maurice pulled them off. He threw them to the ground as he took a deep breath. He had decided that enough was enough. They would live without the lights again this year.

Nancy, who was inside the kitchen baking some Christmas cookies, heard Maurice shouting and came running outside to see what had happened. What now? she thought.

He told her the story. "Something's trying to kill me," he said.

"I'm scared, Maurice," she said, helping him into the house. "I want you to be careful. Promise me?"

Maurice, still smarting from the falls and the strangulation attempt, just nodded. "Yeah, I'll be careful," he said.

But he wondered how he could protect himself from an unseen enemy.

■ ■ ■

After Christmas Maurice and Nancy vowed that the new year was going to be better. After all, it couldn't be any worse, could it?

To start 1985 on a positive note, they toasted at midnight with a bottle of sparkling wine and made plans to take a vacation—their first in years. They decided to drive to Florida, soak up some sun, and leave all this weirdness behind them for a while.

They visited Orlando, Tampa, and St. Petersburg and enjoyed quite a pleasant trip—except for one day when they went out on a boat ride in the waters off St. Pete.

It was a picture-perfect Florida day. The sun was shining bright, without a cloud in the sky. The temperature was in the high seventies, and the winds were not much more than a gentle whisper. The beautiful blue gulf waters couldn't have been calmer.

Although he had grown up in Maine, Maurice lived all his life inland, far from the famous rocky shores. He wasn't used to being out on the high seas. At first he was reluctant to take the boat out, but when he saw what a beautiful day it was, he just couldn't think of an excuse.

They weren't offshore more than half an hour when it happened. Out of nowhere the skies darkened, and waves began to pound against the side of the little motorboat. Maurice was scared. "Let's get the hell out of here," he said.

Rain began pouring down on them as they raced back to shore. The drops felt like icy bullets on their bare skin. It suddenly felt like winter. It was a harrowing ride. Maurice didn't really know much about operating a boat, but he figured it wasn't much different from driving a car or a tractor. He got it back safely, but it was more difficult than he had thought. There aren't any waves on a road or in a field. He and Nancy were dripping wet when they turned the boat back in.

"No more boats," he declared. "I'm a landlubber and I'll always be a landlubber." As they walked to the car the sun came back out again. "Just our luck," Maurice said. Inside, he wondered if the freak storm might have been another in the string of strange events that he had been trying to escape by coming to Florida.

He decided it was just the changing nature of Florida's weather. He remembered what the boat-rental agent had said to him when he'd left the dock: "If you don't like the weather in Florida, just wait five minutes." Maurice thought it an odd thing to say, with the weather having been perfect at the time, but he hadn't let it bother him. Now he wondered if the man had known something.

Oh, what the heck! Maurice thought. Maybe he was making too much of an innocent comment. And he couldn't really complain. They had enjoyed perfect weather the entire time they were in Florida. One bad day hadn't ruined what had been a terrific vacation. The change of scenery had done him and Nancy good. Maybe when they got back to Warren things would be different. They decided they would try to make them different. To start with, they'd go to church more often. And they'd begin right away.

On their first Sunday back they dressed in their best clothes and drove the three miles to St. Paul's. They were a few minutes late, so they scurried from the parking lot to the church, not wanting Father Beardsley to notice their tardiness. They hadn't seen him much lately and they were embarrassed. When they got to the steep flight of stairs leading up to the front door, Maurice began climbing two steps at a time. He could already hear the organ music playing. Mass was under way.

"Come on, Nancy," he shouted, looking back at her as she climbed the steps one at a time behind him.

"I'm coming, I'm coming," she said.

Suddenly Maurice was falling backward toward her—as if he had been pushed. But they were the only people on the steps.

Nancy stumbled but managed to move aside. Maurice rolled down about four of the stone steps before coming to a stop. He was scraped and bruised a bit, and his pants were ripped at one knee, but other than that he was all right. He looked up at Nancy as if to say, Why me?

"You all right, Maurice?" she asked.

"Yeah, I'll live," he said. "But I'm gettin' tired of this." Maurice blessed himself not once but twice with holy water as he entered the vestibule. And as always, Maurice fidgeted throughout the entire Mass. But Nancy spent the hour deep in prayer. Maurice could hardly believe it. He had never seen her pray so hard in all his life. "Ain't you goin' to come up at all for air?" he joked just before Holy Communion was about to be given.

But Nancy was dead serious. "Maurice, this is important," she snapped. "Why don't you pray too?"

When Mass was over, Nancy looked Maurice right in the eye. "Listen to me, Maurice," she said. "And listen good. Something's rotten in Denmark. I don't know what's going on with you. But I can't believe it's my mother's spirit that's doing this to you. I think there's something evil here. And I'm afraid. I think we ought to talk to Father Beardsley again. And this time we have to tell him everything."

As was his custom, Father Beardsley walked outside and stood on the front steps after Mass to greet his parishioners. When everybody else had gone Nancy walked up to him. Maurice remained by the church entrance, fidgeting with the Sunday bulletin.

"Hello, Nancy," Father Beardsley boomed. "Haven't seen you in a long time. Glad you could make it today. Hope to see you every Sunday from now on. Is that Maurice hiding up by the door? Come on over and say hello, Maurice. I won't bite."

But Nancy was in no frame of mind for small talk. Father Beardsley could see that. "Is something the matter?" he asked, taking her hand.

"We've got to talk to you, Father," she said. "We've got to talk to you right away."

The elderly priest recalled the last time Nancy and Maurice had sought his help. "The spirits again?" he asked, with his hand on his chin.

"I don't think it's my mother's spirit anymore, Father," Nancy said. "It's...it's something worse."

"Well, it's a little bit chilly out here," said the priest. "Why don't we go into my office."

Once inside, Father Beardsley fixed them a pot of coffee. "My housekeeper is off today," he said, apologetically. "Just clear those papers off the couch and have a seat."

They sat down next to each other, and Father Beardsley sat down at his desk. In a kindly way, he asked his visitors, "Now, why don't you start at the beginning?"

As usual, Nancy did most of the talking. And talk she did. By the time she had finished, it was nearly three o'clock. They had been there almost three hours. And by the time she had finished telling her stories, she was crying her eyes out.

"You've got to help us, Father," she said, dabbing at her eyes with a tissue. "We don't know what's going on. But things aren't right. I think maybe Maurice is haunted or something."

Throughout the three hours Maurice remained quiet, staring down at his hands. He nodded from time to time, confirming things that Nancy was saying.

"This is quite disturbing," the priest said. "I don't have much experience with these matters. But it's possible your house is haunted. I'll come out tomorrow and bless the house with holy water. Maybe that will put an end to these strange happenings. In the meantime you go home and pray."

* * *

The next day, right after Mass, Father Beardsley got into his black Buick and drove out to the Theriault farmhouse. He was a little bit frightened. He had blessed plenty of houses and people before, but never for any reason like this.

He remembered the story of a priest in a neighboring town who had gone out to sprinkle holy water around a house whose owner was thought to be possessed. That priest died an early death.

Father Beardsley had taken a large bottle of holy water with him, and by the time he was through, he had used it all. Using a sprinkler known as an aspersorium, he went through every room. As he did it he prayed.

When he was finished, he tried to reassure the Theriaults. "I think this may do the trick," he said. "If you have any more problems, call me. There may be other things we can do."

"Thank you, Father," Nancy said. "Thank you so much. I know this is going to work. I just know it."

Father Beardsley wished he were as confident. But he truly had no idea if what he had done would be of any help at all. From the things that Nancy had told him, he feared that the Theriaults' problems might require more than just a sprinkling of holy water.

The next day he decided to drive to the mall near Worcester to browse in the bookstore there. They had a lot of books on the supernatural and paranormal. Maybe he could find something to help the Theriaults. Looking through the section on religion, Father Beardsley came across a book that jarred his memory. It was called *The Demonologist*. He remembered it from a TV program he'd once seen about a couple from Connecticut who had devoted their lives to fighting demonic possession.

He decided to shell out the two ninety-five for the paperback. It seemed a small investment if it could teach him something he might be able to use to help the Theriaults. But when he got back home, Father Beardsley put *The Demonologist* up on his bookshelf and promptly forgot about it. He was growing old and sometimes things just slipped his mind. He didn't give the book another thought until a couple of weeks later when he received a frantic call from Nancy Theriault.

"Father, things are happening to Maurice again," she said. "He was in two places at once."

Father Beardsley didn't understand. "Two places at once?"

"Yes, it's happened before. This time, me and my brother Hank, his wife, Melissa, and my daughter Lori were standing around the kitchen table, and Maurice comes out of the hallway. Hank asks him where he's going, but Maurice doesn't answer. He just went right out the door, like he was a robot or something. He didn't even have any clothes on. But I knew Maurice would never walk out like that, stark naked. Besides, I had seen this thing happen before, where he turns up in two places at once, but before I thought maybe I was crazy, even though I knew in my heart that I wasn't. So...so I asked Lori to go into the bedroom and see if Maurice was still there. Well, she goes in there and I hear her scream. Sure enough, he's in there. He's sitting on the edge of the bed, taking his boots off. Blood is seeping from his eyes."

Father Beardsley listened intently to the eerie story. And then he remembered the book he had purchased a few weeks earlier. "Can you hang on a second?" he asked Nancy. "I'll be right back." It only took him a few seconds to find *The Demonologist*. It was right on the shelf where he'd left it. He paged through it until he found the names of the couple he had seen on TV that time.

"I think I know some people who can help," he told Nancy when he returned to the phone. "I'm going to call them right now. Just sit tight until you hear from me."

"Okay, but please hurry, Father," Nancy said. "I don't think I can take any more. I'm so worried. I'm at my wits' end."

After hanging up, Father Beardsley gazed out the rectory window for several minutes. Then he picked up the phone again and dialed information for Connecticut. "For Monroe," he said to the operator. "Do you have a listing for Ed and Lorraine Warren?"

NINE

ED AND LORRAINE WARREN had just entered the carriage house behind their charming Monroe, Connecticut, home, where they were about to teach their weekly class at the New England School of Demonology.

The students, mostly high school and college kids from nearby towns, were already seated, ready to be captivated by the lecture Ed was about to deliver on the subject of demons and possession. The candles were lit and a tape of a Gregorian chant was playing softly in the background. Everything was in its place: a crucifix, a skull, a sword, a book on the supernatural, a statue of a saint. Dozens of these kinds of objects dotted every available bit of wall and shelf space.

A jovial, husky man of fifty-eight, Ed, with his khaki vest, green plaid lumberjack's shirt, and blue jeans; his down-to-earth sense of humor; and his absolute lack of pretense, hardly fitted the image of his profession. Especially since the release of the popular movie *Ghostbusters.*

But Ed and his wife, Lorraine, are the nation's foremost demonologists. They've been at it for more than forty years. And although they saw the movie and thought it funny, they are dead serious about their work.

Ed, born just down the road in Bridgeport, is one of only seven practicing demonologists in North America. And he's the only one who is not a clergyman.

His wife is a trance medium, with strong powers of both clairvoyance and ESP. An attractive, dignified-looking woman just a few months younger than Ed, Lorraine usually wears her black hair piled up high and has a penchant for wearing large pieces of ornate jewelry. Her eyes have a knowing, calming quality about them that can instantly soothe a troubled mind.

Ed first became interested in the world of ghosts and demons as a youngster growing up in a haunted house. Since the 1940s, he and his wife have investigated more than two thousand cases of the supernatural all over North America, Europe, and Australia. More than fifty of those cases involved demonic possession.

Just as they approached the lectern, the telephone rang once. The call had been quickly intercepted by the answering machine that Ed had turned on just before leaving the house, to make sure the class would not be interrupted.

Since they had not yet started the class, Lorraine leaned over to Ed and whispered, "Honey, do you want me to get it?"

Ed frowned. "That's why we've got an answering machine. We'll return the call as soon as class is over."

Lorraine knew Ed was right. Their phone was constantly ringing off the wall. Half the time it was just some crank. Ever since the release of *Ghostbusters,* everybody and his brother was seeing ghosts. But that didn't mean they didn't have to take each call seriously. Any one of them could be real. And Lorraine felt that this call might be one of those. She sensed that someone was in deep distress and that she and Ed might be the only ones who could help. She let out a little sigh, thinking she'd go ahead with the class, but she'd probably be distracted, unable to get that phone call out of her mind.

Ed took off his vest and placed it over the back of a chair. Lorraine lit two more white candles. Then Ed began to pray to St. Michael the Archangel and St. Theresa. The students prayed with them.

"Now, I'm going to talk a little about demonic possession," Ed began. "People don't become possessed by devils or demons by accident. Doors have to be opened. Once you try to communicate with them, you open the door."

Sometimes, he said, that happens when a person starts playing with a Ouija board. The Ouija board is a definite way to invite spirits in, he said, and you don't know what kind of spirit you're going to get. It's like going into a crowded street and asking a total stranger to come into your house, he explained. "You're likely to run into trouble." Other times, he noted, a person can be singled out as a victim by a deceased relative.

And it's not always "the devil" who possesses people or houses, Ed told the transfixed audience. "Rather, it is usually one of millions of demons. These are the angels who were cast out of heaven."

Possession, he matter-of-factly explained, is the fourth stage of demonic activity. First comes encroachment, where a negative spirit is given an opening to a human being, either through voluntary means, such as a satanic ritual, or through involuntary means, such as a curse or the performance of an unholy act. The second stage is infestation, when the demons first haunt a person's house. The third stage is oppression, when the spirits begin trying to take over the person living in the house. The final stage, after possession, is death.

"We're not talking about fairy tales or ghost stories," Ed told his audience. "When diabolical energy takes over, it has full command of the body. The person doesn't realize what happens. He can't use his own faculties." Sometimes, Ed added, a person can be possessed by more than one spirit, and spirits can be both human and inhuman.

"To get rid of the spirits, an exorcist must command them to leave in the name of Jesus," he went on. Ed said that he was not an exorcist—only an ordained priest can be one. But he described his work with exorcists to help drive out the evil spirits.

Then he took a shot at some of the scientific parapsychologists who also study so-called "paranormal" phenomena. "We'll work with them," he said. "But we also work with priests. They don't. We believe there is only one person who can deliver a man or a home from a demon. That is an ordained minister of God."

A young woman in the front row put up her hand.

"You have a question?" Ed said.

"Do weird things really happen like in *The Exorcist?*"

Ed smiled. "You mean do objects fly around the house? Do strange voices call out? Do possessed people really perform superhuman feats of strength? Can they speak foreign languages they have never studied? Do they bleed? Vomit in grotesque colors?"

A few students laughed.

"Don't laugh," Ed said, his expression turning serious. "All those things have been known to happen. But that's not the half of it. I have been cut and slashed. Spirits have carved out marks and symbols on my body. I have been tossed around the room like a toy. Demons are very serious. And fighting them is very serious business."

Ed explained that when he is called by someone seeking help, his first task is to determine if the disturbance is being caused by a spirit. Like the scientific parapsychologists, he wants to find proof. Unlike them, however, he sometimes finds it.

"Spirit manifestations are orderly and observable," he said. "When they are genuine Lorraine and I work with the clergy to bring an end to the torture that a person or family may be going through."

One thing that must be determined, Lorraine said, is whether the spirit is human or inhuman. "When a spirit is causing phenomena to occur in a home, it's usually being caused by a ghost," she said, explaining that a ghost is the spirit of a human being who died a sudden death and is stuck between worlds. They simply may not realize they are dead. Or they may not be emotionally ready to leave this plane. The spirit, she noted, will attempt to make the earthly world aware of its presence by trying to manipulate the physical environment—making sounds, knocking on walls, that sort of thing.

"Basically, the ghost is calling out for help," Lorraine said. "So we help them. We help them move along to the next dimension. They're not evil, they're just unhappy."

Then Ed stepped back up to the lectern. "But there's another type of spirit we encounter in our work," he said, his voice louder than before. "It's the inhuman spirit. That's an entity totally unworthy of life. And because it is so unworthy it has been prevented from taking on a physical existence. This is the demon. The name comes from his eternal hate of both man and God. The demonic spirit is another thing altogether from the human spirit. It is dedicated to death and destruction. It can manipulate the physical environment easily, whereas the human spirit usually cannot. The demonic spirit's goal is fear, injury, and, if possible, death."

The students were riveted to their seats, but one young man looked at Ed skeptically. Ed could feel a challenge coming on.

The young man wore a bulky black wool sweater under a faded blue-jean jacket. He was probably no older than nineteen. He had long blond hair and a faint trace of a beard. He rolled his eyes as Ed finished his last sentence. "Come on. How do we know any of this is true?" he blurted out.

Ed just smiled. "I'm glad you asked that question," he said. "First of all, let me ask you if you believe in God. Do you?"

The young man fidgeted in his seat. "Well, not really. I'm an atheist or maybe an agnostic. I'm not really sure. I have to have proof. If God actually showed Himself to me, then maybe I'd believe."

Ed pointed to the young man. "It's atheists like this who never believe," he said. "But it's not just me who says this is so."

He explained that demonology—the study of demons—is a legitimate category of theology, with its own literature. Cases have been studied extensively over many years, he noted. The Roman Catholic Church teaches classes in the subject at its seminaries and universities in Rome.

In 1975, Ed told the class, a conference on the subject was held behind closed doors at the University of Notre Dame. The conference was entitled "A Theological, Psychological, Medical Symposium on the Phenomenon Labeled as Demonic."

"Papers that came from the conference confirmed the reality of demonic oppression and possession," said Ed, speaking firmly and punctuating each syllable by tapping his pointer finger on the lectern.

"But, of course, if you don't believe in the Almighty, then you don't believe in the devil either," he concluded. "If that's the case, you probably don't belong here tonight. You may stay, but I ask that you try to keep an open mind. You may learn something. Any other questions?"

"What was your most frightening case?" asked an innocent-looking blond woman in her mid-twenties.

"That's easy," Ed said. "We were involved as the chief investigators of a haunting on Long Island that you might have heard about. It became the subject of a best-selling book and movie. Anybody here remember *The Amityville Horror?*"

A few jaws dropped. Obviously that had struck a familiar chord.

"To this day, that remains one of the worst cases that we've ever been involved with and certainly one of the most controversial," Ed said.

In the Amityville case in the mid-1970s, George and Kathleen Lutz and their three children had been forced to flee from a house they had purchased two years earlier in the Long Island suburb of Amityville. They fled after having been victimized by what they said were supernatural forces. It turned out that a year before they bought the house the eldest son of the previous owner had murdered the six sleeping members of his family. After investigation, the Warrens concluded that the house was haunted not by ghosts but by inhuman spirits.

But the Amityville case was only one of many highly publicized cases in which the Warrens had been involved. There was the case of the hauntings at the U.S. Military Academy at West Point in 1972. The Warrens were called in to investigate a haunting at the home of the Academy's commanding general.

And of course there was the highly publicized case of demonic possession in Brookfield, Connecticut, in 1979–80. In that case, a young man by the name of Arne Johnson was charged with stabbing another young man, Alan Bono, to death. Johnson's defense? Not guilty by reason of demonic possession. Unfortunately for Johnson, the judge wouldn't allow the unusual defense and he was found guilty of manslaughter. But the Warrens, who investigated the case, were convinced Johnson was possessed and had become possessed.

"That was our most shocking case since the one in Amityville," Ed said.

The young man who had challenged Ed earlier seemed to be more accepting of what Ed was saying now that he'd heard of the many famous cases Ed had been called in to investigate. But when he snickered and leaned over, whispering something to the girl sitting next to him, Ed knew he hadn't yet convinced him completely.

"Is something still bothering you?" he asked.

The young man nodded. "Yeah," he said. "How come you publicize your cases so much? You seem like a couple of publicity hounds to me."

A big smile came over Ed's face. "You can call us whatever

you like, but the truth is that we positively want notoriety and exposure for our cases," he said. "It is only through the exposure of these case histories that others who suffer the same diabolical fates can be enlightened about the existence of the preternatural world. And we expose cases only with the full consent of the people involved. There are literally hundreds of cases that we have kept from the public's eye because the people involved didn't want any publicity."

Ed explained that the publicity also spreads the word about the New England Society for Psychic Research, a Christian ministry he and Lorraine direct. The society is a metaphysical organization that bases its beliefs upon Christian doctrine and the teachings of Jesus Christ. "We've got dozens of volunteers who help us," Ed said. "They receive no compensation. Their only reward is helping these victims of diabolical attacks."

Ed then turned on a tape recorder that sat on a table next to the lectern. "I think you might be interested in hearing this," he said, chuckling just a little.

On the tape, an elderly woman talked about a haunted house across the street from her. After a few minutes Ed stopped the tape and warned the students to pay special attention. "The sounds you will hear in the background could not have been made by a human voice," he said.

He restarted the tape as the students strained to hear. In the background a voice seemed to be laughing. But the voice sounded as if it were coming from the bottom of a well. And it was deep, guttural, and had a sinister tone. The disturbing laugh was repeated several times. Then the tape abruptly stopped.

"If that isn't diabolical, I don't know what is," Ed said, turning off the machine.

As he headed toward the door, several of the students just stayed in their seats, stunned by what they had heard. Others charged after Ed and Lorraine to ask questions.

Ed stood by the door, attempting to accommodate the students as much as he could, but Lorraine was tugging at his jacket.

"Remember, we've got a message on the machine, and I have the feeling it may be an important one," she whispered into her husband's ear. With her ESP abilities—proven in tests at UCLA—Lorraine was rarely wrong about a hunch or intuition.

"Jeez, I almost forgot," Ed replied.

Then he turned to the students surrounding them. "Sorry, kids, we've got to go," he said. "We may have a new case."

They walked briskly into the house and headed directly to the telephone-answering machine.

Ed hit the Play button and wandered over to the refrigerator to pour himself a glass of juice.

An elderly voice played back on the little answering-machine speaker. "Hello, this is Father Galen Beardsley in Warren, Massachusetts. Ah, a couple in my parish has been having trouble recently. Strange things have been happening to them. Terrible things. I fear their house may be possessed. I read about you in a book and thought you might be able to help. But hurry. The situation is deteriorating rapidly. Please call me as soon as possible. And God bless you."

Ed and Lorraine looked at each other.

"Did you hear the way his voice was quivering?" Lorraine said.

"He's frightened," Ed said. "We better call him right away."

It was after ten, but the Warrens knew the priest would be anxiously awaiting their call.

Ed picked up the phone and dialed the number the priest had left on the tape.

Father Beardsley was still in his office, sitting by the phone, paging through *The Demonologist*. Nancy Theriault had called again since he had made his call to the Warrens. This time, she reported, Maurice was sitting in his easy chair, a faraway look in his eyes, reciting phrases in a language she didn't understand.

At first Father Beardsley suspected he was simply speaking French, his native tongue. But Nancy insisted it wasn't French. She had heard him speak French hundreds of times. This didn't sound anything like French. She said it sounded more like the language the priests used to use to say Mass, before everything had been changed by Vatican II.

"Latin?" Father Beardsley asked.

"Yeah, Latin," Nancy said. "I think he's speakin' Latin. But he's never said a word in Latin in all the years I've known him. He was never an altar boy or nothin', and he's never gone to Mass all that much. How come all of a sudden he can speak Latin?"

Father Beardsley was dumbfounded. "I don't know, Mrs. Theriault," he said. "I don't know. There are some things going on here that I can't explain. But I've called the people that can help, and I'm waiting to hear from them."

He hung up the phone and opened his prayer book. He decided to say a few prayers in the hope that it might hasten a return phone call from the Warrens.

Father Beardsley had dozed off at his desk after about five minutes of prayer. It was late and it had been a long day. When the phone rang about ten minutes later, it almost knocked him off his chair.

"Father Beardsley here," he answered.

"Father, this is Ed Warren. Sorry I'm calling so late, but I just got finished teaching a class. You sounded anxious. How can I help?"

The priest told Ed what had been going on with Maurice Theriault. He gave him a pretty good rundown on what he knew, trying hard to remember everything that Nancy had told him. He told Ed of Maurice's bleeding eyes, of his sudden ability to speak Latin, about how he was pushed down the church stairs by an invisible force.

Father Beardsley may have forgotten some things, but he figured he had remembered enough to give Ed an idea of what was happening. "I fear their house may be haunted or possessed," the priest said. "But I'm no expert in the field. That's why I called you."

Right away, from what Father Beardsley had recounted, Ed knew he'd have to go up to Warren and investigate. "Father, give me their number. I'll call them right away. I think Lorraine and I will have to drive up there tomorrow."

After hanging up with the priest, Ed called the Theriaults and spoke to Nancy. She recounted some of the things that had been happening. Some of the incidents Ed had already heard from Father Beardsley. Some were new, such as the two Maurices, the car driving by itself, the messages scratched into Maurice's back.

"I'd like to come up there tomorrow, if the weather's good," Ed said. "Is that okay with you?"

"Of course it's okay," Nancy replied. "I wish you could be here right now. I can't take much more."

"Don't you worry," Ed reassured her. "We'll do everything we can to help. And tonight make sure to say your prayers."

Nancy was so relieved. Now they were going to get some real help.

When Ed hung up the phone he turned on the television to get the weather forecast. It was February 17, and there had been some talk about a snowstorm. Fortunately the forecast was for clear skies until later in the week.

"Let's plan on getting up early," Lorraine said, closing up the large road atlas she had been looking at. "It's a pretty long drive and I think we ought to get there with a few hours of daylight to spare."

"Sounds good," Ed said, heading off into the bedroom. Then

a thought came to him. "Honey, what do you think about asking Karen Jaffe to come along with us. She's been wanting to help us investigate a case, and it might be a good idea to have a police officer with us."

Lorraine agreed right away. "That's a great idea," she said. "I don't think she's working tomorrow. I'll give her a call."

Karen Jaffe was a detective with a police department in Connecticut about forty-five minutes south of Monroe. In the course of her job she had investigated many occult-type crimes and had developed an interest in the subject. She had even lectured on it to other police departments. Over the years she had crossed paths with the Warrens several times, and they had come to be friends.

When Lorraine called, Karen jumped at the invitation. And Lorraine was glad she had. Bringing a police officer along couldn't hurt. And the gun she carried would serve as a form of protection in case things got out of hand.

Lorraine told Ed the good news that Karen had agreed to come with them. "I told her to be here by ten o'clock," she said.

"That's good, because I don't want to leave much later than that," Ed replied.

As they got into bed, Ed reached over and picked up his well-worn Bible. "I think I'll read a few passages before dozing off," he said to Lorraine.

"What do you make of this?" she asked.

"It sounds pretty frightening," he said. "I have a feeling we're going to have our work cut out for us." Then he looked into Lorraine's worried eyes and grinned. "Hey, who ya gonna call?"

She laughed and felt better. Whenever Ed repeated that line from *Ghostbusters* she always laughed. It helped to ease her anxiety. But she had a feeling there would be no joking when tomorrow rolled around. She said a prayer as her head hit the pillow.

. . .

Ed and Lorraine were up bright and early the next morning. Lorraine prepared a hearty breakfast of bacon and eggs, and while they ate they plotted their route to Warren on a road map.

Monroe is in rural southeastern Connecticut, halfway between New Haven and the New York state line, about a two-hour drive from New York City. They'd head north on a couple of back roads until they could pick up I-84, the new interstate. Once on I-84, Ed figured they could make good time heading northeast toward Massachusetts. The I-84 would take them past Waterbury, Bristol, and also New Britain, the city where Maurice had lived years before. At Hartford they'd take I-91 directly north toward Springfield, where they would catch the Massachusetts Turnpike east to the exit at Palmer. From there it would be only a few minutes on two small roads, Routes 32 and 67, until they got to Warren. The day was bitterly cold but the skies were clear, so weather wouldn't be costing them time. In all, the ride would take a little more than two hours.

They were so busy planning the trip and thinking about what they might have to confront that Lorraine almost forgot that it was February 18, the anniversary of her father's death seventeen years earlier.

The realization called for a slight change in plans. "We'd better go to Mass," she told Ed. He agreed, and they hurried to get dressed and rush off to nearby St. Stephen's Church for the eight A.M. service.

At Mass, Lorraine prayed not only for the soul of her beloved father but also for that of Maurice Theriault. She could feel that something terrible was going on in Warren and that she and Ed were going to be in for a battle—maybe the battle of their lives.

After Mass was over, Ed and Lorraine headed back home to wait for Karen and to pack up their beige Chevy Chevette with everything they would need to investigate the goings-on at Maurice Theriault's house: a bottle of holy water, a tape recorder, camera, a special crucifix that Ed took with him on all their cases, and relics of several saints, including Padre Pio, the venerated saint who was known for his stigmata—the near-constant bleeding from his hands, feet, and left side—just like Christ on the cross. Padre Pio was also celebrated for innumerable miracles of healing. The relic had been given to the Warrens by officials of the Church in Rome. Ed and Lorraine also made sure to wear medals of the Blessed Virgin around their necks. They never went on a case without them.

Karen arrived shortly after ten. Thirty-eight years old, she looked trim and sturdy in her jeans and V-neck sweater. Her curly brown hair was pulled back in a ponytail. After a quick cup of coffee they hit the road. On the way, they filled Karen in on as much as they knew about the case of Maurice Theriault.

They had been driving about two hours and fifteen minutes when they saw the sign on Route 67 that said "Entering Warren."

When they got to Brimfield Road they began looking out for the farmhouse. Lorraine didn't need to check the number on the mailbox to know that they had arrived. As soon as they were within eyesight of the Theriault property, she pointed and said, "That's it. That's the house. I can feel it." Sure enough, it was. As they pulled into the driveway, the Warrens saw a modest farmhouse that was badly in need of repairs. It was perched on a knoll surrounded by several other buildings, including a makeshift greenhouse with plastic over it and a number of pieces of old farm equipment. The gravel driveway was the only evidence of any landscaping. The front yard was patrolled by a big German shepherd surrounded by half a dozen kittens.

As they got out of the car Nancy Theriault opened the kitchen door, popped her head out, and said, "Welcome to our home. I'm glad you're here."

She looked almost exactly as Lorraine had imagined her. She was wearing jeans and an untucked corduroy shirt. Her red-brown hair was curly and she wore no makeup. She was a real country girl. And Lorraine could see that this country girl had been under incredible stress. Her darkened eyes and the lines on her forehead attested to that.

"Come on in," Nancy said. "Maurice is at the table. I'm going to make some coffee."

Inside, the room was heated by an old pot-bellied stove. Maurice sat at the table, staring into space. He wore coveralls and a corduroy shirt that looked a lot like the one Nancy was wearing. He had a pencil-thin mustache and his brown hair was thinning a bit at the top. His leathery face evidenced a lifetime of hard work.

But more than that, the aura Lorraine saw surrounding him was dark and muddy. Terrible. He's scary to look at, she thought.

Ed sized Maurice up quickly, too, and saw that, despite his small size, he was a strong man. He had muscles on top of muscles. Ed glanced over at Karen Jaffe. He knew she had her gun in her purse and he was glad of that. If Maurice was a nutcase, they might need it. And if he wasn't, well, they still might need it.

They sat down around the table, sipped coffee, and talked for the next couple of hours. Nancy again did most of the talking, telling the Warrens of Maurice's lifetime of incredible incidents. She told the Warrens what she had once told Father Beardsley—that she thought Maurice or the house was somehow being haunted by the spirit of her mother.

But right off the bat Ed doubted that was the case. If the things Nancy was telling them were true, there was no way they could have been caused by a human spirit.

What happened next only helped to confirm that feeling.

As Nancy talked, Maurice mostly just sat there, nodding and staring blankly into space. But at one point, when Nancy spoke of Maurice's mother, Maurice put his hand to his brow and began to cry.

Karen noticed it first, and when she did she almost fell off her chair. Maurice was crying tears of blood!

The veteran police detective had seen plenty of blood in her thirteen years as a cop, but never anything like this. She nudged Lorraine to look. Simultaneously, Nancy and Ed had noticed the bleeding too. Nancy jumped up to get a box of tissues and handed one to Maurice, who dabbed at his eyes to soak up the blood.

Once the bleeding had stopped, Ed began asking questions. "How often does this happen, Maurice?" he asked.

"It happens often enough," Nancy answered. "Usually when he gets angry or upset."

Ed mulled the possibilities over in his mind. Either Maurice had a rare medical problem, or the bleeding was a case of stigmata—a manifestation of the bleeding wounds of Christ.

The bleeding stopped when Maurice stopped crying, but it would start up again several times before the day was over, whenever the discussion re-created some difficult and disturbing time in Maurice's troubled life.

Ed had a sense that Maurice might have come under demonic possession, but that would have required an entry. Maybe there had been an incident that could have provided an entry point.

By delving back into Maurice's past, Ed hit on a couple of matters that might explain what was happening. The first was the incident with Maurice and his father in the barn, back when Maurice was just a youngster. That unholy act, Ed figured, definitely could have opened a door for evil to enter.

There was also the time when, as an overworked youngster in the fields, Maurice asked for the help of an invisible force—and seemed to get it. That could have provided another point of entry.

And then there was the curse put on Maurice by old Hubert Emery. If the door was already open, that might have opened the door even wider, Ed thought.

When they were through, Ed didn't say anything to Maurice or Nancy about what might have caused the unusual occurrences. Instead he just told them that he would be in touch with Father Beardsley and would be sending some researchers up to the house at a later date to do some investigating.

Ed, Lorraine, and Karen then drove off to the Salem Croft Inn in nearby West Brookfield to get some dinner and listen to the tapes of the conversation they had just concluded with Maurice and Nancy.

Karen was shocked by several of the things she had heard. But she just couldn't get over Maurice's bleeding eyes. "Do you think there's a medical explanation?" she asked.

Ed swallowed his last piece of apple pie, put down his fork, and leaned back in his chair. "If only there were," he said.

"Then what do you think is going on?" Karen asked.

"I think something terrible is going on there," he said. "I suspect Maurice is possessed. But we won't be able to say for sure until we conduct a full investigation. We've got to get a team in there right away."

■ ■ ■

Back home again in Monroe the next day, Ed began calling some of his most trusted assistants, lining up a team that could assist in the investigation into the Maurice Theriault case.

In addition to Karen, Ed would ask two college students—both named Chris—who often worked together on these cases: Chris McKenna and Chris Finberg. They were trusted assistants who never shied away from a frightening case. When Ed needed people to spend the night in a haunted house or with a person who was suspected of being possessed, "the two Chrises" were usually the first ones he would call.

Kent Burch, a police detective with the Hartford, Connecticut, police department, was another valuable assistant. Kent usually worked with his friend Ryan Dufrain.

Joey Taylor and Fred Salvio, two friends who worked in a nursing home in Bridgeport, not far from the Warrens' home in Monroe, also usually worked together. Joey would later become a sub-deacon in Danbury.

Rounding out the group would be Sonny Berryhill, a muscular weightlifter; Benjamin Massey, a student of the Warrens'; and Jessica Spellman. Ed figured Sonny's strength might come in handy.

But before Ed sent his troops up to observe, he decided he would need to return to Warren once more, to talk with Father Beardsley. He and Lorraine decided to drive up on the weekend.

They met with Father Beardsley in the rectory of St. Paul's Church at noon on Saturday. Ed and Lorraine had gotten a good feeling about him from their conversation on the phone that night, and their meeting in person only confirmed that feeling. The Warrens found the priest not only willing to work closely with them but also willing to call on his friend and former classmate, the Most Reverend Timothy J. Harrington, a bishop, for help if necessary.

That was good news as far as Ed and Lorraine were concerned. After talking at length with Father Beardsley, they had a feeling that the bishop might be needed—but for more than what the priest had anticipated.

Father Beardsley had been out to bless the house, thinking it might be haunted or possessed. But Ed suspected something more hideous.

"Father," Ed said, "I'm going to level with you. I think that Maurice has come under demonic possession. We haven't proven it, of course. We still have to do our investigation. But that's my suspicion. If it turns out to be the case, exorcism may be needed. And as you know, the only one who can authorize an exorcism is the bishop. We may need your help there."

"You've got it, Ed," the priest replied. "If we need it, I'll call the bishop personally. But I hope to God we won't."

Ed could see the apprehension in the priest's eyes. "Frightened?" he asked.

Father Beardsley sat down at his desk, swung his chair around, and looked out the window to the street below. "I still shudder when I think about the day the priest who preceded me here told me of his encounter with Satan," he said. "He was pushed around for six hours. He was exhausted. He said he didn't ever want to do it again. He said he was in the same room with a demon. That priest died the next month at the age of fifty-five. Does that answer your question?"

Ed realized he had asked a stupid question. Of course the priest was frightened. Who wouldn't be? "I'm frightened too, Father," Ed replied.

"Why don't we go over to the church and pray?" the priest said.

The two men walked slowly out of the rectory and over to the church. As they walked together they didn't say a word.

The battle was about to begin.

TEN

POLICE CHIEF JERRY SEIBERT was still reeling from the events at the Theriault farmhouse two days before. He couldn't shake the image of Maurice, sitting there at the kitchen table, dazed and bleeding, out of his mind.

He really preferred not to think about it, and usually he was good at shutting out the terrible things that happen to people, things that a cop sees in the normal line of duty. But this Theriault case was difficult to ignore.

When Seibert had first become aware that there was something odd going on at the farmhouse on Brimfield Road, he simply figured he had an arsonist on his hands. But then that suspected arsonist, Frenchy Theriault, had come into the station and turned in his guns, making the incredible claim that he was possessed and was seeing a psychic.

The normally unshakable ex-marine could deal with that. Frenchy, he had concluded, was concocting a story to cover up having set his own place on fire to collect the insurance money. And he was probably paying a fortune-teller to back up his story.

As a nine-year veteran with an associate degree in criminal justice, Seibert knew that arson was the hardest crime to prove. But the forty-year-old cop also had confidence in himself and State Fire Marshall Dan Prescott. He figured that if they couldn't trip up this dim-witted farmer, they ought to turn in their badges.

But then he and Trooper Kerns had been called to the farmhouse. Seibert didn't know what the heck had taken place, but he knew what he'd seen. He'd seen Frenchy covered with blood and Nancy screaming hysterically.

And then Father Beardsley had told him about the pair of demonologists that he'd called in. Psychics and demonologists! What next?

Although Seibert had been brought up in the nearby village of West Brookfield, he'd been around. During his four-year stint in the marines, Seibert had been stationed in Scotland and in Guantanamo Bay, Cuba. In addition to being widely traveled, he had studied for two years, pursuing an associate's degree in psychology.

He could usually spot a con a mile away. And as much as he liked old Father Beardsley, he knew that the priest was getting old and wasn't as sharp as he'd once been. Seibert was determined to make sure that he and the town of Warren weren't going to be exploited—either by Frenchy or by these "demonologists."

Seibert decided he'd better take a drive up to the farmhouse to see what he could see. He parked his cruiser out on the road, out of sight, and scoped out the driveway to the Theriault home. There he saw something that bothered him.

There was a black Ford Elite parked in the driveway—a car he had never seen before at the Theriault home. Moreover, he could tell from a distance that the car had out-of-state plates. The plate was blue—from Connecticut.

He walked up the steep slope until he could make out the license plate. Seibert couldn't believe his eyes. The plate read: GHOST.

He didn't know whether to laugh or cry.

But he knew what he would do as soon as he got back to the station. He'd run a check on that plate to see who he was dealing with. Seibert made it back to the station in record time. It didn't take long for the check to be completed. The car was registered to a Lorraine Warren of Monroe, Connecticut.

The chief drove back out to Frenchy's the next day and confronted the farmer about the car with the GHOST license plates. Maurice was just getting ready to leave for town and was surprised to see Seibert. The police chief approached Maurice without saying a word. Seibert, wearing mirrored aviation-style sunglasses that threw Maurice's image back toward him, folded his arms over his chest.

"Frenchy, who's driving that black car with Connecticut plates?" he asked. "I saw it parked in front of your house the other day."

The farmer glanced up and raised his eyebrows as if to ask, What were you doing, spying on me? But he decided against baiting the imposing officer.

"Those are the psychics I told you about. The ones I'm seeing for my problem. The ones who told me to turn in my guns. They're helping me get rid of this thing that's haunting me."

Seibert assumed a look of disbelief. "Psychics?" he said.

"Yeah," Frenchy said. "Father Beardsley calls 'em demonologists."

Seibert nodded. "Mind if I come by and meet them sometime?" he asked.

"Suit yourself," Frenchy replied. "I don't care. They'll be back up on Saturday." Maurice wasn't crazy about having Seibert poking about, but maybe it would be good if he understood, he thought.

When Saturday rolled around, Seibert decided to go and meet these so-called demonologists.

Ed Warren was walking down the path leading from the Theriaults' side door when Seibert pulled up in his cruiser. As soon as he saw the police car, Ed turned around and began heading back to the door, pretending not to have noticed.

"Hold it a second, pal," the chief barked from his open window. He turned off the engine. This guy is starting to irritate me already, he thought.

Ed didn't turn around but kept on walking.

Now Seibert was getting irritated. This guy's not going to

make it easy for me, he thought. "Excuse me, fella," the police chief said, getting out of the cruiser, "but I'd like to ask you a few questions."

Ed stopped and turned to face the cop. The usually easygoing demonologist didn't like what he saw. Look at this guy, Ed thought. He thinks he's General Patton. That uniform. Those boots. That shining brass. That condescending attitude. That stiff macho body language. However, he said, "Hello, officer. My name is Ed Warren. Is there something I can do for you?" Ed, figuring he had better show some respect, added, "Why don't we go in and have a cup of coffee?"

"I just want to know what you folks are doing here," Seibert said. "I like to know what's going on in my town."

Ed Warren had faced police officers before. They never seemed to believe. He wasn't going to let General Patton interfere with his efforts to rid Maurice of the demon that was making his life insufferable.

"I said, I just want to know who you folks are and what you're doing here," Seibert said. "Just a matter of routine."

Maybe, Ed thought. Maybe not. He decided to take the initiative.

"Hey, Chief," Ed said, touching his arm lightly, "I can tell by your attitude that you are a nonbeliever."

Seibert didn't flinch and Ed continued.

"But you are involved in something here that you don't understand and that you are not willing to accept. And that's because you don't want to accept it. But to truly comprehend what's happening to Maurice Theriault, you'll need some understanding of what this is all about."

Ed wondered if this was registering at all.

Seibert shrugged. Actually Ed was getting through, but Seibert simply hated thinking about stuff like this; the whole subject frustrated him.

"Now, come on, Chief," Ed said. "Let me explain everything that's happened here."

With that, Seibert relaxed a little. They walked together into the farmhouse. Nancy was half expecting Chief Seibert to show up, because of his little interrogation of Maurice the day before. She quickly poured two cups of coffee and then went into the bedroom to tidy up.

The chief listened to Ed for ten minutes. Although impressed with Ed's professionalism, he knew that he and this "demonologist" were there for different reasons. Seibert knew that he was there for a criminal investigation. This psychic investigator was there for something else, the chief thought. Maybe money. Maybe sensationalism. Maybe religion. Whatever, their interests weren't the same.

Seibert knew he wasn't going to get any help from the Warrens; that was obvious. He just hoped he wasn't going to be hindered too much in his investigation.

"Well, I'd appreciate it if you'd keep me informed," Seibert said on the way back to the cruiser.

"Sure thing, Chief," Ed replied. Just as much as you need to be, he thought.

Seibert knew that he was being shut out. He walked back to his cruiser and drove off, still trying to put his finger on just what was going on. He promised himself he would continue to investigate until he was satisfied that Frenchy Theriault was— or wasn't—an arsonist.

■ ■ ■

One might think that the Church would be eager to perform exorcisms. After all, what could be greater proof of the power and efficacy of the Roman religion than the ability to cure what can't be otherwise cured—or understood. Aside from miracles, what greater example of the ultimate power for good?

But, as is the case with miracles, the Church, afraid of the sensationalism and exploitation which inevitably accompany such cases, is often reluctant to step in. One of its requirements, in the case of exorcism, is that the person believed to be possessed undergo a psychiatric evaluation.

During the ordeal of Maurice Theriault, the Reverend Walter Harris, a spokesman for the Boston archdiocese, expressed that reluctance in an interview printed in a Boston newspaper on the subject of demonic possession. "In my twenty-one years in the priesthood I've never heard of a genuine case of possession," he said. "The advance of psychology puts a whole different perspective on these cases."

So there was much rejoicing in the Theriault house when the diocese agreed to furnish a Catholic psychiatrist to evaluate Maurice. This could be the first step toward freeing Maurice of the demons that were making his life a living hell, they thought.

Ed, Lorraine, Nancy, and Maurice were sitting together at the kitchen table on a sunny Monday morning discussing the news the Warrens had brought. "Now they'll see that it's not his imagination or some trick he's playing," said Nancy.

Ed Warren, who had seen hundreds of cases of demonic possession, was less sure. He knew that if the Church is reluctant to acknowledge cases of possession, then the psychiatric profession is a hundred times more reluctant. He was trying to appear confident for the Theriaults' sake, but his concern was mirrored in his body language. He sat stiffly, chin in hand, looking out the window.

He mulled the situation over in his mind. The problem, from a doctor's point of view, is that many of the symptoms attributed by the superstitious to demonic forces can often be equally well assigned to chemical and psychological disorders. A doctor is aware that people who suffer from what is now known to be epilepsy, for example, were once thought to have been possessed.

"Let's hope we get one who has an open mind and who can admit that there are things he doesn't understand," said Ed as Lorraine nodded agreement.

Maurice stared at the crumpled napkin in front of him, saying nothing. For him, this meeting might be the beginning of a cure, an end to the bizarre occurrences that had haunted his life since childhood and that were now tearing it apart. He wondered if he would ever feel "normal"—not that he knew what that was, exactly.

The group sat in silence at the kitchen table, each person speculating about the upcoming meeting with the psychiatrist. The ring of the telephone shattered the quiet. Nancy jumped, then quickly moved in the direction of the phone.

"Hello," she said, her voice showing a mixture of anticipation and trepidation. "Yes, Father. He's here. Just a second."

She turned to the table and looked at Ed. "It's for you," she said. "It's Father Beardsley."

Ed got up and took the call. After speaking quietly for a minute or two, Ed hung up and turned back to the table. "He wants us to come up to the rectory," he announced. "That's where the doctor will meet Maurice."

In the car on the way over, the silence persisted. Even talkative Nancy was deep in thought. Maurice stared out the window, expressionless. He had a suspicion of psychiatrists—"head-crackers," he called them.

What if he was crazy and they locked him up, but he was still possessed and didn't have Nancy there with him? The usual sensations of helplessness and trepidation were becoming magnified under all the official scrutiny. He prayed silently to the Virgin Mary.

Maurice had a childlike belief that Father Beardsley, having a special connection to God, could somehow interpret his good side and convey it upward. So he wore a large smile when he saw the priest sitting behind his desk at the rectory of St. Paul's. He trusted the old country priest. Father Beardsley had given Maurice a large gold crucifix, and Maurice carried it with him now at all times, even slept with it clutched in his hand. It was a relief to Maurice to have a physical object that offered protection.

Seeing the priest now, Maurice reached for the crucifix tucked in his belt. "I have my friend with me," he said, a little sheepishly.

As he drew it out the crucifix suddenly flew from his hand and went flying across the room, narrowly missing Father Beardsley's left eye. He cried out in surprise. It crashed into a glass case behind him, shattering it instantly.

Father Beardsley recovered quickly and picked up the cross. Maurice was staring at his outstretched hand. Ed, Lorraine, and Father Beardsley looked at Maurice's palm in wonderment, seeing what looked like a burn mark where he had handled the cross.

A remaining glass shard tinkled to the floor.

Ed knew that it was essential that Maurice and the others be calm for the psychiatric evaluation—the demonologist didn't want the doctor walking in to find a distraught Maurice and immediately conclude that he was mentally unstable—so he did his best to put the conversation on a normal footing. After all, he pointed out, such an incident was the very reason the group was assembled today in the rectory, and in many ways, the cross flying out of Maurice's hand was the least of what they had seen in recent weeks.

Twenty minutes later the doctor arrived. He looked exactly as Maurice had imagined—tall, sturdy, square-jawed, with piercing gray eyes and glasses. It was more than his classic Germanic features, though, that bothered Maurice. With just one glance he could tell that this man was without compassion. He exuded no warmth at all. On the contrary, he had a disturbing coldness about him. Maurice just figured that came with the territory though. After all, he's a head-cracker, he thought.

The doctor introduced himself, shook hands all around, and quickly closeted himself with Maurice in Father Beardsley's private office. The group waited in silence. After a short time the psychiatrist opened the door. "Ed, would you join us please?" he asked.

When the three men were alone the psychiatrist began to question Ed closely regarding Maurice and his friendship with him. How did Ed feel about Maurice? What was his interest in Maurice's case? How did the two men get along? And on and on. The doctor seemed intent on proving that Maurice was in some way sexually deviant.

Finally Ed impatiently interrupted. "Look," he said, his face reddening. "We came here to help because of the things that have been happening in Maurice's home."

"Well," replied the doctor, "I'm afraid I don't believe in any of that stuff."

"Would you call yourself a Catholic?" said Ed.

"I'm not here to discuss my personal beliefs with you."

"Hey, now, wait a minute. Don't you even believe in God?"

A little religious indignation was rising up in Ed. "There you go asking questions," the psychiatrist interrupted, speaking in a condescending tone of voice.

Pointing his finger, Ed said, "You say you wanna ask us questions. Then I'm gonna ask you questions. You say when you're dead, you're dead. What about Christ, if you're such a good Catholic? The Bible says on the third day He rose."

"I simply don't want to talk about that stuff."

"The reason we wanted to see you was to get help," Ed snapped.

He rose to leave and Maurice, seeing his friend get up, followed suit. Beet-red, Ed stormed out and grabbed Lorraine's hand in front of the astonished eyes of Father Beardsley.

"Come on, honey, we're leaving," Ed said firmly. "Father Beardsley, we'll call you."

The Theriaults certainly hadn't expected this to happen, and their heads were spinning from the sudden drama.

They all piled into the car and drove off quickly, gravel flying out behind the tires. But as they were pulling onto the steep road that runs between St. Paul's Church and the rectory, Maurice cried out.

"Ahhhh! My back! My back!" He was moaning in pain.

"Maurice, honey, what is it?" Nancy asked.

Ed slammed on the brakes, ran around the car, and yanked open the back door. "Help me get his shirt off, Nancy," he instructed.

As the pair struggled to peel off Maurice's plaid hunting shirt in the chilly March air, the car became silent. There, across Maurice's shoulder blades, was an enormous cross that looked as if it had been burned into his flesh.

Ed grabbed Maurice by the hand and started down the driveway.

"What are you doing?" Nancy sobbed as Ed led Maurice by the arm toward the rectory.

"We're going to show this doubting Thomas proof," Ed shouted over his shoulder.

As the twosome climbed the stairs to Father Beardsley's office, the now breathless Ed turned Maurice around in front of the priest. Father Beardsley's jaw dropped open.

Ed called out to the psychiatrist. "I think you'd better come have a look at this, Doctor," he said.

The doctor was on the phone. When he hung up and emerged from Father Beardsley's office, Ed demanded, "So what's your explanation for this?"

The doctor looked speculatively at Maurice's back. "Okay, Maurice," he said. "How did you do this to yourself? I've been honest with you, now you have to be honest with me."

Ed Warren felt the hair stand up on his head. He was so angry he was shaking. He knew this so-called scientific type had a completely closed mind and there was no getting through.

Ed's eyes narrowed. "Listen here, you," he said through clenched teeth. "I hope that when you're by yourself something comes up and smashes you right in the mouth as has happened to this poor man you refuse to help. If he needs a psychiatrist, it's not gonna be you."

Turning to Father Beardsley, Ed fought to control himself. "I'm sorry, Father, but we came here for help," Ed said. "Now we're leaving."

As Ed backed the car out of the driveway for the second time, Father Beardsley turned to the psychiatrist. "You know, sir," he said. "I think you're a nasty man." The priest was so upset that he left the rectory and went for a walk to calm himself.

■ ■ ■

The case of Maurice "Frenchy" Theriault was now public property. The police report of the incident at the farmhouse, when Chief Seibert and Trooper Kerns responded to Nancy's frantic call for help after Maurice had cut himself in the bathroom, was picked up by a local newspaper. Like most news-gathering organizations, the paper had a police scanner operating twenty-four hours a day. The police blotter the next day carried some details of the stop Trooper Kerns had made.

On Thursday, March 21, the Springfield *Morning Union* carried a story by reporter Sandra E. Constantine with the headline: CHURCH CONSIDERS PERFORMING EXORCISM IN WARREN.

The story quoted Father Beardsley as saying that an investigation was under way. Bishop Timothy Harrington was unavailable for comment. While the story did not identify Maurice Theriault by name, it did give the town where he lived.

By the next day, the Boston *Herald*, a racy tabloid owned by Australian publisher Rupert Murdoch, had jumped on the story. ARE DEMONS AT WORK HERE? screamed the *Herald*'s banner headline.

The story in the *Herald* also did not give Maurice's name. Although a *Herald* reporter was able to track him down, Maurice would not comment and the paper's editors decided to withhold his name for the moment.

The story reported that a team of demonologists had been called in to study the man identified only as a Warren man, and that the church was considering performing an exorcism.

The next day, the *Herald* followed up with another story. FARMER BATTLING THE DEVIL screamed the headline. A subhead added: EXORCISM IS THE ONLY ANSWER: PSYCHIC.

The story by ace reporter Joe Sciacca detailed the strange phenomena that had plagued Maurice, this time referred to not by name but by occupation—a farmer. The story revealed that the farmer bled from the eyes and that objects flew about his home, defying the laws of nature.

It also quoted Ed and Lorraine Warren as saying that the only way the man could be freed was through exorcism. And in this story, for the first time, the office of Bishop Timothy Harrington confirmed that the matter was officially under investigation by the Church.

In other words, this was no joke.

By now, of course, the story of Maurice Theriault was the talk of the town of Warren. Many people in the small town had already heard something of what was going on in the farmhouse on Brimfield Road. After these stories came out everybody knew about it. And Maurice's already magnified fear was increasing with each newspaper story. Only wishing to be free of his affliction, he had no idea that he would have to become the center of a media-fed frenzy.

On Monday, the *Herald* followed up with a reaction from the townspeople of Warren. The headline: SATAN ISN'T IN OUR TOWN.

The story, by reporter Timothy Clifford, quoted neighbors and Warren residents who doubted Maurice's story, although many expressed compassion. Most of the comments in the story simply revealed people's misconceptions about exorcism. "From what I hear," said one woman, "if a possessed person goes near a priest or holy water, he goes completely wild..."

The next day another *Herald* reporter got Warren's Police Chief Seibert to comment for the first time about the case that had his little town making news in the big city of Boston.

POLICE CHIEF DISCLOSES DEMON CASE was the headline in the *Herald* when Seibert broke his silence. The story quoted the chief as saying, "He had evidently just come out of a seizure. But I didn't see any convulsions." Seibert did confirm seeing a cross or X on Maurice's back.

Then Seibert said something that tantalized the reporter. "There are some things about this case that I just can't talk about right now," he said. "But if you treat me fair, I'll tell you everything when the time is right. And there are some things that I'll tell you that will make your hair stand on end."

The reporter promised he wouldn't betray the chief's confidence and continued to pursue the story from different angles.

By the next week, the *National Enquirer,* the granddaddy of sensational tabloids, was on to the story in a big way. And so was the *Weekly World News,* another supermarket tabloid.

POSSESSED MAN BEGS FOR EXORCISM shouted the headline in the *Weekly World News.* EVIL POWER TEARS HIS FLESH AND FLINGS HIM THROUGH THE AIR.

The *Weekly World News* may have lost points with journalism professors on style, but they had the incredible facts right: Maurice was being tormented by a diabolical force. And with the sensational coverage in the press, he was also being tormented by mockers, thrill seekers, and heartless neighbors who would drive up to the house, honk their horns and scream "devil worshipper!" or "The devil lives here!"

Others would call the house at all hours to hiss "Get out of town!" Church services at St. Paul's in Warren seemed to be composed half of curious onlookers and half of newspaper reporters. Maurice hardly dared show himself.

It was too much for Father Beardsley. In the church's weekly bulletin on Palm Sunday, he lashed out at "merciless and cruel reporters who...called the rectory at all hours...and had the gall to try to see the person involved...looking for sly comments from individuals in town completely unaware of any facts."

From the pulpit that very day the usually gentle priest also made the Maurice Theriault case the subject of his sermon. He accused the media of "trying to make a weirdo and a freak" of the poor farmer.

Outside the church, *Herald* photographer Jim Mahoney focused his telephoto lens through a window and snapped a picture of the priest as he railed against the media. It was the type of "sneak" shot that the tabloid specialized in. The *Herald* ran the photo the next day, along with a story headlined: CHURCH WEIGHING EXORCISM.

After Mass, Father Beardsley talked to *Herald* reporter Joe Heaney about Maurice. "I know him and he is a good church-going man who needs our compassion," the priest said. "I don't know why people would want to go out and hurt him. This is not a freak show."

But it was a cartoon that appeared in the *Herald* that proved particularly upsetting to Maurice and Nancy. It showed an old farm couple in the style of Grant Wood's *American Gothic*, standing in front of their house, with demons and ghosts crowding the background. "Nice folks," says one police officer to another. "Kids are ugly as sin though!"

This was just too much. Maurice and Nancy were crazy about their grandchildren, and the cartoon hurt.

After the cartoon had appeared, cartoonist Don Bailey received a strange phone call from someone purporting to be Maurice. The caller angrily warned him that he didn't know who he was messing with, and to expect disaster. Less than a week later Bailey's father suffered a debilitating stroke.

■ ■ ■

By the time Holy Week came around, the Maurice Theriault case had become Chief Seibert's nightmare as well. He had to go out to the farmhouse often to drive off the tourists and hecklers who had been driving up and down Brimfield Road trying to spot the "devil." All the publicity had suddenly made Warren a tourist destination. The chief saw this as the worst kind of publicity his town could receive, a negative that could be hard to undo.

Seibert himself had been getting his share of attention from the media. That was another thing he didn't care for. After a couple of interviews, in which he gave only the barest threads of information, he decided to clam up.

Besides, he had some more investigating to do. He'd go out to the house under the pretense of wanting to protect Frenchy from the hecklers. In fact, he might actually be needed for that purpose. It was Monday of Holy Week, the day after the Boston *Herald* had interviewed Father Beardsley at Palm Sunday Mass. The creeps usually came out in force after a newspaper story.

When he got there, things were quiet. A couple of cars drove by and honked, but fortunately there was no trouble. Seibert spotted Frenchy out in the yard and drove up to him. "How's it goin', Frenchy?" he asked. "Anybody giving you any trouble?"

Frenchy figured Seibert was there to pry, as usual, and wanted to answer, Nobody but you, Chief. But he held his tongue. Better to be friendly, he thought. "It's quiet today," he said. "But I never know when something's going to happen. The hecklers—I can handle them. It's this other thing that's got me licked."

Seibert chuckled. "Still after you, huh?"

Maurice glared at him. "You still don't believe, even after what you and that colored fella saw?"

For all his cynicism and suspicion Seibert had never actually closed his mind completely to what Maurice and Ed were saying. Sure, it was farfetched and probably a crock. But there was that small part of his mind—the part that had been brought up Catholic—that was willing to at least entertain this stuff about demons and possession.

"Let's just say I'm skeptical," Seibert replied.

"Well, why don't you come over and spend the night one night this week?" Maurice asked. "You'll see."

Seibert raised his eyebrows. "You want me to stay overnight?"

"Sure," Maurice said. "I ain't got nothin' to hide. You'll see. Then maybe you'll believe me."

"Okay," Seibert said. "You got it. How's tomorrow night?"

"Fine with me," Maurice said.

So at seven the next evening Chief Seibert, armed with a camera and a bottle of holy water Father Beardsley had given him, came prepared to spend the night at the Theriault farmhouse. He kept the visit a secret from his wife, telling her only that he would be out all night on surveillance. No need to scare her unnecessarily. No reason to tell her he was planning to spend the night with the devil, he thought to himself with a little laugh.

He rang the doorbell promptly at seven. But when Maurice opened it, he stared at Seibert as if he was the last person on earth he was expecting. "What do *you* want?" he asked.

"Well, Frenchy, this is the night you invited me to stay over, and I'm here," said Seibert.

Maurice started twitching. He had a certain look in his eye. Seibert noticed it right away. Maurice looked different, like someone else.

"I don't think this is a good idea," Maurice said. "I don't think you should spend the night."

"Now, look, Frenchy, you invited me and I'm here. Why don't you let me see for myself and be convinced?"

"Uh, I don't think so," he said. "It's too dangerous. I better call the Warrens."

Oh, Jesus, thought Seibert. They'll put the kibosh on this for sure.

Frenchy closed the door on Seibert and went off to call them. Sure enough, when he opened the door a few minutes later, he told Seibert that he couldn't stay the night.

He explained that the Warrens had suggested another night—not during Holy Week. That would be better, since Holy Week is the worst time for psychic phenomena and it could prove danger-ous. But they said they would leave it up to Maurice and Seibert.

"Well, I'm willing to take the risk," Seibert told Frenchy.

But Frenchy insisted that he couldn't stay. "If you do, I'm going to sleep at a motel," he said.

Seibert knew he couldn't force him, so he backed off. "Okay, Frenchy, have it your way. Maybe we'll do it another time."

But he knew that Frenchy would never let him. The offer was another crock.

As he pulled out of the driveway Maurice peered out his living room window and watched the cruiser leave. His eyes began to tear blood and his mouth began to drool yellow phlegm. His face contorted into a hideous shape and he started breathing heavily.

"Heh, heh, heh," he muttered, more a growl than a laugh. "That bastard will never catch me. If he tries, I'll kill him."

Then he passed out, falling to the floor with a thud. He stayed there, sleeping, until Nancy came home about half an hour later with some groceries. "What happened, honey?" she said, drop-ping her bags to run to his side.

Maurice came out of his deep sleep slowly. He shook himself awake. "I dunno," he said. "I must have passed out. I was just going to answer the door for the chief. He was supposed to spend the night here tonight."

"So where is he?" Nancy asked.

"I dunno," Maurice replied. "I guess he changed his mind. Must have gotten scared off."

"Just as well," Nancy said. "I don't trust that guy. I think he's trying to get you, Maurice."

● ● ●

The next day Maurice and Nancy received a visit from an old personal friend, Robert Manning. Robert was a landscape contractor and had been a guest of the Theriaults on many occasions over the years. When the publicity storm broke, Robert wasted no time in getting to his friends' house. Unlike the neighborhood gawkers, he was there to offer comfort, not taunts.

"Why didn't you tell me you needed help?" he said to Nancy as she took his jacket and led him into the kitchen, where Maurice was sitting. As he pulled out the yellow flowered vinyl chair and sat down, he said, "I brought something from St. Joseph's in Canada, and I want you to have it." He pulled a vial of holy water out of his jacket pocket. "I got this 'specially for you, Maurice."

Maurice had not even greeted his friend yet. He was just staring out the window. But Nancy, delighted with the gesture, took the bottle and proferred it to Maurice. "Look, Frenchy, look what Robert brought from Canada!"

"I don't want it," Maurice said, speaking in a monotone and still staring into space.

Nancy pushed the vial forward again. "Come on, Frenchy, take it."

"No, I don't want it now," he repeated.

Nancy looked nonplussed. "I'll put some on you, then," she

said, and with that, sprinkled some of the holy water on Maurice's forehead.

The instant the first drops hit his head Maurice's body went stiff, and blood began to seep from his mouth. Then the holy water itself, running down Maurice's forehead, turned blood-red. Before Nancy and Robert could react, Maurice rose, zombie-like, and went into the bathroom. The stunned Robert now had confirmation of what he had been reading in the newspapers. His face was white. Several minutes later Maurice emerged from the bathroom and sat down at the table as if he were entering the room for the first time that evening.

"Oh, hi, Robert," he said. "When did you get here?"

Robert was shaken but tried to stay cool and calm, mostly for Nancy's sake. He stayed at the Theriault home for dinner and there were no further incidents during the meal, though he kept looking at Maurice to make sure.

When it came time for Robert to leave, there were warm words all around, and the Theriaults' friend assured them he would be there if they needed him. He was sure that Maurice's problem must be a physical one that was being misunderstood.

Just as Robert reached the bottom of the Theriaults' driveway, he was hit by a tremendous rush of nausea, then by burning stomach pain such as he had never before experienced or believed possible. His head was spinning and aching so badly that he thought it might explode. Immobilized by the pain, he stopped the car and prayed for it to pass. Everything had turned white before his eyes. A terribly foul smell was filling the car.

After what might have been an hour, he managed to open a window. The cool air helped clear his head. He considered trying to drive back up the driveway to the Theriaults' house for help, but decided he'd try to drive home instead. He managed to navigate slowly out to the street, hanging on to the steering wheel, fighting the urge to black out again. He felt stronger and stronger as he got farther and farther from the house. When he finally reached home he vomited all night.

"You're not to go back to that house. *No way!*" his wife said. "Whatever is in there didn't like you bringing that holy water. It's much too creepy for you to deal with, Robert!"

Robert wasn't about to argue. He was scared to death.

Later, Ed Warren explained it all to the Theriaults. He was of the same opinion. "It's the fear factor," he said. "Anytime you pose a threat to a demon, that is what it fears. And Robert definitely posed a threat because he came here to help you with something of a spiritual nature, the holy water."

Although Robert later agreed to appear before the bishop to testify to what he had seen, he never went to the Theriault home again. Maurice was an old friend, but Robert wasn't going to risk his life to help him.

■ ■ ■

For Nancy, trying to sleep that night was difficult. Maurice lay oblivious with his face in the pillow, and she kept turning the day's events over and over in her mind. Then she heard a sound that bothered her. At first she thought it was a dripping sound, perhaps from the bathroom. But the sound was eerie, and it wasn't coming from that area. Slowly she realized that it seemed to come from the foot of the bed. She couldn't place what it was. Then it came to her. It sounded exactly as if a starving animal was gnawing a piece of raw meat, "chomping and chewing," as she described it later.

Frozen with fear, just as at the time the car had driven itself, she couldn't move or speak. So she feigned sleep and waited for the sounds to cease. She felt the hairs on her arms stand up as the eating sounds were followed by animal-like howls.

There would be no sleep for Nancy Theriault. Not that night. Not anytime soon.

■ ■ ■

Ed Warren knew that the strange incidents were bound to intensify around this time of year. It was the Lenten season—a time when psychic activity usually increases. That's why he was pushing so hard for a quick exorcism.

He told a Boston *Herald* reporter that week that Church officials were "doing their best to get things under way. This is Holy Week—the time when these cases seem to explode."

Ed promised that the exorcism would be over by Good Friday

at the latest. But Good Friday came and went without an exorcism. So did Easter Sunday.

So when Maurice and Nancy received a call from Father Beardsley two days after Easter, they were wary at first. He asked them to visit him in the rectory that afternoon. Maurice was convinced the Church had ordered another psychiatric evaluation, and he'd had his fill of doctors who were unwilling to believe in the torments he was suffering. The farmer would dearly have loved exchanging places for just a day with one of these learned men to see what his attitude would be afterward. He was fed up with the whole approach, but knew there was no other plan.

It was with much reluctance that Maurice and Nancy agreed to go to the rectory again with Ed and Lorraine Warren. Ed asked Maurice's friend Robert Manning to come with them to recount his experience.

When the group arrived, they were surprised to see another Catholic priest with Father Beardsley, and they were even more surprised to hear him introduced as Bishop Timothy Harrington. While Ed and Lorraine had talked with the bishop on the phone several times, they had never met him in person.

Bishop Harrington had a certain calm way about him, and Maurice felt comfortable with him. He could tell instantly that the bishop was a man of compassion and kindness.

After Father Beardsley's many calls and the publicity about the case, the bishop had decided to meet Maurice himself. Nothing seemed out of the ordinary about the meeting as the group sat and made conversation about—of all things—buying snow tires.

Suddenly the bishop seemed to make up his mind. "Maurice, I'm going to say a prayer for you," he announced. He asked Maurice to stand and Ed Warren and Robert Manning stood on either side of the tormented farmer.

Ed was gravely concerned that this spontaneous exorcism could go horribly awry. "The bishop didn't know it, but he was in grave danger," he said later to Lorraine. "Maurice could have knocked his block off."

Putting his hand on Maurice's head, the bishop began saying a prayer to St. Michael. Nancy, staring up at him, silently mouthed the words of the prayer in unison.

"St. Michael the Archangel, defend us in battle. Be our protection against the wickedness and snares of the devil."

As the prayer began, Maurice's face began to change, his forehead swelled, and his eyes took on a sadistic gleam. He began to mutter in a deep, guttural voice that was no longer his own.

"I am in the depths of this man's soul," the creature inside Maurice growled and sputtered. "And I will have it!"

Bishop Harrington continued to pray while the creature bellowed, "You cannot destroy me! You cannot make me leave!"

Bishop Harrington flinched but continued to pray.

"May God rebuke him, we humbly pray, and do Thou O Prince of the heavenly host by the divine power of God cast into hell Satan and all evil spirits who wander now throughout the world, seeking the ruin of souls."

Suddenly Maurice pitched forward onto his knees. The bishop took a bottle of holy water out of his cassock and began to sprinkle it furiously on Maurice—so liberally that when Maurice came to some minutes later, he was ashamed to think he had wet his pants.

The bishop kneeled and placed his hand on Maurice's shoulder, looking at him straight on. "You are my brother and I want to help you."

Maurice shook his head groggily and asked for a cigarette. The bishop, obviously shaken too, joined Maurice in a smoke.

"I hope my prayers will help," he said.

"I hope so too, Bishop," said Nancy. "Thank you so much."

Lorraine, terribly moved by what she had seen, also spoke words of praise. "I have never seen anyone of your position, totally unprepared, attempt a thing like that," she said.

Although Ed did not want to discourage Maurice and his wife, he had his doubts. Cases of genuine possession call for a formal exorcism, he knew, not a few prayers, however well intentioned.

Maurice and Nancy seemed so cheerful on leaving the rectory that Ed suggested lunch, and the two couples were soon seated around a table at a local restaurant. Maurice, who had seemed very tranquil on the ride down, sat silent through most of the meal as the others chatted of inconsequential matters.

"The bishop's such a nice man," Maurice gushed at one point. "He's just like a regular Joe." Suddenly he leaned forward and hissed at Ed, "I'd like to spit in both your faces!" His voice had completely changed.

No one said anything. Ed and Lorraine looked at each other knowingly.

It wasn't over yet.

ELEVEN

ALTHOUGH ED AND LORRAINE were hopeful that Bishop Harrington's spontaneous exorcism might calm Maurice and slow the pace of the possession, it was clear from his behavior in the restaurant immediately afterward that the prayers the bishop had said were not going to be enough.

For the next three days at the end of March 1985, things were calm in the Theriault household. A group of trained observers and students from the Warrens' New England School of Demonology were often at the house, either in pairs or larger numbers. The group included Assembly of God minister Jack Berman, police officer Kent Burch, Ryan Dufrain, Joey Taylor, seminarian Fred Salvio, college students Chris McKenna and Chris Finberg, Matthew Chase, handyman Benjamin Massey, Sonny Berryhill, and Jessica Spellman.

Some had never before witnessed preternatural phenomena. Others had worked with the Warrens for years. All were trained observers.

It was the two Chrises, Chris Finberg and Chris McKenna, who were in the house the night it became evident that the forces tearing at Maurice had certainly not been banished from his life as yet.

Lorraine Warren took the phone call late that night as a snoring Ed slept soundly beside her. Chris Finberg was on the phone. In the background Lorraine could hear Nancy screaming, "Oh, my God! Oh, my God! Stop these things from flying around!"

Finberg said that Maurice had been lying quietly on the bed with his granddaughter, when the two young men heard crashing sounds and Nancy starting to scream. Racing for a camera, then to his room, they found a hysterical Nancy, who managed to choke out that objects were flying about the room and smashing into the walls. Shards of shattered vases and pictures lay scattered about the room.

Lorraine told the two young men to try to calm the Theriaults—and themselves—but to get out of the house if anything further happened. She promised that she and Ed would be over in the morning. "Above all, someone must remain awake at all times," she counseled.

Ed and Lorraine had wanted to spend more time at the Theriault house, but they were distracted by another case, a haunted house, in the town of Tewksbury, Massachusetts, about two hours from Warren, in the Bay State's Merrimack Valley, north and west of Boston.

That case, involving a classic poltergeist, was demanding more and more of their time, as another family—a mother and her young children—was being scared out of its wits by unexplained knockings, noises, and flying objects that had smashed nearly every mirror, window, and other breakable object in the home. The case had forced Ed and Lorraine to split their time in Massachusetts between Warren and Tewksbury and caused them to send some of their researchers to Tewksbury to stay up all night in the possessed house to observe the strange phenomena there.

As bad as things were in Tewksbury, Ed realized that Maurice needed most of his attention. He continued to spend the bulk of his time with the poor farmer.

The day after the things had gone flying around the room at the Theriault farm, Nancy sent all the children to stay with friends and relatives. Whatever was torturing Maurice, it was a force far more powerful than anything she could imagine. Far more powerful and far more evil. The children could not be around until this thing was finished— one way or another.

• • •

Despite Lorraine's advice, there was little danger of anyone's going to sleep, not with the increasingly nightmarish events that had become commonplace around Maurice. Although the occurrences were terrifying for everyone, perhaps the most scared was Maurice himself.

The following morning Maurice was getting ready to shave. He filled up the old porcelain sink with hot water and wiped the steam off the mirror. As he looked he was aghast to see not one but two images of himself. It was the doppelgänger again! So many times in his life he had been told that he was in two places at once, but seeing it himself was something else again. He'd always thought that people were just mixed up. Maurice shook so hard he didn't dare hold a razor near his neck. He simply put the shaving utensil down and wiped the shaving cream off his face. He'd do without a shave that day.

. . .

Even in the face of the demonic infestation, life on the farm had to go on as usual and work had to go forward. Even the horrifying events of that month didn't mean that anyone would give the hard-working couple groceries—or any other of life's necessities—for free. On the contrary, people who used to extend credit now demanded cash. Most people assumed that "Frenchy" had gone crazy, and crazy people are not considered good credit risks.

So the days immediately following Bishop Harrington's impromptu prayer service for Maurice found the farmer and his wife working hard in the greenhouse, preparing the fields for spring planting and refurbishing the vegetable stand for the summer trade that would follow.

One bright morning Nancy was working with the small pots of tomato shoots in the greenhouse. On the other side of the long building she heard her husband pounding a nail into a board.

Bang! Bang! Bang!

"Frenchy, you want me to help you?" she called.

No answer.

"Frenchy?"

Nancy crossed the greenhouse to where she'd heard the banging sounds. The greenhouse was empty. There was no one there. And there was no sign that anyone had been there. No hammer, no nails. Just a pile of two-by-fours stacked in the corner where they had always been.

Oh, God, not another thing, Nancy thought. Stepping outside into the crisp March air she called for Maurice again.

"Frenchy!"

As she stood there frantically scanning the fields, Maurice's truck rolled up the gravel driveway with a crunch of pebbles. She turned around, and out of the driver's side popped Maurice, looking as if he'd just come back from a pleasant drive around the block.

"Maurice, where were you?" Nancy said, her face drained of color.

"Down at the stand," he replied.

"Well, I was working in the greenhouse and I kept hearing this banging and I was sure it was you."

"Oh, that son of a bitch again, eh?" Maurice said. "I'll show him." Maurice had forgotten that one of the strictest admonitions the Warrens had given him was to avoid challenging the evil force that was tormenting him. He raced into the greenhouse with Nancy right behind him, clutching his arm.

"No, Frenchy, no!" she cried.

But Maurice broke loose and stood defiantly in the middle of the greenhouse. "Come and get me now!" he shouted at the top of his lungs.

At that moment, as a horrified Nancy looked on, one of the two-by-fours flew as if it had been hurled fifty feet across the greenhouse and smashed Maurice square in the head, knocking him to the floor.

Screaming, Nancy managed to grab her husband by the collar and drag his dazed form out into the light snow that still covered the path to the house.

The crisp March air seemed to revive Maurice. He had a nasty bump on his head and blood was seeping from a minor cut on his scalp, but miraculously, he seemed otherwise unhurt.

■ ■ ■

Saturday morning Ed Warren couldn't sleep. He couldn't stay beside Maurice and Nancy every minute, yet he knew events were escalating and that a final reckoning was still in the future. The best he could do was make sure a team of researchers was at the house every night and that he and Lorraine visited almost every day.

On impulse, Ed decided to drive up to Warren right away. Skipping breakfast, Ed covered the one-hundred-twenty-mile distance between Monroe and Warren in record time. Something was telling him the situation was urgent.

When he pulled into the Theriault driveway, the first thing he saw was Maurice sitting silent and immobile in his running truck. Ed recognized the unnatural stillness about Maurice and approached the car slowly.

Peering in the window, he saw that the farmer had tears streaming down his face. He tapped lightly on the glass. "Maurice, what is it?" he said.

Maurice looked piteously at his friend, his eyes brimmed with tears. "Last night I wanted to hang myself," he said.

Ed knew that one of the signs of possession is the demon's desire to kill the body created by God in His image.

"I was too scared last night," Maurice said. "But then I was going to do it this morning. Just now I was goin' to do it. I would have if you hadn't driven up."

Ed could see a piece of thick rope beside Maurice on the front seat. "You're going to come out of this all right, Maurice," he said compassionately. "The Church will save you."

"They already tried, and nuthin' happened!" Maurice shouted. "You've got to stop this thing!"

"I promise you, we won't leave you alone," said Ed. "I promise you help is forthcoming."

Ed's promise seemed to calm Maurice, and Ed led him back to the house, vowing to himself that he would redouble surveillance on Maurice by his trained observers.

■ ■ ■

Sunday, Maurice followed Ed's advice and went to Mass at St. Paul's in downtown Warren. Sitting in the pew with Nancy as they listened to Father Beardsley intone the Mass, Maurice suddenly heard his name called out in a deep and powerful voice:

"Maurice!"

And again:

"Maurice!"

Looking around to see who might play such a malicious trick, Maurice saw nothing but the congregation sitting silently with heads bowed. It was clear that no one but him had heard the voice.

■ ■ ■

Chris Finberg kept notes on that night's events, notes that give some idea of the atmosphere inside the Theriault farmhouse during that terrifying period:

> 10:30 P.M. *Maurice's body aches all over. Every muscle in his body hurts. There is a smell of dog mess in the house. The room is so cold, and then it is so hot that you feel sick to your stomach... Maurice's son-in-law Rick said that each time the family comes to the farm, something happens. The family experiences tremendous pains in their bodies, unnatural pains. The researchers are also complaining of severe toothaches or pains in their bodies.*

As for Nancy, she didn't know what to do. Part of her wanted to leave this whole thing behind, to be with her children or just leave the state, maybe go to stay with her father. But she knew in her heart that she had to tough it out with her husband and listen to what the Warrens told her to do. She did have faith in God and believed that there had to be a good outcome.

The Warrens had given her several prayers to say, and she said them constantly as she walked around the house. Before she'd sent the children from the house, she'd said prayers over them, as well, to keep them safe. On one occasion, after having experienced a good night's sleep for the first time in many weeks, both Maurice and Nancy woke up to find rosary beads clutched tightly in their hands. Neither had any idea how they'd gotten there. Nancy was seized by an overpowering conviction that the Lord was trying to protect her and Maurice.

■ ■ ■

After the incident at the greenhouse Maurice and Nancy were reluctant to venture out there again, but there was no getting around the amount of work that had to be done.

Because of the cold weather the greenhouse windows were blacked out and wrapped in plastic, giving the structure a solitary and menacing atmosphere.

The next morning an apprehensive Maurice went down to the greenhouse to work, while Nancy busied herself with household tasks. The normal, everyday nature of sweeping the floors, making the bed, and starting the laundry was reassuring. Whistling to herself as she did the dishes, Nancy could almost imagine that she was just like all the other housewives caring for their families and that her house was no different from theirs. She remembered when she used to be bored and frustrated by having to do the housework and shook her head. Housework seemed like a pleasure now, she thought.

Lost in her thoughts, Nancy failed to notice how long Maurice had been gone. It was almost lunchtime, but he hadn't even come back up to the house for a cup of coffee. Suddenly she became worried.

Hoping for the best, Nancy ran down to the greenhouse. The door jamb that Maurice had placed to keep the greenhouse door from flapping open was still in place, indicating that Maurice must be elsewhere, but Nancy was seized by a premonition that he *was* in there.

"Frenchy!" she called.

No answer.

Removing the door jamb, Nancy entered the gloomy greenhouse. Maurice was standing in the middle of a long row of sawhorses, with a paper cup in his hand.

"Oh, honey, you *are* in here," exclaimed Nancy.

Maurice didn't reply but bent over suddenly and straightened up. His face was twisted into a sadistic leer. His brow became distended, apelike. His eyes were infernal. The greenhouse was filled with that terrible odor.

Nancy gasped. Whatever was staring at her was definitely *not* her husband. Instinctively she reached for the cross she now carried at all times and brandished it in front of her. "I command you to leave in the name of Jesus Christ," she cried.

At the sound of the words "Jesus Christ" Maurice grabbed his head and screamed in pure agony.

"Arrrrghh!"

His head drew back and he opened his mouth, which to Nancy's horror, did not form a circle as anyone's mouth would have, but made the form of a square. Blood gushed forward out of this bizarre opening, spraying the floor of the greenhouse and splattering the sawhorses. Maurice collapsed in a heap, shaking as if he had malaria.

Whatever had taken hold of him had let go. But not for long.

■ ■ ■

If others, including the police, now seemed to shun the Theriault family, their relatives continued to visit and to lend emotional support. They came despite the fear that invariably gripped visitors as soon as they approached the house—a house that, in addition to Maurice, Nancy, and the Warrens' team of investigators, now seemed to harbor an evil presence. All who entered felt it. None of them would have come again were it not for family loyalty.

The night after the second greenhouse incident, Maurice's daughter Nicole, her husband Rick, and Maurice's three grandchildren had stopped by to help create a family atmosphere they felt might help distract Maurice. Worried about the children,

Nancy tried to dissuade them from coming. But they insisted on showing their support. Maurice's sister Anne had called and was also going to drop in. Four of the researchers working with the Warrens were staying at the house with Maurice and Nancy. I hope there's safety in numbers, thought Nancy.

Anne drove up the familiar driveway, parked, and got out of her light blue Volkswagen bug. As she approached the farmhouse she thought she saw a large black form emerging from the shadows around the side of the house. Anne laughed nervously.

"Okay, Maurice, don't try to scare me," she said, pulling her hat down over her ears.

But the form was not Maurice, and as it swept over her Anne felt spasms of fear and nausea. She paused in the driveway for a moment, then sat on the steps until she had collected herself.

The family was gathered around the kitchen table, unaware that Anne was outside. Inside the living room, at that same moment, the four researchers scrambled to start a tape recorder to capture loud knocking and rapping noises that were reverberating throughout the house. As soon as Anne entered the house, however, the noises stopped.

Later that evening, as they sat around the table, the children chattered gaily about their friends and their latest activities. But Maurice was silent and morose. Picking up little Julia, his granddaughter, he seemed to gaze into the distance.

"I'll be glad when this son of a bitch leaves, so I can play with you," he said.

As the words came out of his mouth, Maurice's body was rocked backward as if he had been dealt a mammoth blow. The farmer landed on his back with a thud, with little Julia still cradled in his arms, screaming in fright.

When Ed Warren heard the story he had little doubt as to who the "son of a bitch" was.

■ ■ ■

Joey Taylor was one of the researchers who often spent the night with the Theriaults during this time. A Bridgeport, Connecticut, resident who taught elementary school, Joey had been fascinated by the work of the Warrens and eagerly participated whenever they asked for help.

He now found himself seated at the Theriault kitchen table with Maurice and Nancy as well as another researcher, Sonny Berryhill. The slender Joey, who weighed just one hundred forty-five pounds and stood five feet five inches, was only too glad to have Sonny with him.

Sonny's hobby was weightlifting, and he looked it. If anything was to go wrong, Joey would just as soon have someone around who was capable of restraining Maurice.

Joey had never been this close to a preternatural experience and he was very excited. Ed and Lorraine had given the young men strict instructions to observe, to take notes, and not to share what they wrote with one another or with the Theriaults.

But Joey couldn't resist a little experiment. He had brought a bottle of holy water with him, and he wanted to see if what Ed had taught in class about a possessed person's reaction to holy water was true. The short little farmer sitting before him certainly didn't seem possessed.

"Hey, Maurice, let's see what happens when you drink this," he said, offering the vial of holy water.

Maurice looked at him hard for a long moment. Joey felt a chill go down his spine. Nancy started to speak but stopped when Maurice's countenance completely changed. With a grin, he obligingly took a sip. In fifteen seconds he went stiff, his eyes rolled back, he clenched his fist, and started to tremble. In front of his stunned observers, his jaw sagged open and he let out a mouthful of blood onto the yellow placemat before him.

Scared and amazed, the two men had enough presence of mind to grab their cameras and take photographs of the scene. Moments later Maurice revived. He looked tired and bewildered.

"Maurice, do you remember anything that happened here just now?" Joey asked.

Maurice shook his head dumbly.

"You don't remember the holy water? Nothing?"

Maurice shook his head again. He seemed exhausted.

Nancy was wiping up the pool of blood and spittle from the placemat.

Joey looked at Sonny. He was white.

"No more experiments tonight," Joey said.

■ ■ ■

Maurice decided he wanted to visit his father's grave. Thinking that his torment was in some way connected to his father and the cruel experiences of his youth, Maurice believed that if he finally made peace with the old tyrant, even forgave him for the murder of his mother, he might gain a small measure of peace himself.

Ed was doubtful but didn't want to discourage Maurice, especially in his fragile emotional state. "Go ahead and go," he said. "But take some holy water and take a camera. If something happens, I want it documented. That will make it easier for the Church to believe us and to help you."

So Maurice and Nancy, equipped with a vial of holy water and a Polaroid camera, set off for Holyoke, Massachusetts, the last resting place of Maurice's brutal father and the woman he had victimized all her life, even to her final moments.

The day was fine and clear, and a temporary warming trend gave a small foretaste of the spring to come. Maurice had rolled down the driver's side window on the pickup truck and was enjoying the snap of the crisp air as it rushed by his ears. Nancy was listening to country music on the radio and humming along. Maurice's eyes began to tear as he thought of the ordinary life he would like to lead, like other people.

Looking compassionately at her husband, Nancy spoke what was on his mind. "We should be goin' to a nice restaurant or for a walk in the woods instead of somethin' like this," she said.

Maurice could only nod his head. On such a beautiful day it was not difficult to find their errand bizarre. But for Maurice, the day and all its beauty were an illusion. Reality was something darker. Something unspeakable.

They arrived at the cemetery about two-thirty in the afternoon and drove directly to the Theriault tombstone. Maurice, dressed in a red hunting cap and red plaid jacket, parked the truck on one of the cemetery's small winding roads and sat with the door open, staring across a small green expanse at the block of granite bearing the word "Theriault." The dates of birth and the identical date of death of his mother and father were inscribed underneath.

Maurice's breath showed white in front of his face, despite the relatively pleasant weather, as he sat there in the driver's seat of the truck, trying to muster the courage to cross the thirty yards between him and his father.

It might have been four years since Philippe had died, but as far as Maurice was concerned he was still alive. The terror in his own early life had always been authored by the brutal figure of his father, and the farmer was sure that the torment that was haunting him now was, in some way, connected to the cruel old man who lay buried here.

"Well, Frenchy, are you gonna go over there?" Nancy asked.

"Yeah, I'm goin'," he replied, and got out of the truck.

Shedding his jacket and hat, he approached the grave dressed in a T-shirt and jeans. Nancy followed with the camera.

When he arrived at the grave that contained all that he had loved and feared as a child, Maurice dropped to his knees in front of the tombstone and began to pray.

Nancy stood beside him and to the side, feeling uncomfortable, not wanting to impose on this private moment.

Maurice, who had been silently mouthing his prayers, now spoke out loud, addressing Philippe. "I want to be a son to you," he said, "and I want you to be a father to me...."

But as he finished the phrase Maurice's body suddenly flew backward and up into the air. It was exactly like the incident at the church door, or the time he had been holding little Julia. He had simply been smashed by an invisible force.

Nancy ran toward him, then remembered what the Warrens had told her. She quickly snapped a photo, then ran to her husband. He was lying semiconscious, bleeding from the nose.

"Frenchy, Frenchy, are you all right?" she cried.

"Yeah," he said groggily. "I'm okay."

But Maurice wasn't okay.

That night, as Nancy sat brushing her hair in the bedroom, she heard him call out, "Nancy, Nancy!"

She ran to the hallway. Gazing down its length— some twenty feet—she saw Maurice lurching back and forth, bouncing off the walls of the narrow passageway. He fell forward onto the floor and began to roll and spin, his feet striking the walls.

"Leave me alone! Leave me alone!" he cried.

His body started to flop about like a fish pulled out of the water and thrown on a dock.

Terrified, Nancy sank to her knees and began to pray out loud. "In the name of Jesus, leave us alone," she intoned. "In the name of Jesus, leave us alone. In the name of Jesus, leave us alone...."

Eventually the convulsions stopped. Maurice lay there, struggling for his breath. He told Nancy that he just wanted to rest there awhile. Inside, he was afraid of another attack and felt he just couldn't handle another. He lay on that spot the whole night.

. . .

A few days later Maurice and Nancy were outside tending to the animals when they heard the crunch of tires in their gravel driveway. Nancy was brushing the dog and Maurice was taking the cow to the barn. Nancy looked over at her husband. "You expectin' anybody?" she asked.

Maurice shook his head.

A white sedan came up over the rise and pulled to within several yards of the house. Maurice and Nancy could see there were several men in the car. One got out on the passenger's side. He was a young clean-cut man with aggressive, hawkish features. He walked straight up to Maurice.

"I feel I've been sent here to pray or to help you in some way," he said.

Nancy didn't like the looks of the young man, without being able to say why. She told him what the Warrens told her to say in case they were bothered by publicity seekers or people with obscure religious motives.

"Look," she said. "We want everybody to just leave us alone. We don't want any outside help at this time. Thank you anyway. Now, please leave our property."

As Nancy was speaking a second man got out of the car on the driver's side. He had a Polaroid instant camera in his hands. Before anyone could react he had aimed it at Maurice and Nancy and started to click off a shot of the beleaguered couple.

As the camera whirred and spit out a color photo, Maurice exploded into action. He grabbed the man with the camera and ripped the photo out of his hands. "Now, you get out of here," Maurice shouted.

The men were already scrambling back into the car. The vehicle was roaring in reverse back down the driveway before the doors were even closed.

Maurice couldn't help laughing a little, despite his anger. Phony faith healers were a lot easier to chase off than raccoons, he thought. "Hey, honey, did you see them take off?" he said, turning to his wife.

Nancy didn't reply. She was looking at the photo that had fallen to the ground when Maurice had torn it from the grasp of the intruder. "Frenchy, look at this," she said, crouching over it, pointing at it with the handle of the dog brush.

Maurice picked up the picture. He was afraid to look at it after seeing Nancy's face. Now what? he thought. He forced his eyes to the little colored square.

In the photo Nancy's mouth was open, obviously in midsentence as she talked with one of the men, and Maurice could be seen advancing toward the camera.

"Yeah, so?" said Maurice.

"Frenchy, look at the ground!"

Maurice looked at the photo again. All around his feet flames were leaping out of the ground.

■　■　■

Before he would consider a formal exorcism, Bishop Harrington sent two Catholic lay healers to meet with Father Beardsley and the Theriaults. Maurice and Nancy were eager to meet with anyone sent by the bishop and anxious to show Father Beardsley and the two healers the remarkable photo.

Maurice and Nancy drove to the rectory and were introduced to the two healers, whose names were Jesse Curtis and Mike Loggia.

"Maurice, Bishop Harrington asked us to come and see if we could help you," said Jesse. "The truth is, we have never experienced a case like yours, as it has been described to us by the bishop and Father Beardsley. We're used to saying prayers for those who are very ill, perhaps with cancer or another life-threatening disease."

"Well, his life is being threatened," said Nancy. "Here, look at this." She thrust the Polaroid photo into Jesse's hands.

He glanced at the photo and quickly passed it to Mike, who blanched as he looked at it. He began tearing it to shreds. "You don't want to look at that," he said, clearly frightened. "You don't even want to think about anything like that."

Although Nancy was shocked by the action, she reassured herself that these men had been sent, after all, by the bishop, and they must know what was best.

"We'd like to say some prayers over Maurice now," said Jesse. "Is that okay with you, Maurice?"

Maurice nodded his head warily.

The two men assumed positions on either side of the farmer, and each placed a hand on his head. Mike began the first prayer.

Immediately Maurice's body stiffened completely, as if his muscles were undergoing some sort of electric shock. Mike closed his eyes and continued the prayer.

Laughter boomed out of Maurice in a deep, powerful voice: "Ha-ha-ha-ha-ha."

The two healers were so startled for an instant that their hands recoiled from Maurice's head, although each quickly replaced his hand.

Blood and a substance that looked like yellow glue was now pumping out of Maurice's mouth, and Nancy ran into the rectory kitchen for a towel, which Mike used to clean Maurice's shirt-front.

The two healers continued to pray for about fifteen minutes. When they were finished, they were anxious to declare victory and go home.

Standing in the driveway as they were preparing to leave,

Jesse tried to reassure Nancy. "I'm sure everything's going to be all right now," he said.

But Nancy knew everything was not "all right."

■ ■ ■

Maurice was doing his best to continue farming, although all semblance of normality in his life had long since been stolen by the evil force that had turned his existence into one long scream for help.

Sitting atop his tractor as it rumbled up and down the long rows that he would soon seed with tomato plants, Maurice thought back to the days when his feet hadn't even reached the pedals, and his cruel father had tormented him with his inadequacies. What kind of world was it, he thought, that chose some for a life of ease and education, and for others poverty, ignorance, and torment?

Speaking aloud in his native French-Canadian *patois*, Maurice addressed the heavens. *"Pourquoi le laissez-Vous m'ennuyer comme ça?"* he shouted. "Why are You letting him torment me like this?"

As Maurice returned his gaze to the earth he saw a stranger standing in front of him. The man, dressed in normal winter clothes, wore his hair long. His gentle face bore a look of compassion. Maurice had never seen the man before, although there was something familiar about him. Nonetheless, Maurice did not like intruders on his land.

"What are you doing here?" he said, in a none-too-friendly way.

"Stop your laboring," said the man.

"What you are talking about?" Maurice replied. "I still got one more turn to do."

"Don't you think you've done enough for today?" the stranger asked. The voice was oddly familiar. Where had Maurice heard it before?

"I've got one more row to do and I want to finish it," he told the man.

"You'll be coming into a lot of money soon, Maurice," the stranger said. "Remember what has happened to you and help people with it. Now, stop. You've done enough for today."

So many bizarre things had happened to Maurice that he didn't know what to make of this man. He might be real or illusion, he might be good or evil. Maurice felt he had no way to judge. He didn't even trust the evidence of his senses any longer.

The stranger's tone was comforting and what he said reassuring, but the Warrens had warned Maurice that evil might show itself to him in an attractive form.

He decided to ignore the man. He put the tractor in gear and depressed the gas pedal, but the machine lurched crazily. Maurice put the tractor in neutral and jumped down. Both front tires were flat.

He was sure that only seconds ago both tires had been in perfect condition! Spinning around to confront the stranger,

Maurice saw nothing but the empty field, freshly plowed. He felt the hair on the back of his neck stand straight up.

Glancing down, Maurice noticed footprints in the newly turned earth. He followed them along the furrows for fifty feet and then stopped abruptly. Staring down at the ground, Maurice could not believe what he saw.

The footprints ended in the middle of the field.

Maurice surveyed the freshly plowed and softened earth in every direction, yet there were no more footprints. It simply wasn't possible. It was as if the stranger had disappeared into thin air. And yet it couldn't have been an apparition. Here were his footprints! It wasn't possible that the man hadn't been there. But it wasn't possible that he had disappeared either.

"Frenchy! Frenchy!"

Maurice looked up to see his son Marc approaching.

"Hey, what was that crazy guy doing out here?" Marc asked.

"You saw him?" Maurice asked.

"Yeah, I saw him. He walked right by the house."

"Why do you say he was crazy?"

"What would you call it," Marc asked, "walking around in March with no shoes on?"

That night, Maurice dreamed of his childhood, of the time when he was twelve years old.

It was snowing. It was snowing very hard. He had to get home to Maman. *She would be worried about him, and his father would beat him. But it was cold and white, so white he couldn't see any-*

thing, and the snow was stinging his face. It was so cold his tears were freezing on his cheeks. Blinded and half hysterical he fell into a snowbank and lay there sobbing as the snow soaked through his patched winter clothes. Suddenly he felt someone pulling him up out of the snowbank. It was a man with a kindly face. "Come, Maurice, I will take you home," he said.

Maurice sat up with a start.

That face! That voice! No wonder the stranger in the field had seemed so familiar!

It had been more than forty years, but Maurice had not forgotten. The man in the field was the same man who had pulled him from the snowbank when he was a little boy.

Sitting there in bed, Maurice began to cry.

TWELVE

MAURICE AND NANCY were never alone in the house now. Either Ed and Lorraine Warren, or one of their team of observers, was with the beleaguered couple at all times. They were used to being together, and the investigators had become a part of the Theriault clan, even helping in the daily activities around the house.

Monday dawned crisp and cool. It had now been two days since Maurice's moving encounter with the mysterious and kindly stranger in the field. The two Chrises—Finberg and McKenna—were on duty at the Theriault house.

McKenna had worked on several cases with the Warrens before. Finberg, McKenna's classmate in college, had been begging his friend to go along ever since he'd first heard about his work with the famous couple.

Everybody had gone to church together the day before, and for forty-eight blessed hours nothing had happened. None of the terrifying phenomena that had turned the Theriault family life into a combination of horror story, scientific experiment, and tourist attraction had made a reappearance. For two days Maurice had been himself, and the Theriault home had settled into the rhythm of farm life. It was now planting season and there was plenty of activity on the farm.

Ed Warren called several times a day, and during that Monday morning's call Chris McKenna told his teacher that he thought the siege might be over.

"The appearance of the stranger in the field might have been a sign to Maurice that it's stopped," the young man theorized. He had a degree in psychology and thought that if Maurice had taken the apparition in the field as some sort of benediction or deliverance, his troubles might be finished.

"No, it's not over," replied Ed. "These kinds of preternatural events don't just stop like that. I'd love to think you're right, and for Maurice's sake, I hope you are. But from everything I've seen, whatever is possessing Maurice will have to be driven out. It won't just leave."

■ ■ ■

It took only two hours for Ed to be proved correct.

After coffee and croissants and pitching in to wash the morning dishes, the two observers split up. Chris Finberg stayed in the farmhouse to help Nancy with the laundry. Chris McKenna went to the greenhouse with Maurice to help him plant tomato seedlings. McKenna liked working with Finberg. For one thing,

McKenna had helped train his friend as an observer. For another, Finberg was a good photographer and that was always useful.

Every passing day was bringing the farmer closer to planting the now sturdy tomato shoots. Maurice was eager to turn out a good crop. He knew that to most people the biblical injunction "As ye sow, so shall ye reap" meant that they shouldn't cause discord or bad actions that would rebound on them. But he also believed it literally, and he knew that a good harvest would depend on, among other things, strong seedlings, well planted in the earth.

He always loved this time of year. The new moon was approaching, the best time for planting. Maurice spent much of the morning showing his young assistant how to care for the young shoots that would later that year bear the ripe red fruit that drew people from miles around to Frenchy's vegetable stand.

Frenchy poked a short finger into one of the damp egg cartons that bore tiny shoots. The greenhouse was a forest of fine green baby plants, neatly planted in endless rows of cartons. Each plant had two or three leaves on its fuzzy stalk. "You got to give 'em just enough water and just enough sun so they'll be strong enough to plant," the farmer explained. "Too much of either and they'll die."

McKenna was less interested in the fine art of tomato growing than he was in the extraordinary paranormal events that surrounded Maurice. Still, he thought to himself, it's always interesting to listen to an expert talk about what he knows best.

So many of the students who studied with the Warrens began by imagining that they would be rummaging through romantic castles in the English countryside, pursuing famous ghosts. They soon learned, however, that manifestations of evil can take place anywhere and are just as likely to appear in a two-story suburban colonial home as in the dungeon of a deserted chateau. Or for that matter, in the simple lifestyle of a Massachusetts farmer.

Some castle, thought McKenna, looking around the plastic-and-Plexiglass greenhouse and smiling to himself.

Despite the lingering winter weather, it was hot inside the greenhouse and Maurice had stripped down to a T-shirt. Chris decided that was a good idea and did the same. When he was comfortable he began watering the cardboard boxes of seedlings as Maurice had shown him.

It was hard work. There were thousands of the tiny plants and the process of filling the watering can, bending over each plant, trying to give it just enough water, and then after watering fifteen or twenty plants, refilling the can and starting all over again was maddening. Chris was on his third refill when he was startled by a strange, menacing voice behind him.

"You put goddamn ice cubes down my back," the voice growled.

McKenna whirled around to find Maurice, his face contorted in an angry scowl, standing right behind him. He was breathing right into his face, and Chris was sickened by the smell of his breath.

"Maurice! You scared the heck out of me," he exclaimed, keeping his cool. "Nobody put anything down your back."

Maurice said nothing but glowered at the young man. Then slowly he turned away from Chris.

McKenna's eyes widened. The back of the farmer's T-shirt was laced with bright crimson lines, some in the form of a cross, others spelling out words McKenna could not understand.

McKenna quickly grabbed Maurice by the arm. "Okay, Maurice," he said. "Let's go up to the house." He began tugging the muscular little man out of the greenhouse. "Everybody needs to see this."

Climbing the steep gravel slope up to the farmhouse, McKenna called out to Chris Finberg and Nancy, both of whom came running to the kitchen door when they heard Chris's noticeably urgent tone of voice. McKenna pulled Maurice into the house.

"Nancy, get a wet towel and another shirt for Maurice," he instructed. She already knew what to do and hurried off to get the supplies.

Then Chris Finberg began to quiz his partner. "What happened down there?"

"I don't know," McKenna replied. "One minute we were watering the tomatoes, the next minute he was accusing me of putting ice cubes down his back. Then I saw this." He gestured at Maurice's scarlet-streaked T-shirt.

"Let's get his shirt off and see what's written there," Finberg suggested, still staring at the bloody garment.

McKenna nodded agreement. "Maurice, raise your arms," he said.

Maurice didn't struggle, but he wasn't making it easy for them to remove his shirt either.

The two men peeled the farmer's shirt up over his head and stood rooted to the spot, staring dumbfounded at his back.

There wasn't a mark on it.

"My God! Look at that!" Finberg exclaimed. "How the hell did he do that? Let me see that T-shirt."

McKenna held it up. It was snow-white. No stains. No lines. Not a trace of red. Nothing.

The two young men looked at each other without a word as Maurice stood shivering between them.

Chris Finberg finally broke the silence.

"Ed was right," he said.

■ ■ ■

Ed and Lorraine arrived late that night. The two Chrises needed some time off and both were shaken up by what they had seen that day. And Nancy was especially relieved to have the Warrens there now. She really wondered if soon it might not be too late for Maurice.

"You guys go on home and rest," Ed advised Chris and Chris. "Sonny is coming in the morning, and we'll call you right away if we need you."

Sitting around the Theriault table that night, it was clear to Ed and Lorraine that an alien presence was not happy that they were in the house. Throughout the evening the conversation was interrupted by the sound of car doors slamming right outside. But each time Ed went to see what was causing the noise, he could find no vehicle or any other cause. And intermittently the lights in the house would dim, then return to their original brightness, then dim again.

After dinner Nancy swung open the door to the dining room, excitedly calling Ed to the kitchen. "Look," she said, pointing toward the ceiling.

Balanced on top of a curtain rod above the kitchen window was a tray with four small cups on it.

"What happened?" Ed asked.

"I don't know," said Nancy. "I was looking for that tray so I could serve some cherry pie. I couldn't find it anywhere. Then I walked in here and looked up and there it was!"

Of course, Ed thought, it could have been put there as a prank by anyone in the house, but he doubted it. No one was treating the frightening events of the past month as a joke.

■ ■ ■

Ed and Lorraine were ever more deeply involved in the delicate negotiations with the Church that might produce an exorcism for Maurice. There was no question in Ed's mind that exorcism was the only answer. But who would perform the rite? The Warrens had some ideas, but the final decision rested with the diocese of

Worcester. One problem was that the Church, historically, has been slow to approve exorcisms. Another problem was that there just weren't that many experienced exorcists around anymore.

The Warrens were keeping several priests informed of the daily developments inside the Theriault home. Sometimes the clergy offered advice, and they always offered prayers. The Warrens welcomed both. But they knew what was really needed was the direct intercession of a priest who was not afraid to do battle with the demon that was afflicting Maurice.

Ed knew of one such priest. His name was Bishop Robert McKenna. He also lived in Monroe, just a mile or so from Ed and Lorraine's house. But Bishop Harrington would have none of it. McKenna was too controversial.

Although ordained as a Roman Catholic priest, McKenna had been expelled from the Church because he continued to say Mass in Latin. He operated his own chapel in Monroe, with no help from Rome. In the eyes of Bishop Harrington, he would never do.

The negotiations with Bishop Harrington continued. It was a sticky political situation and Maurice's case was in limbo because of it.

■ ■ ■

The day after the cups appeared on the curtain rod, Ed and Lorraine returned home and Sonny Berryhill came up from New Britain, Connecticut. It was his shift of duty. A student at Central

Connecticut State College, Berryhill was trying to study for mid-term exams at the same time he was working on the Theriault case for the Warrens. He sat comfortably spread out on the sofa with his Polaroid camera, tape recorder, and a pile of textbooks. Berryhill knew from experience that he might need to record any unusual happenings and always kept the camera and recorder within reach. In the meantime he bent his head over an anatomy book and tried to study. If anatomy were as exciting as life in the Theriault farmhouse, he thought, he'd ace every exam.

Berryhill's thoughts were interrupted by Maurice's heavy step at the front door as the farmer came in from his work to have lunch.

"Whatcha readin'?" Maurice asked.

"Anatomy," the young man replied. "I'm supposed to know how the muscles work, where strength comes from and so on."

"Strength comes from the spirits," said Maurice, with a wink.

"What do you mean?"

"Come on, I'll show ya." Maurice marched down the hall and out the front door.

Berryhill was about to follow when he remembered his camera. "I'll be right there," he called, and ran back to the living room. He hurriedly attached the flash cube while running back. When he got to the front door, he stopped dead in his tracks. Looking out, he could see Maurice in front of the house, and what he saw was hard to believe.

Several times, coming up the driveway, Berryhill had noticed a life-sized statue of a saint, although Sonny couldn't say which saint, leaning propped against the house. Solid cement, enough to withstand the winter and the high winds that blew across the exposed hill, it must have weighed hundreds of pounds, in Berryhill's estimation.

What had stopped Berryhill in his tracks was the sight of Maurice, his two hands delicately wrapped around the base, holding the statue in the air. What was even more shocking was the expression on his face. Maurice showed no sign of exertion at all.

The Warrens' observer quickly snapped off a photo and placed the camera on the kitchen counter, then ran out to join Maurice, who was just replacing the statue. The farmer straightened with a little smile on his face. He wasn't sweaty or even breathing hard.

Without a word, Berryhill, whose weightlifting had left him capable of bench-pressing one hundred fifty pounds, grabbed the statue and heaved with all his might.

It didn't budge.

"How'd you do that, Maurice?" he asked, after giving up on his own efforts.

"I just call on the spirits," the farmer said, looking upward and chuckling. "I done that all my life, ever since I had to lift heavy logs and sacks for my father when I was a kid."

■ ■ ■

Two weeks had passed since Bishop Harrington's spontaneous effort to rid Maurice of his torment, and Ed Warren hadn't yet been able to arrange for a formal exorcism. Finally the bishop and the Warrens agreed on a man: Father Neil Delaney.

Although not an exorcist *per se*, Father Delaney, a faith healer, was no stranger to the power of prayer, since he held regular healing services at his church in nearby Auburn. He was a Roman Catholic in good standing, well-known to Bishop Harrington, and a friend of the Warrens as well.

The Warrens had met him under unusual circumstances seven years earlier during a legendary storm referred to throughout Massachusetts as the "Blizzard of '78." They had been on a speaking tour of New England and were on a stop at Keene State College in New Hampshire when they saw a feature on the television news about Father Delaney, a Catholic priest who performed faith healing. That got their attention because they had not known many Catholics who believed in the practice. It was usually more the province of fundamentalist Christians.

A few days later the Warrens arrived in Worcester for a talk at Worcester State College. But along came the "Blizzard of '78." It snowed for days. People were stranded everywhere. Drifts of six feet were the rule. Travel was absolutely impossible. The state of Massachusetts, in effect, had shut down.

Ed and Lorraine sat in their room in the Holiday Inn in Auburn, waiting for the roads to be cleared so they could return home to Connecticut. As they sat on their bed reading, Lorraine turned to Ed. "Honey, remember the report we saw on the news the other day about that Catholic faith healer?"

Ed peered up from his book. "Yeah?"

"Well, I just remembered that he lives in Auburn."

"So?"

"Well, why don't we give him a call?"

"We?"

"Okay, I'll do it."

Lorraine pulled the phone directory out of the nightstand and looked up Father Delaney's name. "Here it is!" she exclaimed.

Ed looked up from his book again. "And just what do you have in mind?"

"I don't know. Maybe we can get together for a chat. He seems like such an interesting man."

Ed chuckled. "Oh, and how do you plan on doing that? The whole city is paralyzed."

"We'll find a way," Lorraine replied, dialing the phone number.

And so began their friendship. Father Delaney invited the Warrens over to the rectory for a private healing service. And it turned out, they needed it, for by the time they had walked a mile through the snow, Ed and Lorraine were exhausted. But it was an afternoon to remember. Lorraine came away a firm believer in the healing power of prayer and the laying-on of hands.

So when Bishop Harrington suggested Father Delaney for Maurice's exorcism, she and Ed approved wholeheartedly.

Father Delaney agreed to try it, but he refused to call it an exorcism. He preferred to try what he called a "deliverance."

Ed raised an eyebrow when he heard that but figured that

if Father Delaney was comfortable calling it a deliverance, it couldn't hurt.

The deliverance turned out to be almost an exact replay of the healing prayers performed over Maurice. Done in the presence of Father Beardsley at the rectory of St. Paul's, the result was virtually identical. As soon as the prayers began, Maurice stiffened. Soon blood and a yellow substance began to seep out of his mouth. Despite questioning by Father Delaney, no sound came from Maurice during the service. Afterward Maurice seemed exhausted and depressed.

"I don't know how much longer he can go on," Nancy reported to the Warrens. She could have been speaking for herself as well. She, too, was feeling completely worn out and down. Maybe Maurice's case was hopeless.

Still, the Theriaults continued to visit with Father Delaney, often having Sunday dinner with the priest, then attending his prayer services afterward.

But the mayhem continued in the Theriault house. Chris Finberg's notes reveal the atmosphere inside where a small circle of people were sharing an ordeal that none could explain and that none would ever forget:

Fire in the greenhouse... Seems to be a car coming... Sonny and Rick went outside to investigate. Could not see or hear anything. Just prior to Sonny and Rick's coming back inside, it happened again... Chris called from the bed-

room, stated that he was very dizzy in one corner of the room... Everyone is becoming weak and light-headed...

Benjamin Massey and Jessica Spellman were on duty as observers. Jessica, more than a little frightened by what she had seen and heard about the Theriault case, asked her boyfriend, Chad, to come to the Theriault farmhouse as well. They were joined over the weekend by several more of the observing team.

Nancy had gone to bed early, but Maurice was still awake. He and several observers, bound together by the extraordinary events of the past two weeks, sat in the Theriaults' cramped living room and tried to speak of inconsequential matters, of school and farming and gossip about friends.

The two young men spent some time dissecting the recent upset victory of the Villanova basketball team over heavily favored Georgetown to win the NCAA championship. Jessica was telling Maurice why the recent announcement by the White House that President Reagan would visit the war cemetery in Bitburg, West Germany, was making so many people angry.

Inevitably, however, the conversation turned to the Warrens and their work with preternatural phenomena. They were, at this very moment, back in Tewksbury, where the haunted house of Marie Wyatt was proving more and more troublesome. By this time the poor family had been driven from their home by the unending barrage of unexplained knockings, moanings, and flying objects.

Much as they wanted to help both families, the Warrens were determined to see Maurice through his ordeal before they took on another full-time case. Still, they had visited the Tewksbury home, and coming as it did on the heels of all the publicity about Maurice, the media were in hot pursuit.

But none of this conversation seemed to be holding Maurice's attention. The frustration of waiting was making him irritable, and as Benjamin, Jessica, and the others chatted away, Maurice began to pace the room like a captured beast whose cage is too small. Back and forth, back and forth he stalked, his movements becoming more and more agitated.

"I'm telling you," Benjamin was saying, now back on college basketball again, "Thompson isn't that great a coach. It was Ewing who—"

Crash!

The noise made everyone jump and brought the conversation to a sudden halt in midsentence. It sounded as if somebody had thrown a rock into the living room.

"What the hell was that?" someone shouted.

Jessica wore an amazed expression.

"L-look," she stuttered, pointing at the coffee table.

Where a glass ashtray had rested only moments ago, there was now a pile of cinders and broken glass. The ashtray had literally exploded.

The three young people looked at Maurice, who had stopped pacing. His eyes seemed to have gone opaque, and it was as if he were no longer in the room. A deep moan came welling out of his chest.

Jessica's boyfriend, Chad, grabbed her hand. "Come on," he said, almost shouting. "We're getting out of here."

■ ■ ■

Chad wound up doing exactly that, but Jessica wasn't about to leave. She had always been fascinated by psychic phenomena and working with the Warrens had left her, if not fearless, at least more familiar with the kinds of events involved in a case of possession.

Jessica was thirty-five years old. Her one hundred thirty-five pounds were well distributed on her tall frame, and the dark-haired, brown-eyed observer had been drawing admiring glances from some of the males in the group, even though most were much younger.

Several times during her own life she'd had experiences that were, she found out, extremely unusual. Starting when she was thirteen years old, she would often have dreams foretelling events that would then take place, often exactly as they had in the dream. Wanting to learn more about such occurrences she enrolled in the Warrens' course and began to discover that her gift, while unusual, did not mean she was crazy. In fact, it was a gift shared by Lorraine Warren.

The Warrens were delighted that Massey had agreed to assist in this case. A twenty-seven-year-old handyman, Massey had taken a course with the Warrens at a local high school and had responded eagerly to their request for volunteer observers. Lorraine told the young man that she had been watching him throughout the lecture. "You have the brightest aura in the class," she said.

Massey was a meticulous note-taker and brought his own recording equipment to the Theriault home. He switched on the machine whenever an unusual sound or event took place.

Neither he nor Jessica could sleep very much. Jessica was telling Benjamin about an incident that had taken place earlier that afternoon. One of the observers had brought a friend along. After several minutes' conversation with the newcomer, it was clear to Jessica that he had come neither to study or learn nor to help Maurice. He was at the Theriault home for a thrill, hoping something spectacular of a supernatural nature would take place.

Nothing occurred for several hours and the young man, whom Jessica had already dubbed "the Skeptic," lectured the others about all the possible scientific explanations for each of the events they had witnessed.

After touring the house and meeting Maurice and Nancy, the visitor became impatient. Jessica was never sure afterward if he did it to show off for her, but the young man announced that he wasn't waiting anymore for these "spirits."

"Watch this," he said.

Walking into Maurice and Nancy's bedroom, he hastily scribbled a note and dropped it onto their bed. Jessica picked it up. She turned pale.

"You don't want to do this," she said.

"Yes I do," the young man replied.

The note read: "Spirits, if you are in this house, show your-selves to me."

It was, as Chris McKenna was to remark later, a foolhardy and dangerous game. Ed Warren had taught all the students that challenging a demonic force—or any phenomenon beyond their understanding—was the worst thing they could do in these cases.

Ten minutes later the reason for Ed's warnings became clear, although it was almost as humorous to the people in the house as it was frightening.

The arrogant newcomer was busy giving the others a lecture about not being afraid of "hocus-pocus" when his belt buckle suddenly popped open. He stopped in midsentence and gazed down with a stupefied look on his face. He was still in that posi-tion when his zipper broke and his pants began to sag down around his thighs.

Jessica didn't know whether to laugh or cry as the young man grabbed his waistband and fled the house.

■ ■ ■

Hearing the story, Benjamin Massey did laugh. "Some people really *are* crazy," he said.

It was then that the sounds started. Benjamin hastily switched on his tape recorder. Directly under the couch on which Jessica was lying came scratching sounds, as if hundreds of rats were scrambling all over the floor. Peering under the couch, Benjamin saw nothing. A quick check of the basement revealed it to be empty. Just as suddenly as the noises had begun, they ceased.

The pair looked in every room but could find no cause for the mysterious scratching sounds. Coming back to the living room, Jessica was surprised to hear the television blaring. It hadn't been on when they had left the room. She switched it off.

Benjamin and Jessica resumed their places on the couch and chair and tried to talk. The silence was frightening, even for people with their training and experience. Each knew that the period between nine P.M. and four A.M. is what investigators of the paranormal call the "psychic hours," when preternatural events are much more likely to occur.

Shortly after one A.M. the observers heard several car doors slam in the Theriault driveway, only yards from where they were seated. They ran to the window, but despite a well-lit driveway, they could see no vehicles. Stepping outside, they confirmed that the driveway was empty. Just then, Jessica heard what sounded like a police dispatcher's radio squawking in the hall. The couple raced back inside, but the hallway, too, was mockingly empty.

"Whatever it is we're hearing, it doesn't seem to want to show itself," said Benjamin. "I vote we try to get some sleep."

Despite the excitement, they managed to fall asleep eventually. Benjamin was in a deep, dreamless slumber when he was catapulted out of his chair by Jessica's screams. Bolt upright on the couch, she stared with horror at a plaster statue of an Indian that stood next to the Theriaults' television.

"What is it, Jessica?"

"He told me to get out, to get out of the house."

"Who told you?"

"The Indian."

"The statue talked?"

"And he hurt me. He hurt my legs."

"How'd he do that?" Benjamin asked.

"I don't know," Jessica replied. "All I know is, my legs ache now and they didn't before."

"Shit," said Benjamin. "I think I'd better just stay up with you the rest of the night."

. . .

In the morning Maurice's four-year-old granddaughter, Sadie, came with her mother to visit. While the adults chatted in the kitchen, Benjamin Massey did his best to amuse the child. "You want to draw?" he asked.

Sadie nodded solemnly.

Benjamin went off to the kitchen and returned in a moment with paper and crayons.

Benjamin sat on the floor with the youngster. "What should we draw?" he said.

Sadie seemed to reflect for a moment, almost as if she were deciding whether Benjamin could be trusted. Finally she seemed to have made up her mind. "Let's draw the monster," she said.

"What monster?" Benjamin smiled.

"The one in the house," the little girl replied.

Benjamin's smile vanished.

Without waiting for further encouragement, Sadie began to draw what she called the "Geesemonster" that she said she saw often when she visited "Papi Maurice."

When the drawing was done, it didn't look like much to Benjamin. Maybe a child's idea of a ghost with a halo around its head.

"Did you see the monster?" he asked the girl.

"Yeah."

"Where?"

"Lots of places."

"Can you show me where he hides?"

"Yeah."

Benjamin took the child's hand.

"Show me," he said.

Sadie led him into Maurice and Nancy's bedroom and pointed at the bed.

"He hides in here?"

The child nodded.

"Where else?"

Sadie covered her mouth and giggled.

"Show me," said Benjamin.

Sadie led him by the hand to the toilet and pointed to the toilet bowl.

It's just a kid's game, Benjamin thought. A variation of boogie man and pee-pee, ca-ca.

Sadie must have seen the look on his face. Tugging his hand, she led him to the cellar steps and pointed.

"He hides in the basement?" Benjamin said.

"Yeah, he lives down there."

Benjamin switched on the lights inside the stairwell, picked the child up, and carried her down the steep two-tiered steps into the basement. Looking around, he could see nothing except piles of boards, a couple of sacks of potatoes, and shelves containing boxes and wooden stakes used to grow the tomato seedlings.

"There's nothing down here, honey," he said.

But just then, Sadie pointed at the farthest corner of the cellar and began to scream.

Benjamin swiveled around but couldn't see anything frightening. Sadie, still screaming, bolted from his side and scrambled up the stairs on her hands and knees.

She was halfway up before Benjamin thought to go after her.

■ ■ ■

The next day, the Theriaults' son-in-law Dennis, married to Nancy's daughter Jenny came to visit. He didn't do that often. Too many strange occurrences took place around Maurice, and Dennis didn't mind admitting that he was terrified of the farmer and his bizarre behavior.

But he couldn't very well keep his wife from visiting her mother, and as long as that was the case, he felt better if he went with her. Given the wild nature of the tales Nancy had been recounting to Jenny over the phone, Dennis's fear of what might happen to his wife if she went to the farmhouse alone was only slightly worse than his idea of what might happen to him if he went with her.

But it seemed to him as he sat rocking on the farmhouse porch that his fears had been exaggerated. The family meal together had been without incident, and everyone was enjoying a sense of closeness that had been too often missing of late.

Content with the enormous meal of fresh farm food tucked safely inside him, Dennis took a deep breath. He was imagining a moment very soon when he could go into the kitchen and say, Honey, don't you think we ought to be hittin' the road? Pulling his down jacket more securely around him against the chilly April afternoon, Dennis continued rocking and idly watched Maurice working to separate a huge tractor tire from the metal rim of its wheel. He marveled again at the muscles on his father-in-law. He's just a little guy, Dennis thought, but I'll bet he could take me.

Just then the young man heard the swinging door to the kitchen slam shut. Glancing up casually over his left shoulder, Dennis almost fell over backward with fright. He leapt to his feet as Maurice brushed by him! Swiveling about, Dennis watched dumbfounded as the second Maurice walked up to the first one, who was still changing the tire, and seemed to walk into his body.

The two Maurices had become one.

That was plenty for Dennis. Like Jessica's boyfriend, Chad, he wanted out of the house, and *now*.

Within three minutes he had Jenny in their pickup and could be seen raising a cloud of dust as he got away from Maurice Theriault as fast as his truck would carry him. Jenny cast him a stricken look, but Dennis was in no mood for a reproach about their sudden rude departure.

"We'll go back there when he gets his exorcism or whatever the hell else it takes," he said. "Because I ain't lettin' you go back there again. Not while he's like that!"

▪ ▪ ▪

Benjamin Massey got a phone call from Ed Warren two days later. He had sent Ed the cassette tapes from the weekend he and the others had spent at the house. Ed wanted to use them to help convince the Church authorities of the seriousness of Maurice's plight.

"I thought you said there were all kinds of strange noises that you heard that weekend," Ed said.

"Yeah, that's right," said Benjamin. "Sounds like rats scratching and car doors slamming and the television and radio. All kinds of stuff."

"Well, there's nothing on these tapes besides people having normal conversations," Ed told him.

"Nothing?"

"Nothing."

▪ ▪ ▪

That night the wind howled as in an old-time Hollywood movie. Outside the Theriault home the animals seemed agitated, the dogs barking continuously as soon as darkness fell.

Ever since the publicity about Maurice's ordeal, the couple had been plagued by anonymous phone calls and visits from jeering curiosity-seekers who would drive by and shout epithets at all hours. But that didn't seem to be the case that night. Each time the dogs began barking, Maurice or Nancy would go out to investigate only to return moments later with a quizzical expression and shrug. Despite his fears of an intruder or perhaps a New England fox, Maurice could find no sign of trespassers, human or animal.

"I dunno what's got 'em going like that," he told his wife.

An hour later, with the dogs still barking, the couple decided to go to bed. It would be difficult to sleep. Between the dogs' howling and the shrieking wind, Nancy saw that Maurice was becoming more and more nervous. She knew she had to do something.

"Frenchy," she said softly in the dark.

"Yeah?"

"How'd you like to learn the Hail Mary in English, and then we could say it together?"

"Okay" came the reply.

To Nancy's practiced ear, her husband sounded depressed and listless. She said a silent prayer that an exorcism would be granted soon, then embarked on the task of teaching Maurice the Hail Mary in English. Saying it out loud would reassure her as much as it would Maurice.

She began: "Hail Mary, full of grace..."

"Hail Mary, full of grace..." Maurice repeated.

"The Lord is with Thee..."

"The Lord is with Thee..."

Nancy continued the prayer to the end, with Maurice repeating after her, then began again. She was on her seventh repetition of the holy words.

"Hail Mary, full of—"

Nancy sat up straight, her words and breath cut off by a strong hand that was clamped around her throat like an iron fist.

"Urgh...urgh," she gasped as she struggled to find the chain on her bedside table lamp, finally finding it and giving it a quick jerk.

The room flooded with light, and through the red cloud that was forming in front of her eyes, Nancy could see Maurice, also sitting up, wearing a strange grin on his face but with both hands folded in his lap.

Maurice faded from her sight as black spots took his place. Her last thought before she lost consciousness was, Too late. Too late for the exorcism.

But as suddenly as it had come the mysterious hand around her throat let go, and Nancy dragged air gratefully into her rasping lungs. Running to the bathroom, she retched for several minutes. After cleaning her face with a towel, Nancy looked at her face in the mirror over the sink. There were livid finger marks around her throat. She looked back in the bedroom. Maurice, now lying down, was sleeping soundly. It hadn't been he who had tried to strangle her.

Now, she said to herself, sobbing. It has to be now. We can't wait any longer or we'll all be dead.

. . .

Ed and Lorraine Warren had come to the same conclusion. It was clear that Father Delaney's deliverance had been about as effective as Bishop Harrington's impromptu exorcism. He knew now that he needed an experienced exorcist. Ed informed Bishop Harrington that he was going to ask Bishop McKenna to do it. He knew that Bishop Harrington could never assign an expelled priest, and he was surprised that Bishop Harrington didn't try to talk him out of it. But he also knew that Harrington didn't have any alternatives.

Ed called Bishop Robert McKenna that same night. McKenna was aware of the Theriault case, of course, and had been praying for Maurice for some time, but until then he had not been asked to intervene directly.

Ed said he needed to talk with the bishop, but wanted to do it in person. McKenna, whose Our Lady of the Rosary Chapel was only a mile or so away from the Warrens' home, invited Ed and Lorraine over for coffee the next morning. But the wise bishop knew instinctively what Ed was going to ask him to do.

Lying in his bed that night, McKenna could feel the approach of an enemy, an enemy as old as man. Tenderly holding the rosary beads around his neck, he began to pray silently. He was asking for strength in the ordeal that he now knew was at hand.

THIRTEEN

BISHOP ROBERT MCKENNA of Our Lady of the Rosary Chapel in Monroe woke early. He had a lot on his mind. The fifty-eight-year-old priest had exorcised evil spirits from houses before but had never performed an exorcism on a person. A sense of foreboding gripped him.

The bishop's approaching confrontation with the dark force that held Maurice Theriault in thrall did not, on the surface, look like a fair fight. McKenna was a frail wisp of a man, standing five feet eight inches tall but weighing only one hundred thirty pounds. His graying brown hair was thinned out. Behind his thick, dark glasses fatigue as well as wisdom were etched in his eyes.

Contributing to his frail appearance was the fact that McKenna had been fasting for days in preparation for the confrontation. It should have made him feel weak, but he didn't feel weak at all. He had prayed long and hard during his fast and he felt strong. Fasting made him feel mentally, physically, and spiritually prepared. An air of isolation and holiness seemed to radiate from the priest.

McKenna was not one to back down from a fight. He hadn't backed down when Rome ordered priests to change many of the holy rituals the Church had always observed. In the 1960s, after Vatican II, the language in which the sacraments was delivered—Mass among them—was required to be the vernacular.

McKenna believed it was wrong to change the way things had always been done, and he, like a small cadre of other priests around the world, refused to go along. For them, Latin always was and still is the proper language for the Holy Mass. They simply would not accede to the order to change.

As a result, McKenna's order—the Dominican Order of Preachers—was no longer recognized by the Vatican. Convinced he was following the path God had ordained, McKenna continued to chant the musical magic of the Mass in Latin. For him and for his congregation, the ancient words had never seemed so precious, so full of meaning.

When Rome declared it would no longer fund their church, McKenna's parishioners paid the bills themselves. Their Mass, and their bishop, were certainly worth the sacrifice. To them, Bishop McKenna was a hero in a time when there were too few heroes. He was following Jesus, not Rome. That took courage.

But the frail prelate had no illusions. He knew that he'd need more than courage to meet Satan head-on.

Earlier that morning, at dawn, there had been a spring shower. It had looked as if it was going to be a gray, gloomy day, but now the sun was shining and reflecting dazzling morning light on the dozens of wet dogwood petals that the rain had pelted to the ground. Bishop McKenna hoped the sun would continue shining for the rest of the day.

Walking to the chapel that morning, he concentrated his thoughts toward God in heaven. He felt strength coming in to him in return; he could almost see it, like a shaft of light shining around him. God's love came through the soft grass and was evidenced in the sweetness of the spring air. He had been repeating a prayer and could still hear the prayer echoing in his head, and echoing in nature, as he walked toward the stone chapel. Kneeling before the altar in the cool stillness, he prayed for God's help.

After an hour, he returned to his office to collect the items he would need for the exorcism, the arms he would wield in the battle to come: the official *Ritual Romani* prayer book, a brass crucifix, an aspersorium used to shake holy water, relics of several saints, and of course his religious habit, including a white waist-length surplice, or loose robe, and a purple stole that would hang around his neck and reach down to his knees.

McKenna packed the items into a small black leather bag and calmly walked over to his desk to phone Ed and Lorraine

Warren, who lived only a couple of miles away. "I'm about ready to leave, Ed," he said.

"We're just about ready too," Ed replied. He thought about asking Bishop McKenna if he wanted a ride but remembered that the priest had said he would prefer to drive alone—so he could have more time to pray.

"We'll swing by in a few minutes and you can follow us," Ed said. "We'll have a caravan. We've got a devoted group of helpers coming with us. And they're a great group, rest assured. They're not afraid of anything."

Kent Burch and Ryan Dufrain would drive up in a van with Joey Taylor and Fred Salvio. Then they'd all meet up with Chris McKenna and Matthew Chase at a rest stop off I-84, near the exit for the University of Connecticut.

The date was May 2. The sun was still shining brightly. Every cloud had disappeared. Lorraine hoped that was a good omen. She said so as they backed the Chevette out over the bump at the end of their driveway. A red cardinal had been watching them from its branch in a birch tree, and swooped down in front of the car as they began their drive to Warren, Massachusetts.

Ed and Lorraine didn't say much as they drove the now familiar route to Warren. Lorraine thought to herself how much prettier the drive was now that it was spring than when they had first made their way up there in the dead of winter. She mentioned it to Ed, but he barely responded. He was deep in thought. He was often this way right before an exorcism. It wasn't hard to understand. He was scared, as anybody would be. She knew he was calling on Jesus to help them through whatever was going to come later that day.

"Don't worry, honey," she said, taking his hand. "Everything's going to be fine."

All was quiet when the caravan pulled into the driveway to the Theriault farmhouse just over two hours later. As the crew made its way to the door of the house, Nancy popped her head out and then turned back to Maurice. "They're here, honey," she said. She went over to him and gave him a hug.

Maurice, who was sitting at the kitchen table, looked up but didn't say anything. He wore a white T-shirt and jeans and was sipping a cup of coffee. When Ed and the others came through the door, he nodded to them and even engaged in a bit of small talk about the weather.

"Well, we better get started," Ed said quietly, rubbing his palms together briskly. "Let's do it in the living room. There's more room there. We'll go in and set up and then we'll call you in when we're ready, Maurice."

From behind the swinging door, Maurice could hear their muffled voices and the sounds of furniture being rearranged.

Kent Burch had brought along his camcorder to tape the proceedings and began to set it up across from the chair where Maurice would sit during the exorcism. Bishop McKenna followed

Kent into the room to put on his vestments and set up a little table next to the chair where he could place the items he would need to perform the ritual.

When everything was ready, the group fell silent. Ed and Bishop McKenna stared at each other silently. For Maurice Theriault and the force that possessed him, the climactic moment had come. By the time it was finished, everyone in the living room of this modest farmhouse would be changed forever, and one person would have come close to death.

Ed called Maurice into the living room. The tension was building. Maurice's mouth was dry and he was nervous, but he tried not to let it show.

"Maurice, why don't you sit down here," said Bishop McKenna, pointing to the chair that had been set up for him.

Maurice walked over without saying a word and sat down. Kent and Ryan stood to one side and Chris and Matthew stood to the other, ready to restrain Maurice. Well versed by Ed in the literature of exorcism, they knew that possessed persons could show the strength of ten, cause objects to move about the room, even levitate straight up in the air.

Nancy stood behind Maurice, next to Joey and Fred, who were there for her in case she needed comfort or support.

Bishop McKenna stood in front of Maurice, his back to him as if he were facing an altar, and began to pray out loud. Everyone was still.

Almost instantly Maurice's eyes began to drip blood. The

bright red drops at first seeped slowly from the corners of his eyes but within a few minutes were gushing down his cheeks in a steady stream.

Ed and Lorraine looked at Maurice and then at each other.

It had begun.

Surveying the room, Ed and Lorraine saw that some of their assistants had horrified looks on their faces. Ed put his hands up in a gesture of reassurance. It wouldn't help to have somebody panic at this point.

As for Nancy, she appeared remarkably composed. Ed figured she had seen Maurice's eyes bleed before and had gotten used to it. But despite her outward calm, she was spinning in turmoil inside. She knew that this was probably Maurice's last chance.

Hovering over Maurice, the priest chanted his preliminary prayers: "Our Father Who art in heaven, Hallowed be Thy name..."

Lorraine was praying along with Bishop McKenna, but her prayers were interrupted by a dark tingling at the edge of her consciousness. It had always been like that when she was about to see something that ordinary people—people who did not possess the gift, and the curse, of clairvoyance—could not see.

She began to discern evil spirits in the room, first just a few, then a few dozen. Before long, her second sight felt the presence of hundreds of devils and demons. There's a whole legion of them here, she thought.

Lorraine shuddered and tried to return to her prayers. With the evil forces this strong, Maurice would need every prayer he could get. And so would Bishop McKenna, Ed, Nancy, and all the assistants. Everybody was in jeopardy today.

Bishop McKenna continued to pray. As he did, a banging noise could be heard coming from Maurice's bedroom. It was as if the headboard of his bed was being slammed repeatedly against the wall. At first the banging was just a minor nuisance. But it kept getting louder, louder, filling the room with what sounded like the blows of a giant jackhammer.

Bang! Bang! Bang!

Abruptly it stopped. But that sound was soon replaced by the unnerving drone of what sounded like human voices coming from the kitchen. The voices were whispering, but nobody could understand what they were saying. It was eerie. Then the voices, too, went silent.

Bishop McKenna, focusing all his force and concentration, had attained the trancelike state the exorcist must reach in his battle, and had not stopped his prayers and invocations, even as the frightening phenomena took place. These were Satan's tricks, he knew, meant to distract him from his holy task.

He recited the Lord's Prayer and the Apostles' Creed three times each before going through the traditional litany of the saints:

"St. John, pray for us. St. Peter, pray for us. St. Paul, pray for us."

The priest continued through the entire list of apostles and a long list of martyrs, confessors, and saints.

He picked up the book entitled *The Roman Ritual of Exorcism*, which would lead him through the exorcism rite and opened the page at the cross bookmark. He began by asking God for His help:

*God, it is an attribute of Yours to have mercy and to for-
give. Hear our prayer, so that this servant of Yours who is
bound with the chain of sins, be mercifully freed by the
compassion of Your goodness.*

*Holy Lord! All-powerful Father! Eternal God! Father
of our Lord Jesus Christ! You Who destined that recal-
citrant and apostate Tyrant to the fires of hell; You Who
sent Your only Son into this world in order that He might
crush this Roaring Lion: Look speedily and snatch from
damnation and from this devil of our times this man who
was created in Your image and likeness. Throw Your terror, Lord, over the Beast who is destroying what belongs
to You. Give faith to Your servants against this most Evil
Serpent, to fight most bravely. So that the Serpent not
hold in contempt those who hope in You, and say as it said
through the Pharaoh: I do not know God, and I will not
let Israel go. Let Your powerful strength force the Serpent
to let go of Your servant, so that it no longer possess him
whom You deigned to make in Your image and to redeem
by Your Son, Who lives and reigns with You in the unity of
the Holy Spirit, as God, forever and ever. Amen.*

It was time to summon the evil spirit. Bishop McKenna turned
to face Maurice.

Unclean Spirit! Whoever you are, and all your companions who possess this servant of God. By the mysteries of the Incarnation, the Sufferings and Death, the Resurrection, and the Ascension of our Lord Jesus Christ; by the sending of the Holy Spirit; and by the Coming of our Lord into Last Judgment, I command you: Tell me, with some sign, your name, the day and the hour of your damnation. Obey me in everything, although I am an unworthy servant of God. Do no damage to this creature or to my assistants, or to any of their goods.

The banging began again, louder and still louder. Ed, Lorraine, and the others could barely hear the bishop.

The unholy din suddenly ceased only to be followed by a loud thud that appeared to come from outside the house. It sounded as if a car door had been violently slammed shut. Ed moved toward the window, but there was nobody near any of the cars. He shook his head and returned to his spot by Maurice.

Maurice began to bleed profusely from the nose. His face was a mask of blood.

Even Bishop McKenna, who had come prepared to see almost anything, had to look twice as he saw the blood running down Maurice's face, staining his white T-shirt. He blinked, but he kept on reading:

I exorcise you, Most Unclean Spirit! Invading Enemy! All Spirits! Every one of you! In the name of Our Lord Jesus Christ: Be uprooted and expelled from this Creature of God.

Sweat started dripping from Maurice's forehead as he twitched in his seat. It wasn't long before his entire shirt was drenched in a foul-smelling combination of sweat and blood.

The bishop glanced up at Maurice again and this time saw that crosses had appeared as if burned into the palms of his hands.

Bishop McKenna was trembling a bit, but continued to declaim the ritual in a strong, powerful voice:

He who commands you is He Who ordered you to be thrown down from the highest heaven into the depths of hell. He Who commands you is He Who dominated the sea, the wind, and the storms. Hear, therefore, and fear, Satan! Enemy of the Faith! Enemy of the Human Race! Source of death! Robber of life! Twister of justice! Root of evil! Warp of voices! Seducer of men! Traitor of nations! Inciter of jealousy! Originator of greed! Cause of discord! Creator of agony! Why do you stay and resist, when you know that Christ our Lord has destroyed your plan? Fear Him Who was prefigured in Isaac, in Joseph, and in the Paschal Lamb; Who was crucified as a man, and Who rose from death.

As Bishop McKenna continued the exorcism address, Ed leaned over and whispered to Kent to try and remove Maurice's boots. Maurice was beginning to shake and Ed feared he might kick the bishop. Kent whispered the message to Ryan, and as if on cue, they dropped to their knees and each yanked off a black cowboy boot.

Their eyes bulged when they saw his white socks drenched in blood—from stigmata wounds on his feet. There was a pool of blood in each boot.

Nancy wept, desperately wanting to go to her husband's aid. But Joey and Fred, on Ed's orders, firmly told her not to move toward him. She sobbed quietly, with her clenched fist to her mouth.

Joey asked her if she wanted to go into the kitchen for a while, but Nancy just shook her head. "I'm not leaving Maurice," she said.

Her husband, transformed into a frightening bundle of bloody clothing, had fallen into a kind of trance. He slumped back in his chair, and his eyes rolled back into his head so that only the whites were showing. The putrid smell of the blood was stifling.

Kent's hands were sweating profusely and he shook as he tried to capture the scene on videotape. Ryan steadied him as he moved the camera to film what was happening from different angles. But Ryan was shaking too.

Lorraine glanced over at Ed and noticed that he was looking unusually pale. She whispered to him, "Honey, why don't you go into the kitchen and sit down. You look white as a ghost."

Ed felt nausea welling up inside, but he wasn't going to leave now. He could tell that things were starting to heat up.

Bishop McKenna made the sign of the cross on Maurice's sweaty forehead and continued to read:

Retire, therefore, in the name of the Father, and of the Son, and of the Holy Spirit. Give way to the Holy Spirit, because of this sign of the Holy Cross of our Lord Jesus Christ, Who lives and reigns as God with the Father and the same Holy Spirit, forever and ever. Amen.

Right before everyone's eyes, Maurice's face began to change. Heavy, animal-like groans came up from his throat. His face got redder, then brownish-gray. His nose got wider and flatter, and deep lines—more like crevices—formed across his forehead. It was almost as if his forehead had swollen and split in two. His brow seemed to expand and hang over his eyes, which were becoming slits. In a matter of a few seconds he'd been transformed. The reptilian face that now regarded the bishop with twisted malice did not look like any human being Ed had ever seen.

As Ed and the others looked at Maurice in horror, he started to get up out of his chair.

"Stop him!" Ed shouted. "Grab him!" Then Ed recoiled, grabbing his chest. He suddenly felt as if he had a one-hundred-pound weight on his breast. He was breathing with difficulty.

Quickly, Kent and Ryan, who were standing to Maurice's left, grabbed one arm, while at the same time Chris and Matthew, who were standing to his right, took hold of the other.

Maurice struggled, grunting and kicking violently as Ed, Joey, and Fred grabbed hold of his shoulders from the rear.

For a moment it looked as if Maurice was going to break free. But the seven men struggled with all their might and pushed him back down into the chair. As he fell backward, Maurice let out a hideous groan and seemed to go limp.

Kent looked over to Ed as if to ask whether it was safe to let go his grip. Ed just shook his head. "Okay, I think he's calmed down, at least for now," Ed said. "Let him go, but remain on guard. He could try it again. And if he does, he'll probably go right for the bishop."

As Ed finished speaking, a lamp, which had been sitting on a table on the other side of the room, fell to the floor and shattered. Ed looked around to see if any other objects might be about to take flight. A painting on the side wall began to rattle. And the hallway light began to flash on and off. But nothing more happened.

McKenna had continued praying throughout Maurice's struggle to get out of his chair and didn't stop even when the objects started to move. If he was frightened, he didn't show it. He knew he had to concentrate on the task at hand. He couldn't show fear.

The bishop called out to Maurice by name. "Maurice," he said. "Maurice, can you hear me?"

But Lorraine knew that the man before them was no longer

Maurice Theriault.

"Father, Maurice is no longer here," she said.

McKenna knew it. He knew that an evil presence was now in their midst. He put down the book.

"I abjure you in the name of God to tell me your name!" he boomed.

The creature that had been Maurice looked up and smiled wickedly at the priest. *"I am what I am."*

The words boomed across the room. The voice was deep, guttural. Sinister. Several in the room felt their flesh puckering into goose bumps.

Bishop McKenna repeated his command. "I abjure you in the name of God to tell me your name!"

"I am what I am" came the frightening reply.

The priest tried it two more times, but each time got the same cryptic answer. He decided to try a different question.

"How many of you are there?" asked the priest.

"I am the only one."

The creature's voice seemed strained, but the message was clear. Bishop McKenna knew what he was dealing with. But he wanted to hear a more direct answer.

He asked again. "What is your name?"

"Dicis supercilius."

Kent looked at Ryan with raised eyebrows. Ryan just shrugged.

But Bishop McKenna recognized it as Latin. The rough translation: "You say I'm proud."

He's still playing games, McKenna thought. Of course he's proud. The devil is the king of pride.

"Why are you here?" the priest asked.

But Maurice didn't answer.

"Why are you here?"

Again no answer.

"How did you enter?"

Still no answer. Maurice appeared to have gone back into his trance.

Bishop McKenna again picked up the exorcism book. As his words swelled out over the room, the listeners were moved by their simple majesty and by the power exuding from the frail priest.

I enjoin you under penalty, Ancient Serpent! In the name of the Judge of the Living and the Dead! In the name of Him Who has power to send you into hell! Depart from this servant of God, Maurice, who has recourse to the Church. Cease to inspire your terror in him. I again enjoin you solemnly, not because of myself, who am weak, but because of the strength of the Holy Spirit: that you go out from this servant of God, Maurice, whom the all-powerful God made in His own image. Surrender, not to me, but to the minister of Christ. His power forces you. He defeated you by His Cross. Fear the strength of Him who led the souls of the dead to the light of salvation from the darkness

of waiting. May the body of this man be a source of terror
for you. May the image of God be a source of fear for you.

As Bishop McKenna chanted the ancient and holy formula, he picked up the crucifix and waved it in front of Maurice, making the sign of the cross. As he did, Maurice stirred. He sat up slowly, as if he were Rip Van Winkle coming out of his long sleep.

McKenna put the book down, but continued with his commands. "I said in the name of God, in the name of Jesus Christ, in the name of the Blessed Virgin Mary to depart," he said. "Stop tormenting this creature."

McKenna picked up the aspersorium and sprinkled Maurice with holy water. Then he took the crucifix and again made the sign of the cross with it in front of Maurice's still contorted face.

Instantly Maurice's face started returning to normal. His nose unflattened and took its former shape, and the deep lines etched across his forehead disappeared. Slowly he sat up in his chair. Within moments he had come completely out of his trance.

Ed, Lorraine, and the others looked at him with expectant silence.

Maurice wiped his face with a wet towel and scanned the room. When he spotted Nancy he got up slowly, walked over to her, and put his muscular arms around her. As they embraced, Nancy broke down. Tears streamed down her face, but for the first time in a long time they were tears of joy. She couldn't remember the last time Maurice had hugged her like that.

As they unlocked from their embrace Maurice looked around the room until he saw Ed. Then he broke into a half grin. It was the first time Ed had ever seen Maurice smile.

"It's over, Maurice," Ed said. "You're finally free."

Maurice felt it. Euphoria swept over him as Bishop McKenna read the final psalm readings and a concluding prayer of thanks:

> *We pray You, all-powerful God, that Evil Spirit have no more power over this servant of yours, Maurice, but that it flee and not come back. Let the goodness and the peace of our Lord Jesus Christ enter him at Your bidding, Lord. For through Jesus we have been saved. And let us not fear any ill, because the Lord is with us, He Who lives and reigns as God with You in the unity of the Holy Spirit, forever and ever. Amen.*

■ ■ ■

Ed was quiet as he and Lorraine drove back to Monroe that afternoon. His silence puzzled Lorraine. Although he was often quiet on the way to an exorcism, afterward Ed would always be jabbering on about each and every little detail. And today's went so well that she figured he'd be talking from the minute they left the farmhouse to the minute they pulled into their driveway at home.

She was so excited about what had just happened. Her heart was still racing, but she felt lifted by the awesome power of the

Lord. From the looks of things, the exorcism had been a success. Of course, it was too early to be certain, but indications were good. Maurice had looked like a man who had been reprieved from a death sentence. Just as important, from Lorraine's point of view, was what she had discerned during the exorcism by her powers of clairvoyance. Lorraine could tell when an evil spirit was present and when one was not. At the outset of the exorcism she could feel the spirit's presence very strongly. By the time it was over, she knew that it was gone.

"I think this one's going to take, honey," she said. "I've got a good feeling about it."

Lorraine knew that Bishop McKenna had been the key. Bishop Harrington, she realized, was not really the right type of priest to succeed as an exorcist. An exorcist must be a pious, holy man. Harrington, in charge of a diocese, had become more of an administrator than a priest in recent years. And Father Delaney, for all his good work as a faith healer, plainly had not been prepared. Lorraine figured he was too busy with his popular healing services to devote the needed time to fasting and prayer in anticipation of the battle.

Besides, she knew it was unusual for an exorcism to succeed the first time around. For that to happen, the exorcist had to be very special—like Bishop McKenna.

She was certain it had been McKenna's piety and holiness that had kept this exorcism from getting out of control. She thought back to an exorcism of a teenage girl she had attended in New Jersey. That one had gotten really violent. The girl had uttered the vilest string of obscenities Lorraine had ever heard. Furniture had gone flying around the room. It was lucky no one had gotten killed.

Lorraine knew that today's exorcism could have gotten violent too. She had feared that would happen when Maurice tried to bolt from his chair. Fortunately seven strong men were there to stop him. But she knew that even they would have been no match for the devil that had taken over Maurice if Bishop McKenna had not been up to the task. Yes, she thought, God had protected him. He had let the bishop get on with his work.

"Yeah, honey, we sure got the right man for the job when we got Bishop McKenna," Lorraine said.

Ed just nodded.

Lorraine looked over and saw that he still looked pale.

"Honey, do you feel okay?"

"I'm just a little thirsty," he answered. "Let's pull over and get a soda."

After the drink Ed said he felt a little better, but when they got home he announced that he was going straight to bed.

The next morning, he again had little to say. He didn't even bother to review his notes as he usually did. When he complained about his lunchtime hamburger having no taste, Lorraine didn't know what to think. That wasn't like Ed at all. And besides, she had one, too, and it was perfectly delicious.

Had something happened to Ed during the exorcism?

After lunch Ed decided to turn on the television, but before he went into the living room he called out to Lorraine, "Honey, is there any of that strawberry shortcake left?"

"Sure is, honey," she answered. Well, that's better, she thought. He couldn't be feeling too bad.

Ed opened the refrigerator and took out what remained of the cake. He carried it to the counter and sliced off a good-sized piece. As he walked out to the living room, it hit him: His chest felt as if it were being crushed. He began to sweat profusely. He felt a sharp pain in his left arm. And it became increasingly difficult to breathe.

He placed the plate of cake down and leaned against the counter for support. "Honey, I think you better get me to the hospital," he said. "I think I'm having a heart attack."

■ ■ ■

Ed Warren did have a heart attack, a severe one. He spent seventeen days in St. Vincent's Hospital in Bridgeport, where doctors said he'd been having the attack for at least twenty-four hours—meaning that it had started shortly after the exorcism had gotten under way.

Word got around the hospital about Ed and the circumstances under which he'd suffered the heart attack. Several doctors and nurses—even the hospital chaplain—came by his room to ask about it. They wanted to know if the devil had caused the attack.

It was a question that was on Ed's mind too. But he was unable to answer it. In all his years of fighting demons and other evil spirits, nothing this serious had ever happened to him. He wondered whether his faith was strong enough. Or whether he had just finally met his match.

Ed decided to leave the answer up to Lorraine. She went downstairs to the hospital chapel to pray and meditate. She stayed in there for hours, looking for an answer. Had Satan finally gotten the better of her husband? Finally she came to a conclusion. She went back up to Ed's room to tell him what she thought.

"Well?" he asked, peering up from his newspaper.

"Honey, I've given this a lot of thought, prayer, and meditation," she said. "And I've come to the conclusion that God caused your heart attack, honey. He caused it to slow you down. You've been working way too hard. We both have. I think we need to take a rest. Then, if God sees fit to heal you, we'll continue our work. If not, then our work will have to stop. We'll leave it up to God."

Within a week Ed was discharged from the hospital. His doctors told him he would have to curtail all his activities for at least six months. It wasn't easy for him, since there were new cases being reported and old cases to follow up. But he had no choice. He had to confine his professional activities to reading.

It was a very difficult and frustrating time for him. He felt he was letting people down. But he tempered those feelings by remembering what Lorraine had told him about God's plan.

When the six months were up, Ed's doctor gave him the good news: He had healed sufficiently to return to work. Ed reacted as if he had been given a new lease on life and returned to his duties with renewed enthusiasm. He and Lorraine decided to return to the college lecture circuit and to begin some preliminary investigations into new cases. But first they wanted to check up on some of the old cases. The first one he wanted to check on was Maurice Theriault.

What Ed learned was enough to have sent a weaker man back to the cardiac unit.

FOURTEEN

CHIEF JERRY SEIBERT sat back in his chair with his hands folded behind his head and his big black boots on his desk, staring up at the ceiling. He was trying to decide what to do about Frenchy Theriault. It had been more than two months since the final exorcism. While there had been no more strange incidents that had come to his attention, he had not forgotten about Frenchy. As he proceeded with his investigation into the mysterious fires at the Theriault farmhouse, he had discovered something much worse than possible arson.

Seibert had uncovered evidence that Maurice Theriault had raped his own stepdaughter, not once but probably a dozen times. A tip from a state child-abuse investigator led him to the thirteen-year-old girl's natural father in upstate New York and then to the girl herself. What she told him sent shivers up his spine.

She said she had engaged in sexual activities with Maurice many times over the course of the previous few years. If that had been all there was to it, then Seibert wouldn't have been sitting here pondering what he ought to do. But like everything concerning Maurice Theriault, this was complicated.

According to the girl, it wasn't really Maurice who had raped her. No, she claimed it was somebody else who looked just like Maurice.

The police chief didn't have to ask who that might have been. He had heard enough by then about demonic possession and doppelgängers and all that bullshit. Now he's got her thinking she was raped by the devil. What next? he thought.

Seibert knew this was going to be a tough case to prosecute, especially with all the publicity in the local papers and national tabloids about Frenchy's exorcism.

Although he was a Catholic and of French-Canadian descent, Seibert thought exorcism was strictly for the movies. Sure, there was about fifteen percent of him that thought the possession business might have been true—maybe. After all, he had seen Frenchy gyrating and his eyes bleeding and a few other strange occurrences—but the other eighty-five percent of him, the logical, police-officer part of him, thought otherwise.

Down deep, Seibert thought the demonic-possession stuff was just a crock of shit, albeit an unusual crock of shit, devised by Maurice to cover up the fires—which Seibert figured he had set to collect on his insurance—not to mention the sexual abuse of his own stepdaughter. Father Beardsley and the Warrens, he figured, had just been suckered in by Frenchy, who was not as dumb as he appeared.

No, Frenchy was quite clever, Seibert thought. He'd proved that the time he'd been called to the state fire-marshal's office to take a polygraph test. Just as the test was about to begin, Frenchy began to go into convulsions. He shook and twitched and fell to the floor, moaning and groaning. When he finally came out of it, Dan Prescott, the fire investigator, decided there was no way Maurice could undergo the test. His heart was racing, he was sweating profusely, and he was still shaking like a leaf. Even if Prescott had given him the test, the results would have been suspect. So he sent Frenchy home.

Seibert had been furious when he heard about it. That bastard, he thought. He did it again. What a convenient time to throw a fit.

So he knew that to pin a rape or child-abuse conviction on Frenchy was going to be tricky. But he was determined to do it. There was no doubt Frenchy had done it. The girl had told Seibert that, even though she was convinced that it wasn't really Frenchy. And her natural father had said he would allow her to testify against the farmer. If there was anything Seibert hated, it was a child molester. He wasn't going to allow Frenchy to get away with this one. No way.

He sat straight up in his chair, dropping his boots to the floor with two clunks. He had made his decision. He was ready to bring the matter to the district attorney's office. He had a tape of his interview with the girl. That ought to be enough to get an indictment before a grand jury, he thought.

He showed the assistant district attorney at the Spencer district court what he had, but the young prosecutor said he'd have to take it to the main office in Worcester. Days went by. Then weeks.

Seibert started to get the sinking feeling that the DA's office wasn't going to take the case.

"Come on," Seibert told him. "This thing is bigger than I am. I want to take this thing to a grand jury. I need some help."

But he couldn't seem to get anywhere. Finally Seibert decided to call the office of the district attorney in Worcester himself. When he did he was put on hold for twenty minutes. When he finally got through to his secretary and explained what he wanted, she put him off. He was being stonewalled. Nobody appeared willing to meet with him.

Seibert called the DA's office repeatedly, but he couldn't seem to get an answer. He knew it would be a tough case to prosecute, but he had the evidence. Yet they didn't seem to want to touch it.

By now it was July. Still no answer from the DA's office. Seibert had a problem. He had never faced anything like this before. He had a decision to make. He was mulling it over in his office at home one steamy night when his wife, Janice, came in carrying a bag of groceries.

"I got a couple of steaks, Jerry," she yelled from the kitchen. "Want to put them on the grill?"

But he didn't answer.

"Honey?"

Janice walked into his office and found her husband deep in thought. He hadn't even heard her.

"I said I bought us a couple of nice steaks," she said. "And I got a six-pack of Michelob. How about firing up the grill?"

Seibert looked up from the papers spread out on his desk. "I'm sorry, baby," he said. "I got a serious decision to make here. I got to think."

"Want to tell me about it?"

Seibert frowned. He didn't usually involve his wife in police-department matters. Of course, she knew about the Frenchy Theriault case. It seemed as if the whole world did. But he had kept his rape investigation secret. Not even his patrolmen knew about it. That's why he had the paperwork on the case at home.

He decided to break with tradition. He told his wife all about the new developments in the Frenchy Theriault case.

"I've been trying to meet with the DA's office for more than a month," he said. "I know I've got probable cause. But they're stalling. I don't think they want to handle it. I guess there's just been too much publicity. So they're backing off and I'm stuck with a problem. I could arrest him and take him to court, but I'm going to get no help. It's all on my shoulders now."

Now that he had started talking about it, his frustrations were all coming out. He paced the room as he talked. "The DA has the prosecuting responsibility," he said. "But they just refuse to prosecute. Normally, I'd have options. Present it to a grand jury or, based upon probable cause of his committing a felony, arrest him. I can't go to a grand jury without the DA, so the only thing left to do is arrest him on my own."

His wife had been sitting on the couch while she listened. She got up and went over to his desk to lean on it and gently put her hand on his shoulder.

"The way I see it, sweetie, is that you've got no choice. You've got to arrest him. You can't let him go free if he raped a little girl. If he gets off on this devil thing, he gets off. But at least you'll have tried. I know it's weird, but you've got to do it. What are you afraid of?"

Seibert drummed his fingers on the top of his desk for a moment and then looked deeply into his wife's eyes. "What if this stuff's true?"

She raised her eyebrows and shook her head. "I thought you didn't believe in that stuff," she said.

"I don't," he said. "It's just that...well, you never know, do you?"

Janice gave him a sideways look and folded her arms. She wasn't going to let him off the hook that easily. "Don't take the easy way out, Jerry," she said. "You're a cop. A good cop. And you've got to do what's right."

Seibert knew it. He'd known it all along. He'd just had to share some of his doubts with someone. And his wife was the only one he could trust. He felt better for having talked to her.

"I know," he said. "I'm going to arrest him tomorrow. Now, what was it you were saying about some steaks?"

■ ■ ■

The next morning, as it turned out, Seibert ran into Nancy Theriault at the post office. She tried to avoid him as she left the lobby, but Seibert came right up to her. "Morning, Nancy," he said.

"Morning, Chief," she said nervously, trying not to look at him. She still hated Seibert for going after Maurice on the arson charges and for the way she felt he had mistreated her husband during a very difficult time. But she tried to act civil toward him. "Nice day, isn't it?" she said.

"Uh, Nancy," Seibert said, not wanting to beat around the bush. "I've got to talk to Frenchy. Could you ask him to come around to the station this afternoon? If he can't, I can come out to the house, but I'd prefer it if he came to me."

Nancy Theriault didn't like the sound of Seibert's voice. "What's the matter now?" she muttered with a half-sneer. "Haven't you caused enough trouble for Maurice?"

"I'm sorry you feel that way, Nancy," he replied. "But I just need to talk with him. Will you please tell him?"

"Yeah, yeah," she said flatly, turning to go. "I'll tell him."

Later that afternoon Maurice Theriault walked into the tiny police station in downtown Warren. Chief Seibert was the only one there. He was sitting at his desk, doing some paperwork.

"You wanted to see me, Chief?" Maurice said as he strode through the door.

"Yeah," Seibert answered. "Have a seat."

Maurice was wearing his work jeans and a white T-shirt. His hands were still dirty from working around the farm. He was smoking a cigarette.

"Maurice, I'm placing you under arrest," Seibert said. "I'm going to read you your rights now."

Maurice was taken aback. "W-what's the charge?" he demanded. "I thought I was cleared on that arson thing."

"Yes, you were," Seibert replied. "But this is a much more serious charge."

When Seibert told Maurice what he was charged with, he seemed puzzled. "I don't know what you're talking about," he said. "I never touched that girl."

Seibert began to pepper him with specific questions, but Maurice clammed up. "I think I better talk to my lawyer," he said.

That said, Seibert knew he couldn't pursue his line of questioning any further. He began to fill out the arrest forms.

As he filled in the blanks, he asked Maurice for some basic information such as the proper spelling of his name, his date of birth, and so on. He was lousy with a typewriter, so he was taking care to fill in the information on the arrest card without errors. He typed out the letters in a slow, halting rhythm.

Finally, with most of the questions answered, Seibert glanced up at Maurice, who was sitting in a wooden chair about five feet away. Seibert's jaw dropped when he saw him.

The farmer was sitting motionless, his eyes staring transfixed on the chief, as if he felt he could control him simply with his eyes. Blood was seeping out the corners of his mouth. Bubbles of blood were popping out of his nose. He looked dazed.

"Jesus!" Seibert whispered.

Then Maurice began to speak in a low, hissing voice that did not sound at all like his own, or like a human voice at all. He said something that scared the shit out of the normally unflappable Seibert.

"You and I are going to be together a long, long time."

Seibert could hardly believe his eyes and ears. He had convinced himself that Frenchy's claim to having been possessed was nothing but a fraud. And now the little bastard was vomiting blood and sounding like something right out of a horror movie!

The part of Seibert that believed that maybe, just maybe, what Maurice and the Warrens had said was true now seemed to overrule the skeptical, rational police-officer side of him.

Just then he got an idea.

Seibert got up and walked into a back room. He remembered that he had put away a bottle of holy water that had been given to him by Father Beardsley. He didn't know what he'd been thinking when he accepted it. Maybe he'd just been humoring the old priest. Maybe he'd thought that someday he might need it. Whatever, he had stashed it in a file cabinet next to the washroom. He fished it out and carried it back into the front part of the station.

Maurice eyed him suspiciously as he approached with the bottle of clear liquid.

"I've been waiting for this for a long time," Seibert said, unscrewing the cap with shaking hands. "I've been waiting to see something."

Seibert was shouting now, almost out of control. It was as if every emotion that he had experienced through this strange, sordid ordeal was coming out at once.

He took the cap off the bottle and began splashing the water all over Maurice. "See how you like this," he shouted as he doused the dazed farmer with the holy water.

Immediately Maurice began to shake and shiver and wriggle all over the chair as if he were having convulsions. He began moaning and groaning and then fell to the ground.

Seibert was frightened, there was no question about it. He was caught off guard and he was alone with Maurice—if this was Maurice.

He had to know the truth. As a police officer he was used to thinking on his feet. He decided to try the plan that had been brewing in his mind for the past few minutes. Maybe, he thought, he could trip Maurice up if he was faking.

"You asshole," he shouted, pointing a meaty index finger at the writhing farmer. "I've been waiting for a chance like this, a chance to prove that you're a fucking phony!"

"That's not holy water," Seibert boomed, scared stiff but feigning laughter. "That's nothing but tap water. And you're nothing but a fucking fake."

He looked at Maurice to see his reaction.

But Maurice didn't react.

He just lay there on the floor, calming down some but still appearing dazed and confused.

"Huh? What are you talking about?" he mumbled. "Where am I? What's going on?" Blood continued to seep from his mouth. He wiped his face with the bottom of his T-shirt.

Seibert sat back down in his chair and placed the bottle on his desk. His plan hadn't worked. Either Maurice was really possessed or he was too smart to fall for his bluff. Either way, his lie about the water in the bottle's not being holy water hadn't proved a thing.

He took a deep breath, picked up the phone, and called the district court. "I've got one coming over," he told the clerk. "Rape of a child under sixteen." Then he pulled his handcuffs off his belt and got up to put them on Maurice. But first Seibert dipped his index finger into the bottle, wet it, and made the sign of the cross. He wasn't going to take any chances.

He cuffed Maurice's hands behind his back and led him to the cruiser. Maurice didn't say a word as they drove the fifteen miles to the courthouse in the town of Spencer. Seibert drove with one eye on the road and the other on his rearview mirror. He didn't know what to expect out of Maurice, but he didn't want any surprises. Fortunately Maurice just sat there, dazed, as if he didn't understand what was happening to him.

Seibert led him into the courtroom and cuffed him to a special bench where he was to await an appearance before the judge. Then the chief went into another room to talk with some friends who worked at the courthouse. They all wanted to hear about the farmer who was possessed by the devil.

Seibert hadn't been in there five minutes when a very pale court officer rushed into the room looking for him. "Sir, you better come in here quick!" he said.

Seibert hustled back into the courtroom. He stopped dead in his tracks when he spotted Maurice.

"Oh, Christ, not again!" he said.

There was Maurice, cuffed to the bench, in the throes of another convulsion. As he twitched and shook, blood seeped from his mouth and his eyes.

"Let's get this guy to a hospital," one of the court officers said. "Call an ambulance."

Chief Seibert sat in his cruiser and watched as Maurice was placed into a straitjacket and loaded into an ambulance for the ride to the hospital in Worcester. He shook his head as he noticed that none of the paramedics would ride in the back with Maurice. Everybody knows about this guy, he thought, and they're all scared shitless.

He wondered how he was ever going to get a conviction.

As Seibert headed back toward Warren, he thought long and

hard about the Maurice Theriault case and wondered if he had done the right thing. He realized that he was as confused as everyone else.

Driving down Main Street, Seibert passed St. Paul's Church, and he realized that it had been a long time since he'd been to church. He made a U-turn at the next intersection.

Seibert pulled slowly into the church parking lot, turned off the engine, and sat there in silence for several minutes. Then he folded his hands, bowed his head, and began to pray:

"Our Father, Who art in heaven..."

EPILOGUE

CHIEF JERRY SEIBERT never did get a conviction against Maurice Theriault. Although the farmer was judged competent to stand trial, the charges against him were ultimately dropped when the district attorney's office got a look at the shocking videotape of the final exorcism. The decision was cemented by the girl's reluctance to testify. Seibert later quit his job as Warren's police chief, although he claims the decision was unrelated to the Maurice Theriault case. He still lives in Warren, works for the National Guard, and is moonlighting as a private investigator. He still carries a medallion given to him by a psychic investigator who told him that it would prevent him from ever coming under possession.

MAURICE AND NANCY THERIAULT lost their farm as a result of the arrest. They had to sell it to pay their lawyer. They are now renting a farm in another small central Massachusetts town where they grow pumpkins, squash, and tomatoes. Maurice has not had anything unusual happen to him since his arrest and is considered free from the demonic possession that had made his life a living hell from the days of his youth. Although he experienced a few strange occurrences after the final exorcism, including the incident when he was arrested, such relapses are not unusual, according to demonologists, and taper off in time, as they did in Maurice's case. According to Ed Warren, it was not Maurice who repeatedly had sexual relations with his stepdaughter, but an incubus, a diabolical spirit that had taken the image of Maurice. An incubus is a spirit of lust that sexually oppresses women. Maurice abhorred the very thought of his stepdaughter being molested, according to Ed. "If you knew him, you'd know he could never do anything like that," Ed said. Maurice himself has no memory of any sexual encounters with the young girl.

ED AND LORRAINE WARREN continue to practice demonology from their home in Monroe, Connecticut. Ed has fully recovered from his heart attack, and he and Lorraine have resumed a full schedule of investigations, lectures, and classes. They have investigated several cases of possession since the Theriault case, although to this day they say they have never seen one as frightening.

FATHER GALEN BEARDSLEY has retired to a trailer park in western Massachusetts.

BISHOP ROBERT MCKENNA continues his pastoral duties in Our Lady of the Rosary Chapel in Monroe, Connecticut. He has been involved in several exorcisms since the one involving Maurice Theriault.

ALSO BY ED AND LORRAINE WARREN

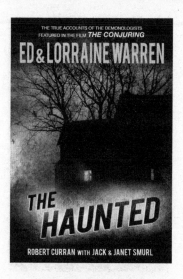

THE HAUNTED

THE WORLD'S MOST FAMOUS DEMONOLOGISTS, Ed and Lorraine Warren, were called in to help an average American family who were assaulted by forces too awesome, too powerful, too dark, to be stopped. Their harrowing encounter with otherworldly evil—supported by dozens of eyewitnesses including neighbors, priests, police, journalists, and researchers—makes for one of the Warrens' most gripping accounts… and one of the most terrifying true tales of the supernatural.

The grim slaughterhouse odors. The deafening pounding. The hoofed half-man charging down the hall. Physical attacks, a vicious strangling, failed exorcisms, a succubus…and the final terror that continued to torment the Smurl family.

In this shocking, deeply absorbing book—rivaled only by the Warrens' most famous case, The Amityville Horror—journalist Robert Curran digs deep into the haunting of the Smurl home in West Pittston, Pennsylvania, and the unshakable family bonds that helped them survive.

ISBN: 978-1-63168-013-7

ALSO BY ED AND LORRAINE WARREN

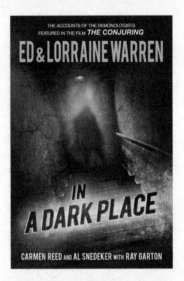

IN A DARK PLACE

THIS STORY OF THE MOST TERRIFYING CASE OF DEMONIC POSSESSION in the United States became the basis for the hit film *The Haunting in Connecticut* starring Virginia Madsen. Shortly after moving into their new home, the Snedeker family is assaulted by a sinister presence that preys upon them one by one. Exhausting other resources, they turn to world-renowned demonologists Ed and Lorraine Warren—the paranormal investigators portrayed in the blockbuster film *The Conjuring*.

But even the Warrens have never encountered a case as frightening as this....No one warned the Snedekers that their new house was once an old funeral home. And their battle with inexplicable and savage phenomena has only just begun. What starts as a simple "poltergeist" soon escalates into a full-scale war between an average American family and the deepest, darkest forces of evil. A war this family can't afford to lose.

ISBN: 978-1-63168-014-4

ALSO BY ED AND LORRAINE WARREN

GRAVEYARD

GHOSTS ARE ALWAYS HUNGRY, someone once said, and no one knows how ravenous they really are more than Ed and Lorraine Warren, the world's most renowned paranormal investigators. For decades, Ed and Lorraine Warren hunted down the truth behind the most terrifying supernatural occurrences across the nation…and brought back astonishing evidence of their encounters with the unquiet dead. From the notorious house immortalized in *The Amityville Horror* to the bone-chilling events that inspired the hit film *The Conjuring*, the Warrens fearlessly probed the darkness of the world beyond our own, and documented the all-too-real experiences of the haunted and the possessed, the lingering deceased, and the vengeful damned.

Graveyard chronicles a host of their most harrowing, fact-based cases of ghostly visitations, demonic stalking, heart-wrenching otherworldly encounters, and horrifying comeuppance from the spirit world. If you don't believe, you will…

ISBN: 978-1-63168-011-3

ALSO BY ED AND LORRAINE WARREN

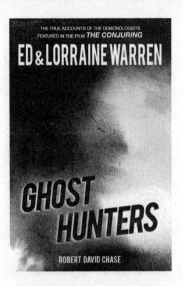

GHOST HUNTERS

GHOSTS KNOW NO SEASON, respect no boundaries, and offer no mercy. Ed and Lorraine Warren, the world's most famous and respected demonologists, have devoted decades to exploring, authenticating, and conclusively documenting countless cases of otherworldly phenomena.

From the grounds of the United States military academy at West Point, New York, to the backwoods of Tennessee, *Ghost Hunters* chronicles their first-hand confrontations with the unknown, the unholy, and the unspeakable. Here are the accounts of teenage girls who trifled with Satanism and séances, only to fall victim to the most horrifying of spirits…A village terrorized by a murderous, unstoppable force too evil to be anything but Hell-born…A family's home besieged by the relentless, destructive fury of poltergeists…The real facts behind the house of horrors in Amityville. In all, fourteen terrifying tales…all the more spine-tingling because they're true!

ISBN: 978-1-63168-012-0

ALSO BY ED AND LORRAINE WARREN

WEREWOLF

THIS IS THE HARROWING *TRUE* ACCOUNT of William Ramsey—a mild-mannered Englishman, loving husband and father, and nearly life-long prisoner of a demonic and primal force inside him…with the horrifying power to erase the fine line between civilized man and vicious animal. World-renowned demonologists Ed and Lorraine Warren brought their unique expertise to Great Britain to investigate the shocking case that captured headlines, terrified the public, and turned one otherwise ordinary man's life into the stuff of nightmares.

What kind of blood-curdling transformation did an ER nurse, a police officer, and Ramsey's own wife behold when something violently untamed and unstoppable raged from deep within to make a man become a monster? And when medical science couldn't help William Ramsey, where else was there to turn…except to the veterans of countless campaigns against otherworldly evil? But even the Warrens would find their formidable skills severely tested confronting the dark soul of a savage beast.

ISBN: 978-1-63168-015-1

ABOUT THE AUTHORS

ED and LORRAINE WARREN both had supernatural experiences when they were growing up in Connecticut. They became high school sweethearts, and on his seventeenth birthday, Ed enlisted with the US Navy to serve in World War II. A few months later his ship sank in the North Atlantic, and he was one of only a few survivors. Soon after, Ed and Lorraine were married and had a daughter. In 1952 Ed and Lorraine formed the New England Society for Psychic Research, the oldest ghost-hunting group in New England. From Amityville to Tokyo, they have been involved with thousands of investigations and Church-sanctioned exorcisms all over the world. They have dedicated their lives and extraordinary talents to help educate others and fight against demoniacal forces whenever they are called. Ed and Lorraine Warren also wrote *Graveyard*, *Ghost Hunters*, *The Haunted*, *In a Dark Place*, *Werewolf*, and *Satan's Harvest*.

MICHAEL LASALANDRA is a veteran journalist who has covered medicine and health care for the *Boston Herald*, *Palm Beach Post* and *Miami News*. He is currently free-lancing and his articles have appeared in the *Boston Globe*, among other publications. He is also the author of *The Sensitive Gut*, which won the Will Solimene Award of Excellence in 2002 from the American Medical Writers Association, New England Chapter. A graduate of the Boston University College of Communication, he also maintains a web site about prostate cancer, www.watchwait.com.

MARK MERENDA was a professional journalist for fifteen years, including five years with *The New York Times* Company. He now owns Smart-Marketing, a marketing firm serving the legal industry nationwide.